KATIE HAMSTEAD

FAIRYTALE GALAXY CHRONICLES #1

PRINCESS OF TYRONE

AF505988

CURIOSITY
QUILLS PRESS

A Division of **Whampa, LLC**
P.O. Box 2160
Reston, VA 20195
Tel/Fax: 800-998-2509
http://curiosityquills.com

© 2016 **Katie Hamstead**
http://kjhstories.blogspot.com

Cover Art by Andrea Garcia
http://andygarcia666.deviantart.com

All rights reserved, including the right to reproduce this book or portions thereof in any form whatsoever. For information about Subsidiary Rights, Bulk Purchases, Live Events, or any other questions - please contact Curiosity Quills Press at info@curiosityquills.com, or visit http://curiosityquills.com

ISBN 978-1-62007-099-4 (ebook)
ISBN 978-1-62007-421-3 (paperback)

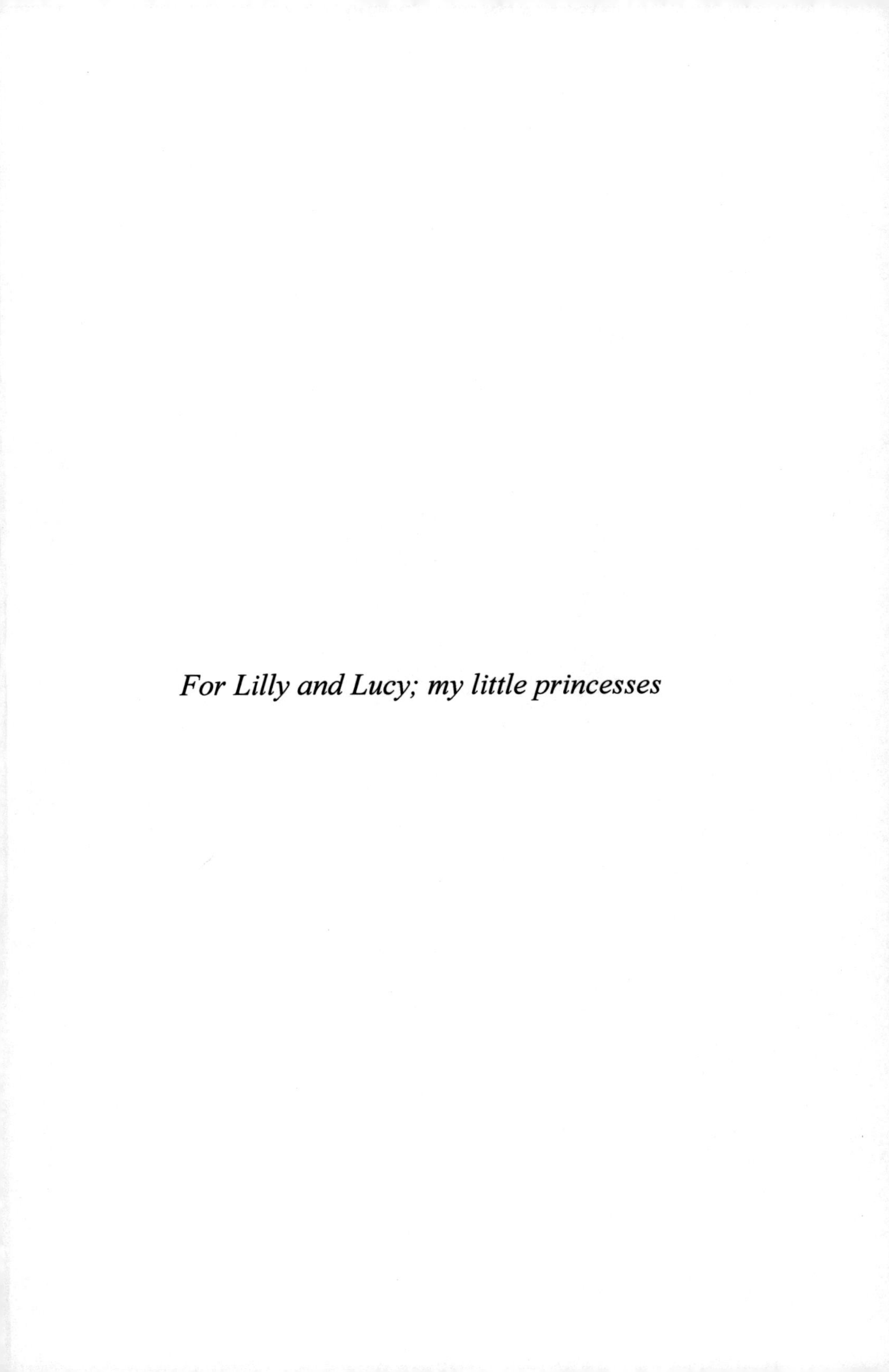

For Lilly and Lucy; my little princesses

PROLOGUE

Apolline giggled from under her bed, watching her Aunt Fantine's feet as she paced the room.

"Apolline? Where has she gone?"

Apolline giggled again.

"I thought I heard something."

Apolline gasped and covered her mouth.

The bed skirt flew back and the round face of Fantine appeared, making Apolline screech and giggle.

"Found you!"

"No!" Apolline dashed out, wrapping her arms around Fantine's wide waist. "I got you, Aunt Fantine!"

Fantine laughed and lifted her up in a tight squeeze. "It's getting late now, dearie."

"Tell me a story."

"All right." Fantine set Apolline on the bed.

Apolline grasped her blankets and wrapped herself up so only her face showed.

Aunt Sophronia, a tall, slender woman with cropped auburn hair, glanced in with a scowl as she twisted two metallic rods in her hand.

"Why is she still awake?"

"Hush, Sophronia," Fantine scolded. "A few minutes of extra play and a story won't hurt."

Sophronia sighed. "Just keep her quiet."

Apolline poked out her tongue as Sophronia moved on.

"I saw that!" Ashlan, the youngest of the three aunts, appeared in front of Apolline with a pinkish glow. She bent over and kissed Apolline's forehead. "Don't sass her, Apolline."

"She's a mean fairy," Apolline responded with a frown. "Fairies are supposed to be nice."

"I heard that," Sophronia called down the hall.

The three of them giggled. Ashlan kissed Apolline's head again. "Don't forget her potion, Fantine."

"I know. I never do." Fantine sat in the chair beside Apolline's bed with a book in her lap, and slipped a small bottle and spoon from the satchel attached to the waistband of her skirt.

"Why do I have to drink that every night?" Apolline pouted. "It tastes awful."

"It will keep the ogres away," Fantine responded as she poured a spoonful.

Apolline shuddered. "Are ogres real? I've never seen one. Joshua from school says they're made up."

"They are very real." Ashlan sat on the end of the bed as Apolline swallowed the potion. "As real as the space-pirates and drunks."

"Gross."

Fantine ran her knuckles down Apolline's cheek. "I'm glad you feel that way. Now, shall I read?"

"No." Apolline shot up. "I want a fairytale."

"Oh, you know I'm no good at those," Fantine said with a twinkle in her eye.

"You're the best, Aunt Fantine. Please, please, please?"

Fantine chuckled. "All right, as long as you lie down and hold tight to that bear of yours. Tonight I'm going to tell you about the lost Princess Elpida."

"I like this one," Apolline said in a hushed voice. She shuffled down and curled up with her toy bear.

"Once upon a time, there lived a handsome young prince named Hernan."

"That's King Hernan now, right?"

"That's right." Fantine touched Apolline's head. "Now, he fell in love with a beautiful young maiden named Cytheria and they married. They were so in love, and the whole kingdom rejoiced when the king and queen discovered they were to have a daughter."

"Because King Brencis and Queen Miriam already had a son," Apolline said, sitting up. "So they all knew their children would unite the twin kingdoms."

"Yes. Apolline dear, would you let me tell the story?"

"Sorry." She grinned and shuffled back under her blankets.

"But, the evil sorceress, Bryanna, was jealous of their love. So she plotted the child's demise before she was even born.

"Now, King Hernan and Queen Cytheria had three fairies bonded to them, and fairies give gifts when a child is born to help the child through life. So, after the birth, the fairies came to give their gifts. The first fairy gave the baby the gift of intelligence, so she could learn quickly and have a clear and thoughtful mind. The second fairy gave the gift of inner strength, so the baby could grow into an independent and unwavering Queen. But the third fairy—"

"The third fairy waited," Apolline interrupted. "Because she felt like something was wrong."

"Fantine is telling the story." Ashlan squeezed Apolline's little leg. "You are supposed to be closing your eyes and falling to sleep."

Apolline closed her eyes tightly.

Fantine chuckled and continued. "And the third fairy was right, too, because in that moment of hesitation, Bryanna appeared and placed a curse on the baby. She said that on the princess' twenty-first birthday, she would prick her finger on a spinning wheel and die.

"Cytheria begged her to take the curse back, but Bryanna disappeared, leaving the king and queen to mourn for their child.

"But the third fairy hadn't given her gift. So she touched the baby's lips with her wand and said that she would not die, but fall into a deep sleep, and rise again with true love's kiss.

"The king made every precaution to prevent the curse reaching fulfillment. He destroyed any spinning wheels he could find, and even changed the way wool was spun to remove the needles from the process. The betrothal for the prince and princess was signed.

"But Bryanna discovered the counter curse, so she set out to kill the baby. Queen Cytheria called the fairies together and ordered them to hide the child until she reached her twenty-first birthday, when she would be required to return and marry the prince."

"Fantine," Ashlan whispered. "She's asleep."

Fantine looked down at Apolline, her face pressed against the teddy bear as she snored softly. "Good night, my little Princess."

She kissed her head as she stood to leave. Ashlan waved her wand to turn out the light.

CHAPTER ONE

Waiting, watching, I lay under the scrub. With the crossbow held firmly, I set the trigger. I ran my tongue over the blade of the dagger clenched between my teeth, ready to slit the deer-like yuckah's throat if I didn't hit it right on target.

A young stag stepped into my line of vision. He sniffed the air and lowered his head to graze on the wiry grass. Resting my finger over the trigger, I lined up my laser point and flicked, releasing the arrow. The yuckah grunted and fell to the ground, bucking for a moment before falling limp.

"Perfect." My dagger fell into my hand when I spoke. Standing, I brushed off the dirt and leaves from my cotton shirt and I headed over to my kill.

The buck released his dying breath as I bent over him. I rested my hand on his side, the soft fur tingling with magic. "Thanks, buddy."

I wrapped a rope around his hind legs and slit his throat to bleed him. Tossing the rope over a branch, I pulled until he hung upside down and rested a bowl beneath him to catch the blood now oozing from the slit in his throat.

I set up traps to ward off scavengers, then whipped out my pad to initiate the sensors. Little green lights flashed onto the screen as a map of the woods I made for myself showed where I had set traps. Nothing out of the ordinary.

I headed back to my earlier kill. Once I poured the blood from the doe into a jar, I retrieved my magic cart from the bushes. I dumped the doe in, setting the jar of blood beside her, and pulled my cart through the woods back to the stag. The wood creaked as it slowly expanded to make enough room to carry both yuckah.

As I approached, a young wolf circled the carcass. Whipping out my revolver, I fired to the right of it. The wolf yelped and scurried away.

"Bloody scavengers."

Taking pity, I sliced the yuckah's belly open and left its stomach, liver, and intestines for the wolf. A wolf on its own was a sad creature.

I hummed as I made my way back to the cottage. I enjoyed hunting. To hunt yuckah was a skill few people acquired, so the work also brought in good money. Every day I felt grateful for Sophronia's impatience with me as a twelve-year-old.

I'd spent almost an hour stomping up and down the stairs of the cottage, reciting my math homework, then my spelling, then the history of Mish, our planet. She grew fed up with me and marched out of her study, grabbing me by the ear.

"I'm trying to work, Apolline!" she snarled. "Your noise is driving me insane."

She took me to the shed where a rifle and a crossbow sat on the table. I screamed and cried, begging her not to kill me.

"I'm not going to kill you. I'm not a sadist."

"What's a sadist?"

She groaned. "Pick up the gun."

She proceeded to show me how to load and shoot the gun. It took me a couple of weeks to be good enough to actually hunt. When she finally did take me out, I cried over my first kill.

"It's just a rabbit, Apolline," she said, picking up the dead, fluffy creature by the ears. "Toughen up."

"But it's so cute."

"And it tastes good, too. Now stop your sniveling."

I forced back my tears with deep, quivering breaths.

"Better. Now, follow me so I can show you how to gut and skin it."

I cried through the whole procedure, making her even more irritated with me.

Thinking back on that experience, I couldn't help chuckling. Unlike Fantine and Ashlan, my other fairy "aunts," Sophronia had never been fond of me, so she tolerated my presence just long enough for me to get a taste for the hunt. I think her patience only lasted because she knew she would get me out of her way in the end.

I stepped into the small clearing in front of the cottage. To my right, the wooden shed sat with its doors still hung open from when I left. Pulling my cart in, I dragged the doe onto my butchering table.

As I worked, the cottage door squeaked open and then slammed shut.

"Apolline!" Ashlan, the youngest of the three fairies, appeared at the door of the shed. Her long, blonde hair shone as she looked around the doorway, her brown eyes sparkling. Then she stared at my bloodied hands. "Oh my."

"Hello, Ashlan."

"That's horrible. Why must you do that?"

"They fetch a pretty kep, and I know how much you love new dresses."

She rolled her eyes and pressed her hand against her hip. "Why don't you buy yourself a dress? Those pants and boots do nothing for you. You are pretty underneath all this... filth."

She pinched my arm, and I slapped her away. She didn't look much older than me, about twenty-five, but she certainly held the position of the most beautiful woman on the planet. With a petite frame, and long, thick eyelashes, she always caused trouble when she went into town. Although, no one ever mentioned how she never seemed to age. She'd looked to be in her mid-twenties for as long as I could remember.

Mind you, no one wanted to bring up that my aunts were fairies and end up having their memories wiped by Sophronia.

"Apolline, sweetie, why don't you try doing something a little more lady-like once in a while?"

"Ladylike?" I sliced the doe's chest cavity open and worked to cut the heart free. "Everyone knows the queen of Tyrone hunts yuckah, as well."

"Yes, but she has servants to deal with them afterward."

"Are you telling me she misses out on the best part?" I lifted the heart in front of Ashlan's face and squeezed it, making blood ooze down my arm.

"Urgh." She scrunched her nose. "Sophronia wants to see you."

"What for?" I set the heart in a jar for Fantine.

"She wants you to go into town to buy some supplies."

I stepped out and turned on the hose to wash my hands. "Lucky I killed two yuckah today, isn't it?"

"Just hurry. You know how impatient she is with you." She turned on her heel and skipped into the house.

Nothing seemed to faze Ashlan. She lived with her head in the clouds. I shook my head and smiled as I wiped my hands. Raising me hadn't been the plan. They told me they found me one night when I was a baby, and Fantine and Ashlan fell in love. Sophronia only agreed to keep me so she could study human growth patterns. The truth is fairies need human bonds to make their magic stronger. So as much as Sophronia hated to admit it, she needed me as much as I did her and the other two as a child. A child's heart is too pure for a fairy to pass up.

I entered the cottage, inhaling the strange scent of Fantine brewing something, probably a new experiment since the odor wasn't familiar. I climbed the stairs and made my way down the hall to Sophronia's office and lifted my hand to knock.

"What took you so long?"

I lowered my fist and opened the door at the sound of her voice. "I had to wash up."

"Mmm." She pursed her lips, no longer interested in me. She turned to the large bookshelf across the wall behind her desk. All kinds of strange things rested on the shelves; pieces of magical creatures, skeletons, magically enhanced technology, boxes full of data chips, and, of course, books. The room in general was dark and sterile, especially since she kept the drapes pulled closed. "I need you to pick up some things for me in town."

She slid a piece of notepaper across the desk for me.

I plucked it up, scanning the list. "It looks like you're making a dress."

"Mmm. Your birthday is coming up."

I huffed. "I don't need a dress. Who wears dresses out here anyway? Plus, since when do *you* make dresses, or anything for that matter?"

Her green eyed gaze turned to me as her brow slowly rose. "Apolline."

"I don't want a—"

She lifted her hand and snapped her fingers shut. My mouth sealed closed so I couldn't speak.

"This dress is for your twenty-first birthday. You know that means you will meet your betrothed, so we need you to look presentable... for once." She tossed a purse of miroans across the table at me. "This should be enough."

She twirled her finger, making me spin and march out the door. As soon as the door slammed behind me, my lips unsealed. I growled. "I hate it when you do that!"

"Hurry up. You need to be home before dark."

I growled again, crushing the paper.

Fantine popped her head out of her lab door. "Apolline, you're going in to town?"

"I am." I walked toward her, curious to see what she'd mixed up.

"Good! I needed a store run. Come in." Her head disappeared, and I darted in after her.

I loved her lab; it appealed to my gory side. She, like Sophronia, had animal parts on shelves, but Fantine's were in jars and cans to be used for her potions. Canisters of powder made from who knows what sat in stacks between the jars, and the table in the center had burns, stains, and scars from failed attempts at all kinds of potions.

She grabbed a notepad and scrawled down a few items. "Do you need any money, dear?"

"Money is always appreciated."

She smiled as she handed me the list. "Of course it is. It's not like you'd help me out by using some trading credits for some of those dead creatures out there."

"Mmm, not likely. I need a new set of arrows."

She smiled that warm smile I knew so well. It lit her whole face, and met me each day growing up as I arose, and when I came home from school. When I looked into her round face and chubby cheeks, it gave me a sense of security.

"Hurry, then. You know the woods are full of predators after dark."

She gave my thigh a slap as I left the room.

I hurried down the stairs and Ashlan appeared at the landing, beaming up at me. "So, what color do you think you'll pick for your dress? I think a deep pink would look divine against your skin. You have lovely skin under this muck."

I brushed by her and headed for the shed.

"I think maybe a trim for your hair might be in order, too. It's pretty long. Don't get me wrong, it's thick and has a healthy shine when you brush it..."

I twisted my hair up into a bun on top of my head.

"And it has a lovely color, too. Chestnut is stunning, and your blue eyes just pop..."

I tuned her out. She always dressed me up like a doll as a child, but now that I'd grown too old for that, she'd just go on and on, begging me to let her play with my hair, or something else to make me look "pretty." I had no desire to look pretty. We lived on an outer perimeter planet where girls who made themselves look pretty usually were whores.

I grabbed a yuckah I'd killed the day before, wrapped it in plastic to keep it clean and frozen, and dumped it into the cart. Quickly collecting some skins while Ashlan continued rambling, I set off down the trail toward town.

Ashlan followed.

I glanced back at her. "I'm heading out now."

"I know. I'm coming too."

"Why?"

She huffed, apparently annoyed that I'd interrupted her rambling. "Someone needs to make sure you don't pick something horrible for the dress. I don't trust your taste."

"Thanks." I turned, rolling my eyes.

She chatted continuously as we made our way out of the woods. We reached the edge of town and I opened the gate, while Ashlan stood back talking away, watching me as I wedged it open, pulled my cart through, and closed it again. I wondered why the fence was even there since anyone other than me and the fairies that entered always ended back at the gate again. Enchanted woods were good like that.

I waved to the elderly people who lived along the way. Not many people lived on Mish. There wasn't much to do, so unless someone inherited a farm or small business, they left to go out pirating or, if they were lucky, an apprenticeship on a more central planet.

We reached the edge of town where the usual drunks sat on the pub porch watching the slow-paced town.

Ashlan waved, batting her eyelashes. "Hello, gentlemen."

They all sat up, straightening their shirts and flattening their hair. "Hello, Ashlan."

I grabbed her arm, irritated. "Why do you always—"

"No, she waved at me!"

One of the drunks hit another and a fight broke out. I scowled at Ashlan. "You know that *always* happens when you acknowledge them."

She pushed me off. "You can be so *boring*. Live a little, flirt a little."

I moaned. "I'm betrothed, remember? You genius' hooked that up before I could even walk."

"Don't complain, Apolline." She pinched my arm. "How were we to know non-aristocrats don't do betrothals? We wanted you to be taken care of. We can't watch over you forever."

"Technically, you can," I said, giving the cart a pull as we headed toward the general store. "How old are you now? Two hundred and eighty something? And Fantine's around the four hundred mark. Who knows how old Sophronia is."

"A lady doesn't discuss her age." Ashlan folded her arms, glancing at me out of the corner of her eye. "And I'm only two eighty-two. Sophronia is the old one. She's six ninety-eight."

I smirked. "Nice."

She grinned. "Just take these in to Charlie. I'm tired of looking at all these sliced up body parts. I'll go to the dressmaker for you."

She tugged the money from my belt and hurried down the street.

I pulled my cart around to the ramp for the store, and headed in. A soft bell tinkled, announcing my entrance. I glanced around at the five aisles. Laser guns and exotic treasures lined the wooden shelving, set there by Charlie after he traded food for them. He had no use for such trinkets, but the pirates and traders often liked to buy them to appear wealthier.

The soft voice of the news announcer played above me on the holo-projector. I glanced up at the man whose head was about the size of my hand. He was covering some kind of celebration on one of the other Oran Kingdom planets.

"Apolline."

I snapped my head around to the counter as Charlie appeared from the food storage room out back. "Hey, Charlie. I brought some stock for you."

"I can see." He stepped around and looked into my cart with his hands on his hips. "A large kill here."

"Yup. That one was a full grown buck. Sophronia took the antlers, sorry."

"That's all right. I'm not sure how I'm going to pay you for all this." His pale blue eyes sparkled. A man in his forties, he'd become like a father to me since he moved to Mish when I was a child. He'd abandoned his position in the Oran courts after his wife and daughter were killed.

I pulled out Fantine's list. "Will this help?"

"Ah!" He smiled and took the paper from me, squinting as he struggled to read her writing. "Brilliant woman that Fantine, but she has terrible handwriting. I'm telling you, you should buy her a pad."

"I've tried," I said as he lifted the frozen yuckah to weigh it. "She goes on about not needing new-fangled toys to get by in life, and all I end up accomplishing is catching a few minutes of sleep."

He laughed. "Sometimes I wish I was a fly on the wall in that cottage." He set the yuckah on the scales and let out a soft whistle. "I'm glad I'm expecting a royal shipment tomorrow. Only the palaces would pay for this."

I stood taller, quite proud of myself.

"Let me tally up how much Fantine's request will cost and I'll take it out of your payment for this. I'd say he's worth five hundred miroans."

I let out a quick laugh. "My best kill yet!"

"You've become quite a good huntress." He lifted the yuckah and set it back in the cart. "I'll check out these skins and organs and pay you when I get back. I'll put Fantine's things in the cart. Can you watch the store while I do this?"

"No problem." I slid up onto the counter as he pulled my cart out back.

I drummed my fingers on the wooden counter, until my attention was drawn to the news broadcast. Images of giants crushing a town made me shoot to my feet and stand below the projector, watching.

"These are the latest images from the lower perimeter of the Tyronian kingdom," the reporter said. "It seems that with the date fast approaching for Bryanna's curse to be fulfilled, she is becoming more desperate. These petty attacks on weaker planets are growing more frequent, but authorities are still unable to catch her..."

The bell tinkled, announcing someone had entered, but I was too enthralled to care.

"Some believe Prince Allard's presence in the royal Tyronian capital over the past year provoked the most recent round of attacks, saying that he visited his soon-to-be in-laws to secretly meet the princess. The royal families have given no comments on the matter at this time."

"Excuse me? Is there someone around who can help me?"

I turned, irritated at the interruption. "What do you want?"

A young man in the black Oranian military uniform glanced over his shoulder at me as he stood by the counter. "You work here?"

"Sort of." I looked up at the projector again. "What do you need?"

"I'm picking up some supplies."

"Like what?"

He stepped up behind me. "What's so interesting?"

I shuffled forward, not liking how close he stood. "News. It's so awful."

"It's actually not as bad as it looks. The media really hypes it up and picks out the worst parts," the man said in a heavy, central Oran Kingdom accent, speaking rounded vowels and precise consonants.

I narrowed my eyes and looked at him. "And who are you, then?"

He laughed lightly. "I'm in the military, and I spent some time in that sector. The people of Tyrone are very afraid. They don't know whether their princess, who was their hope, has died, or will ever come back. And if she does, will the sorceress return to attack and seek her revenge?" He wiggled his fingers in the air for dramatic effect.

I groaned. "Who wants some weak little pampered princess who's probably been hiding out in a convent anyway? How is some girl who has been isolated all her life supposed to suddenly step up and lead the two kingdoms by the side of prince what's-his-name?"

"Prince Allard."

"That's the one. I mean come on, I could probably do a better job, and I'm a simple huntress and trader."

"A very opinionated huntress and trader."

Blood rushed to my cheeks. "I'm sorry. I really do let my mouth get the better of me sometimes."

"That's all right, it's quite refreshing. Most women in the central planets are quiet and dull, rarely showing any sort of conviction on any topic except their hair."

"Ah, yes, you should meet my Aunt Ashlan. She's probably worse than all of them."

He grinned. With a slight dimple in his cheek, combined with his dark hair and brown eyes, his good looks made my heart skip a beat. I stepped back, uncomfortable in the presence of someone so attractive. "So, what do you need?"

His eyes twinkled as he handed me a pad. "We're heading into Oran and were sent orders to pick up the shipment the palace ordered."

"Oh." I looked at the pad that displayed a substantial order for yuckah meat. "Oh! You're keeping me in business." I motioned to a stuffed buck's head on the wall.

"You're not just any old huntress then. Yuckah are difficult to catch."

I shrugged. "It doesn't seem too difficult." I slid over the counter and opened the door for the back storage area. "Charlie! The palace order came early! I'm sending it through to your computer so you can bring it out when you're ready!"

"Okay!" he hollered back.

I entered Charlie's computer code and the receipt sent. I looked up to give the man his pad back and found him smirking. "What?"

"That was... impressive. Very classy."

I rolled my eyes. "Look around you. This isn't a ballroom."

He took his pad and slid it into his pocket, then stretched out his hand. "Allard."

"Ahh, so that's why you remembered the prince's name. I guess it *was* popular for a while there." I slid over the counter again. "There's a ton of Theo's among the elderly here, and of course Brencis is popular among the forty-something's. I knew a handful of Allard's at school, but they're all gone now."

"You know how people are, naming their kids after royals." He stuck his hand in front of my chest. "And you are?"

I stared at his hand, unsure if introducing myself was wise. The fairies always warned me against giving personal information to strangers. But when I looked up into his eyes, something about him, a certain kindness within, told me he was harmless. I grabbed his hand. "Apolline."

"It's nice to meet you, Apolline." He squeezed my hand.

I pulled free, my belly fluttering. "So, what brings you out this way?"

"My vessel has been traveling around, keeping the peace. This is our last stop before returning to Oran."

I looked him over in his uniform with the Oran Kingdom crest over his heart. Then I noticed the stripes on his shoulder. "An officer?"

He nodded, his stare locked on my face.

I turned away from him, his gaze making me uneasy. "How's that peace-keeping working out for you?"

He sighed. "Not so well. The Tyronians unfortunately saw our presence as a threat to their crown. They believe Oran is eager to take the kingdom rather than unify."

"I thought that was likely if the princess remains... lost."

I looked back over my shoulder at him staring up at the projector. "It is, but the king doesn't want that. King Brencis trusts King Hernan, and he believes him when he says the princess is alive and well."

The bell tinkled again and Ashlan entered behind Allard. She glanced around and set the new fabric on the counter. Her focus turned to Allard quickly, then to me. Our eyes met and she grinned, mouthing, *He's cute, flirt a little.*

Allard turned to follow my gaze, but Ashlan darted behind a shelf and out of sight. I scowled after her before looking back at Allard. "You know a great deal about the royals."

He shrugged. "Only what I see on the news. Occasionally we get extra top secret information about them from our ranking officers, but that's rare."

"Well, I don't care what they do, as long as I can keep doing what I'm doing."

He laughed. "Sounds fair; this seems like a pleasant enough planet."

"It is, I guess." I gestured toward the treasures on the shelves of the store. "If you don't count the pirates and drunks."

He laughed. It felt good to have someone my own age talking to me. Growing up, there were very few people my age. The planet had one school and most of the children were farmers and teased me about being an orphan who lived in 'the haunted woods'. Along with everyone being superstitious about fairies and not mentioning their presence, I was avoided like the plague.

"So, what do you do around here? You don't strike me as the pirating type."

I gestured at the yuckah head again. "Hunt, mostly. Nothing much else to do. Luckily, I enjoy it."

He grinned. "I have to say, I'm impressed. Most women would be horrified by the thought of killing an animal."

I clasped my elbow, again feeling uneasy. "Ah, well, I do what I need to."

He leaned closer. "May I—?"

Charlie banged a box down on a crate hovering an inch from the floor, making both me and Allard start. "There you are, sir. That will be three thousand, five hundred and twenty-four miroans and four kep. We have a free teleport service, too, if you would like?"

"No, thank you, good storekeeper."

Allard handed Charlie a card, nodding politely, and Charlie swiped it on the register. "Royal guard, eh?"

"Yes, and we must return quickly. Thank you for your goods." Allard placed a teleport signal on the crate and it vanished, then he turned to me. "I will try to visit you soon, Apolline. It is nice to have a conversation with someone who doesn't have an agenda."

He pressed a button on his wrist pad, then he, too, disappeared.

"Hoity-toity, rich, central planet scum. They think they own the place," Charlie muttered as he put the miroans in my pouch.

Ashlan appeared beside me, grinning. "He was cute though, right? *I* thought he was adorable."

"I don't think it matters," I answered, trying to force back my fluster as I took my pouch.

Charlie waved a finger at me. "You be careful with those sorts, Apolline. Young, handsome, charming... they're the worst!"

I laughed. "I know they are, Charlie. But don't worry, I'm betrothed, remember?"

CHAPTER TWO

Allard straightened his official Prince of Oran coat. The deep blue with the royal crest —a deeply rooted tree forming a circle in the shield, with a mermaid around its trunk—embroidered over his heart was tradition, going back several hundred years. Although forward thinking and advanced, the people loved tradition, especially when it came to the royal family.

He sighed, running his hand over his dark, cropped military hair. He'd grow it back now that his time in the service was done—another one of those traditions, serving in the military for a year after completing his Master's degree.

"Highness," his guard, Donald, said over the intercom.

Allard looked at himself in the mirror, seeing the discouraged look in his eyes where only a year ago, they'd been so bright with hope. "Yes, Don?"

"We have docked at the space station for Oran."

"Thank you. I'll be out in a moment."

Allard sniffed and straightened his shoulders, then left his quarters. Donald stood by his door as he stepped out, and gave him a quick salute.

Allard nodded. "Good to be home."

"Yes, sir."

Even Don, who had served at Allard's side every day since he turned eighteen, treated him with complete respect. Allard thought about the huntress, Apolline from Mish, and how she didn't realize who he was. He wished more people would talk to him like she did; without pretense.

"Shall we?" Allard said.

"Yes, sir."

Allard marched down the corridor and disembarked from the ship. The space station hallways cleared to make way for the prince as he headed for his shuttle home. This didn't faze Allard in the slightest. He'd become used to everyone making way for him, pausing their daily lives as he passed by. In fact, he barely even noticed.

They landed on the palace platform. Allard's father, King Brencis, waited in the doorway, a huge grin stretched across his face. Allard looked nothing like his father who once had thick, blond hair, but now thinned at the top, with flecks of silver. He reached Allard's nose in height, and was about twice Allard's width around the middle.

Allard hurried out of the shuttle and embraced his father. "It's good to see you again."

"And you, my boy." Brencis patted his back. He looked up at Allard with his wide grin and proud blue eyes. Brencis was known for his jovial nature, and the only times that smile vanished was when he entered the courts.

"We have so much to catch up on," Allard said.

"Indeed." Brencis squeezed his shoulders. "But you should freshen up first. I know how those military vessels are."

Allard smirked. "Yes, awful. But I have so much I want to talk to you about."

"All right, a compromise. I sit in your lounge while you freshen up, and you tell me everything through the bathroom doorway."

Allard chuckled. "Sounds great."

They made their way to Allard's chambers, and once Allard showered and dressed in comfortable pants and a shirt, he sat in front of his father on an armchair. "What a trip."

"It was a big deal for you." Brencis stretched his arms across the back of the couch. "You've never spent so long with Hernan and Cytheria. Did you enjoy them?"

"Very much," Allard responded, relaxing back. "I always liked them when they came here, especially Cytheria; she is so much fun."

"And that was why Hernan fell in love instantly."

Allard smirked. "I'm sure her beauty helped with that."

Brencis' eyes darkened. "Hernan isn't like that."

"I know," Allard said with a sigh. "Hernan is remarkable. He's under so much pressure to bring Elpida home early because everyone is so afraid, but he refuses. When he enters a room, you can feel his presence. People who meet him are in awe of him. If I could be a king like that..." Allard shook his head, letting out a soft whistle.

"He has been my best friend for many years, and every moment I've respected and admired his courage."

Allard looked into his father's eyes. "My time there made me think about Elpida a great deal."

Brencis' face lit up again. "I bet."

"I've never really thought much about marrying her. It was just something I knew would eventually happen, but being with them, getting to know them on a deeper level, made me wonder what she's like. There's barely a few months left until I marry her, and I don't even know what she looks like."

Brencis' arms dropped to his lap as he leaned forward. "You understand why."

"Of course I do, it's just..." He groaned. "She's going to be my *wife*. What if she's been locked up in a convent and is duller than all the courtiers combined? What if she drives me crazy?"

"Son." Brencis leaned over and grasped his knee. "If she's as beautiful as her mother and as clever as her father, she will be a prize catch. Trust that some of their traits will be in her. I see your mother in you every day, why wouldn't Elpida be the same way?"

"Yes, I'm just nervous." Allard lowered his voice. "What if she doesn't like me?"

Brencis laughed loudly. "She will adore you! You are handsome and charming and women fall at your feet. Hernan had that gift, but not me. You must have inherited it from your mother; she was remarkable like you."

"Father." Allard scowled. "You are remarkable too."

Brencis smiled proudly. "You're a good son. Trust your heart and everything will be fine."

They continued talking for over an hour about everything Allard did while in Tyrone. Their conversation only ended when Brencis received a call. He slipped out his pad, unfolding it to answer, and the prime minister popped up on the screen.

"Majesty, your guests have arrived."

"Ah! Perfect. Thank you, Gerald." He disconnected and stood. "Well, Allard, would you like to join me?"

Allard's eyebrows shot up. "Like this?"

The king's gaze swept over his son's casual attire. "Hmm, yes, get changed and meet in me the lobby." He patted Allard's shoulder. "It's good to have you back."

Allard smiled as his father left. Once the door shut, he flopped back, letting out a long sigh. He shut his eyes and Apolline's face popped into his mind. He enjoyed her ignorance of his identity. But more than anything, he wanted to enjoy her easy conversation again.

That thought made him feel guilty. He'd never had a problem with his betrothal to Elpida. It happened when he was only three, so he never knew any differently. But with the marriage fast approaching, he thought about it more and more.

Apolline had appeared right when he least wanted it. No other woman had ever sparked his attention, but all other women he'd met swooned in his presence. Did wanting to kindle a friendship with her dishonor his betrothal?

He shook his head as he stood. He could be friends with whomever he wanted; it didn't mean he was breaking anything.

He pressed his intercom. "Don."

"Yes, sir," his guard responded.

"Send someone to Mish for me and find a huntress named Apolline. Find out when she goes to town for trade."

Don hesitated. "Sir..."

"Don't worry, she's just a friend." Allard paused, shaking his head at his own words. "Just do as I say. I won't break any oaths."

"Yes, sir."

As he changed into his dress pants, shirt, and vest, he thought about Apolline again. He shook his head again. He needed to stop.

Once dressed, he headed down to the lobby. As he reached the grand stairway, the voices of his father and Hernan drifted to him. He slowed his pace and peeked around the corner.

On the black leather couch sat King Hernan, with Queen Cytheria beside him. Hernan ran his fingers through Cytheria's long, blonde hair, and his hand rested on her waist. Allard moved out slowly, watching the three of them, and like everyone else, marveling at Cytheria's beauty. In her late thirties, Cytheria didn't seem to be touched by age. Her skin and hair looked as flawless as ever.

"Allard!" Brencis shot to his feet.

Allard paused as the three of them stood to look at him.

Cytheria beamed and rushed over. "Hello, Allard. I bet it feels good to be home." She grasped his hands, her dark blue eyes sparkling up at him. "How were the perimeter planets?"

He stared at her, momentarily dazzled. "Yes, it is good to be home." He cleared his throat. "The perimeter planets were rough and wild, but they didn't seem as war torn as I expected. In fact, most could probably fend off an attack on their own."

Cytheria let out a soft laugh, the sound of it making him tingle. He knew she hated how much men admired her, but the years of excessive fairy magic exposure had seeped into her skin, permanently altering her to make her stunning in every way.

Hernan stepped beside her, offering his hand to Allard. "It's good to see you again."

Allard shook his hand. "And you, sir."

Hernan laughed. "Sir? Allard, you don't need to speak to me so formally."

"Sorry."

Cytheria looked up at Hernan, smiling warmly. She touched his chestnut hair, now flecked with silver, then spoke to Allard. "These two are talking politics again. Shall we go for a stroll in the gardens?"

"Of course," Allard answered, offering her his arm.

She grasped it firmly. "The maze?"

He grinned.

Hernan kissed Cytheria's head. "Don't cause too much trouble." He turned to Brencis. "Shall we?"

"Of course." Brencis grasped Hernan's shoulder and they made their way to a conference room.

Cytheria patted Allard's hand. "Let's go."

She pulled him, and they hurried out the glass doors to the gardens. As they strolled around the pond, Allard said, "I've been thinking more and more of Elpida of late."

Her arm tightened around his. "Oh?"

"Mmm." He stared at the water. "There's less than three months until we marry."

"It's gone fast," she said airily.

"Tell me honestly." He looked into her eyes. "When did you see her last?"

She smiled, but a tear glistened in her eye. "She was a year old. I know many think we see her in secret, but we don't. Bryanna watches our movements too closely to risk that. No, I am as anxious to see her as you are."

"My father says if she is as beautiful as you, and as clever as Hernan, I shall be a lucky man."

"Bite your tongue." She slapped his hand. "No one should be cursed with as much beauty as me. Men constantly watch me, desiring me. Several times, I've almost been abducted. Even Bryanna's hate is fueled in part by it. My hope is that Elpida looks like her father. He is a handsome man, and his face would look pretty on a young woman."

Allard nodded. "But what if we don't get along? What if she's never seen a man? I wish I could talk to her just once before we marry."

Cytheria gazed off as they paused outside the entry to the maze. "I wonder similar things. What if she resents me for sending her away? What if she wants nothing to do with me? But I must trust the fairies. They are wise and will do what's best for her and the kingdoms."

"Three months," Allard said on a sigh as he stared into the maze. "After a lifetime of waiting, it feels surreal."

She patted his arm as she kicked off her shoes. "I completely understand. Now, I will beat you this time." She darted into the maze.

He smirked and kicked off his own shoes, setting them and hers to the side, before darting into the maze after her.

Bryanna ran her fingers over the crystal ball. Allard wasn't even trying to beat Cytheria. Everyone always pampered her. Bryanna growled and waved her hand over the crystal, making the image vanish. Only three months left and the princess continued to elude her. She had found her several times in the beginning, but then Sophronia removed Bryanna's planet, Mahkba, from the galaxy, then vanished.

Now, in the darkness, Mahkba moved in the drag of the galaxy's gravity.

A mirror lit up. Turning to face the rows that filled the dark room, Bryanna watched the mirror's surface shift and quake as it changed into a portal.

A rat leaped through. It scrambled onto her desk, sitting up on its haunches. "Good news, my queen."

"Yes?" She leaned forward, hoping for some sign of Elpida.

"The prince has sent men out to watch a maiden, a huntress, from the agricultural planet of Mish."

She sat up, her green eyes glowing. "The prince?"

"Yes, my queen."

She waved her hand over her crystal again, and a serpent appeared. "Serpent."

It lifted its head. "I hear you, my queen. How may I serve?"

"I need you to go to Mish and watch a huntress named..."

"Apolline," the rat squeaked.

"Apolline. Tell me what kind of interest the prince has in her."

A different mirror, further back in the room, lit up, and the serpent slithered through, searched the room quickly, then slid into another mirror.

Bryanna stroked the rat's back. "Very well done. We could use this to our advantage. If he returns to the planet, I want to know immediately. Keep a close eye on him in the palace, and if he even hints that his loyalty to Elpida is shifting onto this huntress, I want to know."

"Yes, my queen." The rat jumped down and scampered back through the mirror from which it came.

Bryanna leaned back, stroking her crystal ball. "Mirror, who is the fairest of them all?"

The mirror directly in front of her swirled with clouds, then Cytheria's face formed as the mirror spoke in a male voice. "The Queen of Tyrone."

Bryanna clenched her fist. She hated Cytheria like none other, the little thief. "Mirror, who is the most handsome of them all?"

The mirror seemed to hesitate, then, Hernan appeared. "The King of Tyrone."

"Did you hesitate, mirror?"

"I cannot answer that question."

"Mmm." Hernan's face had appeared instantly for many years. The mirror's pause showed that his aging was finally catching up with him, and another man would soon appear in the mirror.

She stared at King Hernan, his brown eyes captivating her. She blinked and shook her head, then looked down at the crystal. "Show me Cytheria again."

Cytheria appeared, sitting beside Prince Allard on the fountain located in the middle of the maze. Her smile made the young prince's gaze dance across her face, dazzling him like every other man who gazed upon her. But he looked away. He fought the urge to stare and gawk at her.

"Noble prince." Bryanna ran her finger down her cheek. "More like your mother than your father."

She scowled, remembering her younger years; Miriam with her dark hair and eyes, charming the entire ballroom with her witty stories and sharp conversation, and of course her voice. No one could sing like Miriam did. Bryanna never understood why she fell for the buffoon, Brencis. Miriam never did things for status, so his royalty wouldn't have done it.

She ran her fingers over the crystal, making the image of Allard's face zoom closer. He smiled, talking quickly, making Cytheria hold her sides as she laughed. He chuckled, and Miriam's dimple appeared in his right cheek. Definitely more like his mother.

Cytheria's daughter didn't deserve him.

CHAPTER THREE

I **fidgeted and the needle pricked me. "Ouch!"**

"Then stop moving," Sophronia said in a threatening tone. She yanked at the fabric, cinching my waist.

Gasping, I rested my hand against the wall. "I have to breathe, and my legs are starting to hurt."

"You complain too much."

Ashlan glided into the room with a tray of sandwiches. "Who's hungry? I'm hungry."

"I am!" I reached over.

Sophronia slapped my arm. "Don't *move!*"

"Oh, Apolline!" Ashlan set down the tray and clasped her hands. "You will look so pretty in it when it's done."

"Hrmm mmm." I slumped.

"Stand up straight!" Sophronia jabbed me with a needle.

"Ouch! Vicious!"

"You want vicious?" She yanked hard on the corset, making me gasp again. "There."

"Sophronia." Ashlan slipped out her wand and loosened the corset.

"We've let her become spoiled," Sophronia grumbled.

Ashlan sighed and looked up at me standing on the wooden soap box. "Oh! You look so pretty! Just like when you were a little girl and I'd—"

"Don't remind me," I said.

"Stop making her talk!" Sophronia tossed her needle down. "This is incredibly frustrating."

Fantine burst into the cottage, muttering under her breath as she stirred her pot, then disappeared upstairs.

"What's she doing?" I asked, stepping after her.

Sophronia grasped my waist. "Hold. Still."

"You should have let *me* do this." Ashlan grabbed the hem, and with two flicks of the wrist, had it pinned.

"I can do menial tasks like sewing." Sophronia sat back, scowling.

"Are we done?" I stared up the stairs, hoping I wouldn't miss Fantine's dramatic, yet undesired, result to her concoction.

"Take it off." Sophronia waved her hand at me.

Ashlan helped me peel the dress back and untied the corset. Once free, I leaped up the stairs, sprinting for Fantine's lab. I leaped through the door just in time to see a hairless dog burst into flames and scream at her.

I laughed heartily as she added a dispersant into the potion. "Well that didn't work."

"What were you doing?"

"Trying to make a puppy."

"Fantine, even Sophronia can't create life." I sat on the stool facing her as she waved her wand to separate the chemicals. "Why are you even trying? Everyone knows you make the best 'medicine' on Mish."

"Healing potions? Ha!" She wrapped her fuzzy hair into a bun and tied it down. "What good are they when Sophronia conjures and manipulates everything, and Ashlan weaves enchantment spells? There's no wonder in potions."

"I don't know about that. You've healed me from self-inflicted injuries, and several people in town have miraculously lived longer than the doctor expected."

She chuckled, shaking her head. "This is why I like you, Apolline. You make me feel like I'm not a useless fairy."

"Far from useless." I leaned forward and whispered, "You're my favorite."

Her rosy cheeks flushed with color. "Apolline."

"Well, you are. How about you tell me a fairytale?"

She rolled her eyes. "Aren't you a bit old for those?"

"No. I love your fairytales. Why don't you tell me... hmm... Snow White?"

"Apolline."

"Please?" I grinned at her with large pleading eyes.

"You're almost twenty-one. I won't be doing this when you marry."

"Yes you will. You will tell my children and I will stand by the door and listen. Now, tell me Snow White."

She chuckled. "Once upon a time..."

I shuffled closer.

"There lived a beautiful young daughter of a Baron. When she was born, her mother looked at her pale skin and called her Snow. While she was still a girl, her mother died and her father remarried. But her step mother was jealous of Snow. She'd become so accustomed to being the most beautiful woman in their sector, that she resented Snow's shiny raven hair and flawless pale skin.

"Now, the story that most people hear says she was saved by a prince, but that's not so. When her step-mother tried to have her killed, she fled their planet and crash landed on the mining planet of the dwarves. Several dwarves raised her, and her father died of a broken heart when a report came in that she'd been killed by a pack of wolves while playing in the woods.

"So Snow grew into a woman, and worked as an administrator over the mines."

"Skip the boring bits," I said.

"Yes, yes, okay. Her step-mother remarried and had a daughter of her own. To celebrate the wedding, a pair of fairies came and gave an enchanted mirror to the baroness. It was intended for good, to show her the joys and blessings in her life, but she corrupted it for vanity. So when she asked it, 'Who is the fairest one of all?' to her horror, Snow appeared.

"Now, the dwarves' planet was owned by a Lord by the name of Timothy White. When he saw that, all of a sudden, the mines were more organized and productive than they had been in years, he visited the planet to investigate. He was shocked to find Snow pushing papers in the office, and sat down with her to discuss—"

"Boring."

"Yes, yes. Okay... so, they fell in love and were engaged. Timothy took her to his home planet for the engagement party, and there, unbeknownst to her, she met her step-mother's new husband. He was a greedy man who only married her step-mother for her beauty—and probably her money too—so when he saw Snow, he coveted her and plotted to abduct her."

"Now it's getting to the good part." I rubbed my hands together.

"How would you know? You'd usually fallen asleep by the time I reached this part."

"Yeah, because you never skipped the boring parts. Continue."

She shook her head. "But Snow's step-mother found out. Full of resentment and rage, she murdered her husband and sought out Snow to kill her, too. So she brewed a poisonous potion and dipped an apple into it.

"She disguised herself as an orphan, not an old hag like everyone seems to believe, and knocked on the door as an apple seller. She knew Snow's kindness would cause her to buy the apple.

"And Snow did, and to make the little girl smile, she bit into the apple and told her it tasted delicious. Then, she fainted. But the dwarves entered, and being able to see magic, several chased her step-mother away, while two stayed behind and made Snow vomit up the apple.

"But, some of the poison remained inside her, and she fell into a coma. When Timothy heard, he came straight to her and wept. A passing fairy felt his sorrow, and came to see if she could help."

"That was you, wasn't it?" I asked.

"It might have been," she said with a smirk. "But I am not bound to the Whites, so let's not get off topic. When I arrived, I saw the magic poison in Snow, so I drew it from her body and isolated it in her lips. I told Timothy to kiss her and the spell wouldn't hold because love conquers dark magic. He immediately obeyed, and as his lips broke away, her eyes fluttered open."

"So romantic." I sighed.

"But the step-mother hunted them for many years as she tried to take revenge. As a result, Snow lived among the dwarves so their magic could protect her. When her step-mother vanished—she probably died—Snow was finally able to join her husband on his planet where they lived and raised their children happily. Their descendants still live there."

I grinned and drummed my feet on the floor. "I just love your stories."

"You know they are all true," she said.

"Yes, I know that, but you tell them better than my history teachers did."

She tapped her temple. "That's because I remember them; they don't."

I laughed. "A plus side to being a fairy."

Sadness filled her eyes. She touched my cheek. "Yes and no."

I grabbed her hand. She loved me like her own child, but she would outlive me. I couldn't even imagine that kind of sadness. "It's a long time until you lose me, Fantine."

She smiled. "Yes, your life has barely begun."

I stood and wrapped my arms around her. "I love you."

She squeezed me. "You're a good girl, Apolline. I love you, too."

I untied the yuckah and it fell from the tree into my cart. As I adjusted it so it lay straight in the cart, movement caught my eye. I froze to listen. The soft rustling of something small to my left pricked my ears. I grabbed my revolver from my holster.

Then I saw it; a snake caught in one of my traps. I relaxed and grabbed a stick, pinning its head down as I released its body from the snare. I grabbed it behind its jaws and lifted it. "It's okay, buddy. I'll set you somewhere safe."

"I know you will."

I screamed and tossed the serpent. "You spoke!"

It shook its head from the impact and looked up at me. "What an astute observation."

I pointed my gun at it. "I've been warned about talking creatures. You're a product of dark magic."

"Aye, I am." It slithered onto a rock and curled up. "But I have been cast out. I am trapped on this lonely, forsaken planet at the edge of the galaxy. I thought maybe I could eat just a piece of your kill since I am incapable of hunting."

"I should kill you right now." I shuffled toward the cart. "But I'll give you one chance. If I ever see you again, I will kill you." I tossed it a dead rat I'd removed from a trap.

The snake slithered down, its tongue flickering over the rat. "You are kind and merciful, huntress. I will not forget."

I hurried to leave while it ate. I knew not to head back to the cottage in case it followed. The fairies had made it very clear never to lead anyone or anything back there. Instead, I headed into town. Being one of my usual days, no one would be surprised by me showing up. I'd have to gut the yuckah and handful of rabbits out the back of Charlie's store.

"Hello, Apolline," one of the younger drunks called as I passed the pub. "You are as pretty as ever."

"And you are as drunk as usual." I smirked at him.

"You're breaking my heart, princess." He clasped at his chest. "I love you."

"Go sober up."

He collapsed back onto his chair laughing. *Moron.*

I entered Charlie's store. He scrunched his nose when he saw the contents of my cart. "Gross. You know I hate it when you bring them here fresh."

"I'll use your butcher's room out back."

"Why didn't you go home?"

I paused. I didn't want to alarm him with the truth. "It's getting late. You know the fairies get crazy about me being out after dark. I didn't have time to go there and come back out again."

He shrugged. "True. Very well, go cut the beast to pieces."

I pulled the cart into the cool room by the freezer and went to work. Barely ten minutes passed before male voices drifted in from the store.

"I should have enough by Saturday," Charlie said in an impatient tone. "I keep telling you, my hunter can only catch so many at a time, and it's coming into breeding season, so the females are becoming scarce."

I silently trotted through the storage area and peeked in the door. Two men stood on the other side of the counter.

"What other magical items do you have in this store?" the taller one asked.

"I don't know. Go look around."

The men disappeared between the shelves.

I slipped out and stood beside Charlie. "They were here on Monday."

"Mmm. They came in yesterday, too. I think they must be the servants of someone wealthy who wants to throw a lavish party. They want to buy five yuckah. The one you brought me today brings me up to three. That royal shipment took all my stored meat."

"That's good. More money for you."

He nodded. "Yes, but I don't like being harassed. I wish they'd just stay at the inn until the time I said I'd have them."

One of the men reappeared, slowly eying me over. "Is this your hunter?"

Charlie stood taller. "That's none of your business."

"She's covered in blood."

I looked down at myself in the bloodied butcher's apron. "Yeah, I'm his huntress. Did you need help with understanding the magical qualities of the yuckah organs?"

His lip twitched. "No, thank you."

"Because if you're looking for magical items, yuckah organs have amazing healing qualities. One liver stewed can end menstrual cramping, not that you would need that, but it helps other severe cramping too."

"Ah, thanks."

"You're welcome. Oh, and tell your friend not to touch that. It will turn him into a frog if he's not careful."

He looked around. The other man pulled his hand away from a porcelain toadstool.

"If you're the huntress," the man said to me. "When will we expect enough yuckah to fulfill our needs? Say, five head?"

"I believe I just brought Charlie his third, so when I come back in on Friday or Saturday."

"Can I be sure of that? Are you regularly here then?"

"It's my routine." I shrugged. "Charlie likes me to be reliable."

"Apolline," Charlie muttered, elbowing me in the ribs. He turned his attention to the man. "I promised you Saturday, so you will have them by Saturday."

The man's gaze lingered over my face. "Apolline, was it?"

"Get out." Charlie patted his handgun on his hip. "And she has one too."

The man frowned. "We'll be back Saturday."

They left the store.

Charlie turned to me. "Why did you tell them that? You don't know who they are."

"Why does it matter? They just want their meat."

He groaned. "They could be connected with pirates, or ogres, or giants—"

"Or even the sorceress herself," I responded sarcastically. "I'm almost twenty-one and you still treat me like I'm ten." I pulled out my revolver. "I could kill someone with this. You know I'm a great shot, so I don't think I need much in the way of protecting anymore."

"Apolline." He pushed down my gun. "You are smart and savvy, yes, but there are things out there you don't understand. Things that can't be handled with a gun."

"Well, if the fairies would just let me leave this planet—"

"You will leave when you are to marry. It's not long now, so just be patient."

"And what good will *that* do me?" I slotted my gun back in the holster. "I don't even know who this guy is. He's likely aristocratic, since only they do betrothals anymore, which probably means he's a boring stiff who will keep me locked up for the rest of my life."

He shook his head. "You are lucky to have this. Look at the other girls who grew up around you. You have been given a better chance at life than them."

I frowned as I thought about the brothel tucked away around the corner. "Mmm. But I'm an excellent huntress."

"Don't you want a family?"

My frown deepened. "Yes. Eventually."

He grasped my hand. "Trust the fairies."

I sighed, slumping. "I know."

CHAPTER FOUR

Sunday. **Allard lay on his bed, enjoying the sleep in. He** glanced at the clock. 10:52 a.m. He yawned, looking across at the tray of food sitting on the small table in the corner of his living room. His first week back in the Oran courts proved busy. Endless overseeing, events, people pleasing, all filled his schedule by day, and with Hernan and Cytheria, balls and formal functions kept him up late into the night. He'd barely had time to sleep, let alone think.

But now he had some spare time, he found his mind on Apolline. He shut his eyes, and realized he couldn't picture her face anymore. He sat up and grunted. Elpida needed to fill his thoughts.

He climbed out of bed and grabbed his food. He turned on his projector and watched cartoons as he ate.

"Even princes watch cartoons."

Allard glanced up at Donald in the corner. "Shoot!"

"Sorry to startle you, sir," he said with a bow. "But you did permit me to enter."

"When?"

"About an hour ago, but you fell back asleep."

"Oh." Allard turned off his projector. "What is it?"

Donald bowed his head again. "The report you requested from Mish."

Allard shot to his feet. "Really?"

Donald stretched out a pad for him. Allard grabbed his pad on the table and accessed Donald's. The report popped up on his screen right away. Allard scanned it over. Apolline kept a regular routine, visiting the town on Mondays, Wednesdays, Fridays, and Saturdays. He tapped the pad, scrolling down. Mish's township was several hours behind the Oran palace, so he could visit her at night, on her Friday and Saturday.

"Thank you, Don."

"You're welcome, highness." He bowed, but paused. "Sir, may I speak?"

Allard nodded, scanning over the detailed report.

"Do you think it's wise to be spying on a maiden so close to your wedding?"

Allard flinched. He already felt guilty about his distraction for Apolline, but he continually justified himself.

"She's an interesting subject," he said calmly. "She has no idea who I am, so she speaks without reservation. I can learn a great deal about the common person's perspective through her."

"So the fact that she's pretty doesn't contribute?"

Allard snorted. "If you could call that dirty mess pretty." He came across an image of her in the report. She was pretty, even covered in dirt and blood.

"Very well, sire. If that is all?"

Allard looked up at him. "Yes, thank you."

Don bowed and left Allard's chambers.

Allard scrolled through the file and found a better image of Apolline, with her whole face visible as she talked with the storekeeper. It wouldn't harm anyone if he just talked to her. Like he said, she could give him a common person's perspective. He nodded and set his pad aside. Friday night, he would be heading out to Mish.

Never in his life had a week taken so long. Each day seemed to move by at a snail's pace. Finally, Friday evening came, and Allard sat at the banquet, waiting anxiously for it to end. His father looked across at him and raised an eyebrow. Allard shuffled, knowing his anxiety must be written all over him.

Brencis made his way over and stood beside him to speak in a low voice. "Hernan and Cytheria head back tomorrow. It will be over soon."

Allard nodded; relieved his anxiety simply looked like his patience wearing thin. "Not that I don't enjoy them, but these endless events…"

Brencis chuckled. "I know. Two weeks straight was enough for even me when I was your age, and I was a party animal."

"So I've heard." Allard nudged him playfully.

Brencis laughed. "Oh yes, your mother and I were always the life of the party."

"I hope Elpida makes me light up like mother does you." Allard gazed ahead at Hernan and Cytheria.

Brencis patted his back. "She will, son."

One of Allard's professors from the university shuffled over, bowing. "Majesties."

"Father." Allard motioned to the small man with round glasses. "This is Professor Pelt. He teaches astronomy at the university."

Brencis bowed his head. "It's a pleasure. In fact, I read a journal by you recently, discussing your theories regarding other galaxies in the cosmos. You believe ours is tiny compared to most."

The professor straightened, his eyes twinkling. "Yes. The fairies in particular have helped me lead to this conclusion, as we all know their home planet, Zethuran, is from another galaxy. They claim our galaxy is only a fraction of the size of theirs, so I decided to look out and try to measure the diameter of other galaxies nearby."

"And what have you found?"

"We are indeed quite small. The fairies' galaxy, the closest to us, would take more than a hundred years to cross its diameter, whereas our galaxy, in our fastest ships, only takes a month."

"Interesting."

"It is. While I was doing this, I also noticed the light emitting from our galaxy, although so miniscule in size, is considerably brighter. I addressed this with some fairies with whom I am in contact, and they explained that it is the abundance of magic within the galaxy."

Allard glanced around. He'd written a paper on how magic affected the brightness of stars within the galaxy, but didn't really feel much like discussing it. Cytheria caught his attention and smiled. The perfect invitation. He excused himself and hurried over.

She caught his arm. "How are you? These past two weeks have been rather hectic."

"As much as I enjoy your company, I'm ready for it to end."

She patted his hand. "I feel the same. Have you thought much of Elpida recently?"

Guilt made his stomach tighten. "I'm afraid I've barely had a moment to think."

"It's probably for the best." She looked around at Hernan as he laughed heartily. "I told him you asked about her. He has contact with the fairies, so if you would like, he can probably answer some of your questions. You know he thinks you're the best thing in this galaxy, so he'd love to ease your mind."

Allard looked over at Hernan. He'd love to know more about Elpida, but right at that moment, Apolline consumed his thoughts. He hoped his guilt didn't show. "I'd like that."

She stroked his arm, and opened her mouth to speak, but a young photographer snapped a shot. "Oh wow! Prince Allard and Queen Cytheria together!"

She popped the hologram up and smudged Allard's face. "We need to protect your identity from the sorceress." She giggled. "Not that it's not a handsome face. Oh, everyone is so excited for the upcoming wedding. The daughter of King Hernan and Queen Cytheria will be a stunning woman without a doubt."

Cytheria touched her hand. "Calm down, dear. This is your first big event, isn't it?"

"Yes. Is it that obvious?" She blushed.

"It's all right." Cytheria's voice soothed even Allard. "We are people too. Let me see what you have."

The photographer giggled as she popped her images up for Cytheria.

Allard glanced around again. At least half the guests had left. He looked to his father still engrossed in conversation with his professor. Then he glanced at Hernan who also was engaged in conversation. No one would notice if he slipped out.

He shuffled toward the door, and dashed into the corridor heading for his private ship.

I knocked on the door of the small house. The elderly woman answered with a huge smile. "Apolline! Did you bring me my medicine?"

"I did." I handed her the bottle of potion Fantine made for her.

"Come and sit for a minute and have some tea."

I glanced back at my cart full of furs, organs, antlers, and hooves. "I have a large load today. They've been building up, so I need to get them to Charlie."

"Very well. Next time." She motioned for me to bend over so she could kiss my cheek. "You're a good girl, Apolline."

I smiled as I pulled back. "Thank you. I'll see you next time."

I trotted down to my cart by her gate and continued on into town. I received the usual wolf whistles and cat calls as I passed the pub, then stopped at the bakery to buy a pastry for breakfast. Being Friday, many farmers had come in from their islands to sell and trade. Hovercrafts lined the main street, weighed down by produce and livestock.

Charlie negotiated prices with a farmer as I entered the store. I pulled my cart in and headed toward the back.

"Hey! Apolline!"

Grinning, I pulled the cart through to wait for him to finish. I returned to the store and decided to check his shelves to see if he had anything new and interesting. Walking up and down the aisles, I found items that had sat untouched for months, and wondered what they were. As I reached the back corner, something tucked away behind a music box glittered. I reached in and wrapped my fingers around a smooth, glass surface.

Pulling it out, a glistening castle sat inside a glass globe, gleaming white with tiny blue capped roofs on all the towers. The windows were gold, and the landing platforms glittered with silver. On the inner walls, delicate vines crept up the surfaces. I couldn't help staring at it as I slowly turned it around and around, examining every little detail.

"That's the Tyronian Palace."

I jumped at the male voice and dropped the ball. I immediately panicked, but a hand appeared beneath it and broke its plummet to destruction.

"Sorry, I didn't mean to startle you."

I turned to see the owner of the hand and voice, and recognized him; the handsome stranger from the military. But it would be weird if I showed that I recognized him. So I tilted my head, pretending as if I'd never seen him before. "Have we met?"

"Yes, my ship passed by here two weeks ago and we stopped for supplies." He smiled hopefully.

My belly filled with butterflies. With slightly longer hair and normal clothes, he looked different, but just as attractive. "Oh, you're that guy in the military with the same name as the prince."

His smile turned into a grin. "That's correct; Allard."

He offered me his hand but, instead of shaking it, I took the ball out of his other hand and placed it back on the shelf. "So why are you here?"

"To collect supplies. The palace was impressed by what we brought, so I've been sent out to collect more."

I eyed him over. That was a great big lie. "Uh huh." I turned away from him, making my way down the aisle. "Charlie should be done soon. Since you have a ways to travel, I'll let you go first."

He followed me. "Couldn't you help me? You helped me before."

"No. It's Charlie's store. He does all the negotiations."

"I just need six yuckah, and you said you were the huntress." His hand brushed my elbow.

I pulled way, swinging to him. "What are you doing?"

"Could I buy the yuckah directly from you?"

He leaned in and I caught a whiff of his cologne. Musky, warm... mmm... I blinked and pushed on his chest. "No. Suppliers sell to distributers. My kills help keep Charlie in business."

He leaned against my hand with a coy grin. "You think I'm flirting with you."

"No." I pulled my hand back, darting to my left as he caught his balance. *Wrong way, now I'm cornered.* "And even if I did think that, it doesn't matter, because I'm betrothed."

He blocked me in, gazing into my eyes. "I'm not, just so you know. Not that I don't find you attractive, but I..." He paused, a light switching on in his eyes. "Hang on; did you say *you're* betrothed?"

"Yes, is that so shocking?" I raised my hand to his chest again, mostly for my own need to keep him at arm's length.

"But you're a commoner."

Rage flared inside me. "I'm a what?"

"Ah..." He glanced around, on edge. "Non-aristocrat."

"You called me common." I shoved his chest. "Well, Mr. High-and-Mighty, we *common* folk, as you put it, are the very backbone of this society which you so obviously enjoy. I am one of the few who provides food, blankets, clothing, and a great deal of other necessities and luxuries you inner planet folk take for granted. Without me and all the other 'commoners' like me, the very society you thrive in would cease to exist and the economy would collapse. A commoner? How dare you insult my station like that!"

His eyebrows shot up. "I meant no offence. I'm sorry. I didn't use good judgment with what I said. I do believe you are far more than common."

I pushed him back, freeing myself from the corner. "What's wrong with regular people being betrothed anyway?"

He followed. "Nothing. But usually I think of betrothal as an arranged marriage, not a love match."

"Mine *is* an arranged marriage." I peeked around the corner at Charlie still with the farmer. *Just seal the deal, Charlie. This man makes me uncomfortable.*

"That's just not the usual thing," Allard said in a hushed voice. "That's usually an aristocrat and royalty thing. Are you secretly noble born?"

I glared at him. "No. I'm an orph... an... I shouldn't have said that."

I dashed into the next aisle.

He followed. "Why not?"

"You're nosey; has anyone ever told you that?"

His smile made my knees quiver. "No, actually."

"Well, you are. Now back off."

"What's wrong with being an orphan?"

I glared at him as his eyes sparkled. "Nothing."

"Hey!" Charlie appeared at the end of the aisle. "The brothel is down the street."

Allard turned to Charlie. "I'm here for supplies."

"What kind of supplies?" Charlie said with dark eyes and a deep scowl.

"Yuckah mostly." Allard pulled his pad from his pocket and slid it open. A holographic image appeared with a list of items. Charlie raised his pad and the list shot to it.

"Leave the girl alone." Charlie patted his handgun on his hip and returned to the counter.

"Well, that was intimidating." Allard turned his attention back to me. "Now, where were we? Yes, orphan."

"Nope." I hurried by him and into the main part of the store.

Again he followed, causing Charlie to give him the filthiest look I'd ever seen.

"Storekeeper," Allard said. "How much for that globe with the Tyronian Castle in it?"

"The what?" Charlie snarled as he worked out the cost for Allard's supplies.

"The globe." Allard disappeared down the aisle and returned with it.

Charlie raised an eyebrow. "I don't even remember trading for it." He raised his hand. Allard gave it to him. "Fine workmanship, I'd say elven made, but just a trinket. Not a drop of magic in it." He seemed to weigh it, then looked at the bottom. "Yes, elven. It's from Durrang. I'd say sixty miroans."

"For that?" I let slip, stunned by its value, and that I'd almost broken it.

"I'll take it." Allard tapped on his pad. Charlie's register beeped. A receipt popped up above Allard's pad, then vanished into it.

Charlie grumbled. I knew he didn't want to discourage Allard's impulsive spending, but he didn't like it either. "Here's your total."

Allard's screen flashed, and he nodded. "Looks good."

"All right. I'll need to go out back and crate them." He glanced at me. "And stay away from the girl."

"Yes, sir." Allard bowed his head.

I stared up at Allard, completely stunned by how he'd just tossed down sixty miroans for a globe like it was nothing. Although he dressed like anyone else—cotton shirt, work boots, tan pants—the way he talked, behaved, and even his position as an officer, told me he was probably noble born.

He looked down at me staring. He lifted the globe. "It's a gift for a friend."

"Lucky friend."

He smiled, lowering the globe. "I'll tell you a secret."

"Nope, you're fine." I hurried out the back and grabbed my cart, glad to find it empty with a satchel of coins resting inside. I pulled it out as Allard watched me.

"I'm betrothed too."

"That's nice." *Definitely noble born then.*

"I've never met her though, so I don't know what to expect. Have you met the man you're to marry?"

I hesitated, put off guard by his genuine expression of interest and concern on his face. "No, I haven't."

"Do you know anything about him?"

"Only that he's from a good family from another planet." The words just popped out like when Sophronia forced me to admit to my mistakes with her spells, except, this time, there was no magic. For some reason, I couldn't help telling him things. "Stop talking, Apolline."

"Don't stop."

I looked up at him and he smiled.

Charlie pushed by me with Allard's crate. "Pay me and leave."

Allard typed on his pad and the register beeped. He bowed, backing toward the door. "Good day, sir, and you, Apolline."

Once Allard had left, Charlie turned to me. "Apolline..."

I moaned. "Geez, Charlie, I didn't encourage him. I even told him I'm engaged." A white lie, but Charlie would give me a lecture if he knew I'd said 'betrothed'.

"Good. Hopefully he won't come back."

I sighed and pulled out a handful of miroans. "Give me some of that jerky."

I chewed on a piece of beef jerky as I left the store. Heavy clouds swirled overhead, and I took a deep breath, smelling the scent of the storm. The rich fragrance of the ocean carried in the wind. This was Mish at its finest. Late summer storms couldn't be beaten by anything.

I turned toward the ramp, starting when I came face to face with Allard leaning against the rail. He smirked. "I felt like I'd worn out my welcome in there."

I pulled my cart by him. "Where's your crate?"

"Transported to my ship. Now, tell me about being a betrothed orphan."

"You don't give up, do you?"

"Not when I've found someone my age who is so candid."

I looked over my shoulder at him. "You like that?"

He nodded. "Where I'm from, everyone has an agenda, so they're very guarded. But not you. It's refreshing. I'd like to be friends."

I stopped walking. "Friends?"

I'd never had a friend before, not my age anyway. Charlie was more like a father, and the fairies, well, they were fairies, guardians of sorts, rather than friends.

"I've never really had much in the way of friends," he said. "I've always been kind of… different."

I drew a sharp breath and looked back at him. It seemed like he'd read my mind. "I know how that feels."

"Really? But you're so…" He paused as I raised my eyebrows. "Well adjusted."

I laughed sarcastically. "Good save."

"Thanks."

I tipped my head for him to approach. He rushed over and I handed him the handle of my cart. "Well then, tell me about yourself so I can decide if I want to be your friend."

He grinned, revealing the dimple in his cheek. I stared at it for a moment, then turned away as I led him down the street.

"Tell you about me, huh?" He gave the cart a tug. "Well, let me see… I grew up on Oran, graduated from the Oran Academy for Gifted Students, then attended the University of Oran where I studied political science."

"Wow." I whispered. He was a genius. Those were the best schools in the Oran kingdom! All I had was a high school diploma from an insignificant outer-perimeter planet. How pathetic.

"After graduation, I joined the military. I just finished my one year tour with them."

"So accomplished," I muttered, cramming a lump of jerky in my mouth.

"I'm a bit of a sports fanatic actually," he said, raising his hand in the air. "Football, anti-gravity hockey, wrestling, you name it, I played it. Some people like the rush of the endorphins, but I just like to hit things without getting into trouble." He laughed.

"You'd like hunting then," I said in a soft voice, feeling incredibly inferior. "You'd probably be better at it than me too."

He stopped walking. "I doubt that."

I shrugged. "Being a great shot doesn't feel like much after all that."

I pulled out my revolver, spinning it on the palm of my hand. "I'd show you, but I'd have to kill you."

He chuckled. "I'll pass then."

"You think everything I say is funny, don't you?"

His eyes sparkled. "Pretty much."

"Oh, I get it, I'm a joke. An ignorant, outer planet sucker."

"No." His face fell. "Apolline, you are very intelligent. You seem to understand things without trying. I think you're funny because you just say what comes to mind. I've never met anyone quite like you."

My cheeks grew hot, so I turned away, heading down the street again.

"Tell me about you," he said, matching my pace.

"Me?" I stared ahead, afraid to admit my inferiority. "Not much here. What you see is what you get."

"I like what I see."

I took a deep breath. *This is insane!* I had just over two months until I married, and *now* I meet a guy who makes me giddy? I shook my head at the universe for its cruel joke. I grabbed my cart. "This is it."

He glanced around. "You live in a tree?"

I pouted. "No. There's a fence here. We live beyond and down the trail a little ways."

"We? I thought you said you're an orphan. Do you have siblings?"

"You're nosey." I gave my cart a tug and pulled it free of his hands.

"Wait." His hand rested on my shoulder. "I want to see you again."

I looked up at him, completely thrown off guard. "Why?"

"I told you; I want to be friends."

"Oh."

"Oh?"

"Yes, oh." I fought back a smirk.

"Well?" He raised an eyebrow.

"Well... the jury's still out on that one."

As I turned away, his face lit up. I smiled, delighted to cause such a reaction from him.

"Goodbye, Apolline."

I waved as I disappeared into the woods.

Back home, I took my cart straight to the shed. Ashlan called to me from the cottage, announcing dinner was ready as I pulled my cart inside. As I turned to leave, something glimmered underneath one of the mesh covers. Pulling it back, I gasped.

The globe with the Tyronian castle.

CHAPTER FIVE

Sunlight flooded the room as the drapes were pulled back. Allard groaned and rolled over.

"Wake up." Brencis yanked the blankets off Allard. "Good heavens, Allard, it's almost noon. Hernan and Cytheria want to see you before they leave."

Allard sat up. "Noon?"

"Yes. Are you sick?"

"No... I stayed up late." Allard rubbed his eyes. He'd arrived back at five a.m., and had slept on the three hour journey, so he wasn't tired, just groggy.

"You left the banquet at nine!"

"I stayed up watching a movie."

Brencis scowled. "That's not like you." He patted his shoulder. "Just hurry up and get dressed. Hernan and Cytheria want to leave no later than two."

Brencis left as Allard slid with a moan out of bed and shuffled to the bathroom. Pressing his forehead against the wall, he relaxed as the shower water ran down his back. Shutting his eyes, Apolline's face came to his mind. He smiled as her look of alarm flashed through his thoughts. He'd enjoyed pushing her buttons, making her uncomfortable. He'd never been on the dishing out end of making someone uneasy. Women always fell at his feet—he's the prince after all—but not Apolline.

He rested his hand on his chest where she'd shoved him. He chuckled, delighted to be seen as any other person and not a prince. He knew she didn't want to like him, but those deep blue eyes gave her away; she liked him too.

The shower entered the air dry cycle, snapping him out of his daydream. Elpida. He needed to focus on *Elpida*. If the plan to have her reach her twenty-first birthday without the curse being fulfilled failed, he needed to give her the kiss. That was his duty.

He made his way out to dress in a traditional navy blue suit, which he would be expected to wear for the departure. With plenty of media present, he'd need to demonstrate respect for the heritage of both kingdoms.

He strode down the hall. In a common area by the stairs, Hernan stood waiting for him. Allard bowed. "Highness."

Hernan's chocolate eyes turned to him. "Allard, please, you know there's no need for formalities."

Allard headed over. "Habit. Sorry."

Hernan motioned for him to sit on an intricate antique style couch by the window. They sat facing each other and Hernan spoke. "My wife tells me you've been asking about Elpida."

Allard nodded. "I'm curious. There's not much time left."

"I know." Hernan smiled, gazing out the window. "I think about her every day."

"It was a great sacrifice to give her up."

Hernan's gaze slowly turned to Allard. "But I don't regret it. The sorceress would have killed her if we hadn't given her to the fairies."

Allard stared at his hands. Hernan's words gave him the sense of being scolded. The princess had to go into hiding. His anxiousness didn't matter compared to that.

Hernan sighed and faced him. "It's been hard on all of us. I can't imagine what it's been like for you. You've been told all your life she is to be your wife, and you don't even know what she looks like. *I don't even know what she looks like.* When I last saw her, she had soft gold hair and blue eyes like her mother, but she also had chubby cheeks and wore a diaper."

Allard couldn't help smiling.

"Allard, don't concern yourself with who she is. My contact says the gifts the fairies gave her are evident as she demonstrates cleverness and courage. She is kind and spirited. How she looks will be the tip of the iceberg for you. Many only see Cytheria for her beauty, but for me, I see those qualities; her strength, her gentleness, her warm heart. She is more than a pretty face, and I know Elpida will give you the same joy in her companionship."

Allard opened his hands, staring down at his palms. "I've been concerned about whether we'd get along or not. If she is what you say— clever, strong, and kind—*I* will have nothing to worry about. But..." He pursed his lips, feeling ridiculous.

"But what?"

He looked into Hernan's eyes. "What if she doesn't like me?"

Hernan chuckled. "Everyone likes you."

Allard snorted. "Because I'm the prince. No one knows or even cares to know *me*. I don't even know if I'm truly a good person."

"You're friends with that White boy, what's his name?"

"Beaumont."

"Yes. He's a good sort."

Allard smirked. "He's a White."

"The point is, if you weren't a good person and interesting to be around, he wouldn't be so fond of you."

Allard grunted.

Hernan patted his arm. "She will love you. You never cease to impress both myself and Cytheria."

Apolline popped into Allard's mind. She impressed him... Guilt swept over him for allowing his thoughts to wander to a different woman. He hoped it didn't show on his face.

"Have I eased your mind at all?"

Allard forced a smile. "A little, but I don't think I'll be completely at ease until…"

"Me too." Hernan clasped his hands together. "Well, I believe we have a farewell ceremony to attend."

Allard jumped to his feet. "I think my father is upset with me for sleeping so long, so we best not be late."

Hernan chuckled and stood, wrapping his arm around Allard's shoulders. "I don't think your father is capable of being upset with you. But you're right; we should get a move on."

They hurried through the palace to the dock on the top floor.

Cytheria stood with Brencis, stretching out her hand as they entered. "Finally! Everyone is waiting."

Hernan took her hand. "We just needed to have a chat."

Cytheria smiled at Allard, but his father raised an eyebrow.

They headed out to the boarding bay, the two kings and the queen in front, and Allard a step behind. The cameras flashed, and he instinctually bowed his head. When he was a boy, his mother told him to do so, and covered his face, but many years had passed since he had needed to.

When he was ten, Bryanna attacked the city, focusing on the palace. His mother came to him, just before the ogres broke into his room. She led him through a secret passageway, but at the end, a pack of wolves picked up his scent.

They attacked, and she dashed him back into the palace. She hid him in a closet, and led them away. That was the last he saw of his mother. They refused to allow anyone other than his father to see her body due to the severity of the mutilation.

Allard shuddered at the memories and forced them aside. To prevent him following a similar fate, his face was no longer allowed to be shown anywhere. Very few people knew what he looked like now. All the media had to blur his face.

Brencis' hand rose and the crowd fell silent. "It has been my honor to have King Hernan and Queen Cytheria here with us. Our good relations are as strong as ever, and we hope to find peace soon, especially for those living on perimeter planets."

He glanced at Hernan, who spoke. "The unifying of the two kingdoms remains on course. This unity will bring great things to our peoples. Trade and industry will open up, a stable economy will be built..."

Allard's mind wandered. He'd heard it all before. He'd been trained and taught for the unifying of the kingdoms his whole life. He was born to be king over them.

He glanced at a group of noblewomen chatting quietly together not far to his left. He focused on them, shuffling inch by inch closer to hear.

"...You should have seen her. I doubt she was wearing any makeup," a slender, curly haired blonde said. "And everything about her was just so... drab."

"Oh my gosh, I can't believe she actually talked to you," said a small brunette.

"I know! And she was so rude too. She looked at me and was all, 'Are you going to pay for that?' I mean, obviously I was, I'm not poor like *her*. So I said, 'Well, since it seems you made it, it's obviously not worth much.' And she said, "It's fifteen miroans.'"

The women giggled. Allard, thinking of Apolline, shuffled closer, disgusted.

"So, tired of her insolence, I said, 'You filthy little commoner. Do you have any idea who you're talking to?'"

Allard had heard enough. He pushed into their circle. "Excuse me, ladies."

They batted their eyes at him and smiled. Why did women throw themselves at him when they all knew he was betrothed to Elpida?

"I couldn't help overhearing your conversation and feeling disturbed by it."

"I know," the blonde said with wide eyes. "The audacity!"

"I agree. Insulting a hard working citizen like that."

"I... what?"

They stared at him, taken aback.

"They aren't common, as you so wrongfully stated. They are more than just common. The common folk, as you put it, are the very backbone of our society, which you obviously enjoy." He gestured at her elaborate, lacey, and over-the-top dress. "They provide food, clothing, and many of our necessities and luxuries we take for granted. Without all the 'commoners', the very society we thrive in would cease to exist and the economy would collapse."

The women stared at him with jaws hanging.

Allard noticed silence around him. He turned to find everyone staring at him. He drew a sharp breath, realizing every reporter, journalist, and person on the dock, had heard every word he said.

"Well spoken, son," Brencis said. "The people of the kingdoms deserve their voices to be heard. I hope my son's words help spread good faith among our people, so they feel secure in their future leaders."

The crowd's attention turned back to the kings, and Allard backed away to hide. He felt like a fool.

Cytheria sidled up beside him. "Well spoken."

"Thanks." He side glanced at the women, red-faced and flustered, making their way to the exit.

"I'm glad you are paying an interest in the working class. They are the majority of people in the kingdoms. I think, in our palaces and lush gardens, the upper class often forget who puts the bread on their tables while they govern."

"I didn't mean for everyone to hear it," he said in a low voice.

"I know, but they did, and it will be a bold statement for the people. You are on their side. It will help when we work on uniting all the laws and legislations. They will know you are thinking about them and looking out for their well-being."

"I do want what's best for everyone." He thought of Apolline. All she wanted was to continue living her life. He hoped he didn't do anything to alter her happiness.

"Keep that hope and you will be a great king."

The rat spy from Oran Palace scampered through the mirror. Bryanna turned from the mirror she gazed into solemnly, and made her way back to her oversized desk. "News?"

"Yes, my queen. Very good news."

The rat leaped onto her desk, sitting up on its haunches. "The prince left the banquet early last night, and disappeared for several hours. His guards spoke in whispers of him visiting a maiden."

"Really?" Bryanna smirked, tapping her chin. "I just received word from my serpent on Mish that he visited our little huntress. Apparently she made it clear his snobbery didn't appeal to her, but her attitude did appeal to him."

"Maybe that's the reason he spoke out in defense of the working class." The rat leaped over to a holo-projector and flicked through the channels until he found a news report.

Bryanna stepped closer, watching the royals and the crowd gathered to listen. She stared at Hernan at first, oblivious to anything else, until the image shifted to Prince Allard. He appeared blurred, as was customary, but his words grabbed her attention.

"Rewind," she commanded, and it played again.

She reached over and tapped her crystal ball. It lit up in a lavender color and she ordered, "Play me the serpent on Mish's memory."

The crystal played through the day in fast forward. When it reached the moment the serpent peered through a crack in the wall of the store, watching the huntress and prince interact, she slowed it. She heard the words that made her smile. "He spoke her words."

The rat twittered. "This is good news, my queen."

"Very good news." Bryanna laughed. "Silly little boy. Keep an eye on him. I want to know every time he leaves for Mish."

"Yes, my queen."

The image in the crystal kept playing. Allard slipped something into the huntress' cart while she wasn't looking. Bryanna rewound, then zoomed in.

"A globe?" She peered closer. "A fancy globe of elven design! An expensive trinket for someone he barely knows." She chuckled. "He's already smitten! I hardly need to do anything, just sit back and make sure she doesn't frighten him away."

She sat in her chair, stroking the rat's back. "Cytheria, Cytheria, did you really think love could best me?"

The mirror before her swirled and its face appeared. The man's eyes stared blankly at her. She hated that. Those eyes once had so much love and life in them. She stood, marching from the room, unable to look at the face. She paced the hallways, startling a pack of wolves, and disrupting the giants' poker game.

She made it to the living room where the last embers to the fire glowed, casting shadows around the room. She fingered the drapes, kept drawn because no sunlight ever shone on Mahkba. She parted the heavy velvet, peering out into the blackness. Outside, a lavish garden once grew, but even if she could see it, the lack of light certainly would have killed it all.

She dropped the curtain, clasping her face. So many memories. She turned to the armchair where Miriam had once sat when she told her of her pregnancy, and again she came just to show her new son.

Miriam.

Bryanna withdrew her hand, the pain too much to bear. She glanced around the room, many more memories coming to life in the shadows. Beautiful memories, painful memories. Hernan smiling at her, then Cytheria betraying her.

She clawed at her face, forcing the memories aside. "Stop."

"You deserve this," her mother's voice echoed in her mind. *"You killed me, after all I did for you. I could have prevented Cytheria—"*

"No!" Bryanna marched from the room, slamming the doors behind her. She turned to the doors, pressing her hands against them, and sealed them shut.

CHAPTER SIX

Sophronia ordered me to get rid of everything I had in storage, so my cart overflowed with meat, skins, jarred organs, and bones. The cart weighed more than usual, so I moved slowly. Charlie didn't like me bringing too much at once, but I figured I'd buy new arrows and rounds for my guns to cover the difference he couldn't give me in cash.

Allard stood waiting by the pub as I turned onto the main street. I paused, my heart fluttering, as he fiddled with his pad. *Don't be silly, Apolline, you're getting married soon!*

I pulled my cart onward, and he looked up, smiling.

In an attempt to look indifferent, I raised my eyebrow at him. "Joining the early birds today?"

"Huh?" He glanced around at the pub. "Oh! No. Drinking isn't my thing. I just knew you would come by this way." He grabbed hold of the cart beside me. "So, how's that jury going?"

I looked at him, baffled. Then I remembered the last thing I said to him, and grinned. "They took a lunch break."

"Typical!" He grinned back. "Right when a man's neck is on the line."

I chuckled. "Well, so far they seem to approve."

His hand brushed over mine as he took hold of the cart. "Good to know."

I pulled my hand away and stepped back, my cheeks hot. "So, why are you back?"

"I'll be back every weekend for a while. For supplies."

Every weekend? "I better make sure I keep up *my* supplies."

"You better."

We climbed the ramp and entered Charlie's store.

Charlie scowled at Allard, but turned his focus on me. "You know all of that is too much."

"I'm sorry. Sophronia had a fit. She said it stinks and is taking up too much space. So Fantine and Ashlan took what they wanted, and I brought you the rest."

He pulled back the mesh cover. "I can't pay you for all this."

"That's okay." I pulled my crossbow and shotgun out of the cart.

"Ah, now those I can throw in." He hurried out the back and brought out five boxes of shotgun rounds. "For all your guns?"

"Yup."

He returned to the cart and pulled out the pile of skins with a grunt. "I'll trade them for these and that crate of jars."

"Deal."

He nodded and disappeared out the back.

Allard tugged at my holster. "You're packing?"

I slapped his hand off it. "Of course."

"It's not a laser gun. Isn't that dangerous?"

I swung around to face him. "No."

He seemed to wait for me to elaborate, but when I didn't, he said, "Why would you use one of those relics over a laser gun? They are nowhere near as reliable, and prone to misfires."

I raised an eyebrow. "We are on the perimeter of the galaxy."

Again, he waited for a moment, his dark eyebrows bunched together. "So...?"

"So projectile guns are easier to come across, cheaper to maintain and buy ammunition for, and work better for hunting and such."

He raised an eyebrow and pulled a small laser gun from a well concealed holster. "Take this for protection. I have some charged rounds—"

"I don't need your gun." I pushed it back.

"It would work better against pirates—"

"No, I—"

He shoved it into my hands.

I growled and slammed it on the counter. "I said no. I'm fine. How do you think I survived this long? Sheer good luck?"

He stared at me with pursed lips, but didn't say a word.

I turned my back on him. "It's yours, anyway. I can't just take it."

"Why not?"

"Because it wouldn't be right. Speaking of which, you left something in my cart yesterday."

"No, I didn't."

I swung back around to look at him and found him smiling. "Yes, you did. I don't have it now. I didn't realize you'd be back so soon."

"I left nothing of mine in your cart."

I put my hands on my hips. "Yes, you did! It was a—"

Gunshots and loud laughter outside interrupted us. We looked out the door as Charlie shoved through, mumbling all kinds of profanity under his breath. He burst out the door, raising his shotgun to his hip. "You hooligans! Joshua Hicks, I'm not surprised it's you."

Joshua cussed out Charlie. I jumped over the counter and ducked down. Joshua was the last person I wanted to see, or worse, to have see me.

Allard leaned over, his brows furrowed. "Apolline?"

"Tell me if he comes this way."

"Um…" He glanced toward the door. "Do you know him?"

I laughed shrilly. "Yeah. We go way back."

His eyes narrowed. "Old friend?"

"You could say that."

His brows shot up. "I thought you said you were betrothed?"

I gagged. "Oh gross, not that kind of old friend. Fantastic, now I have that image burned into my mind. Excuse me while I throw up."

He smiled, grasping his laser gun. "He won't come near you."

Charlie and Joshua argued loudly in the street, but soon, Charlie forced Joshua and his cronies to move on.

I slowly stood, letting out a breath from relief as Charlie reentered. We had a moment of eye contact, exchanging a clear understanding—his concern and my thanks. Then he looked at Allard and his expression darkened. He pointed at him. "You! Get out."

"Yes, sir," Allard replied, but when Charlie turned his back, Allard tipped his head to signal that he would meet me outside. I nodded. He left while I finished my transaction with Charlie.

I stepped outside and Allard rushed to me, taking the cart out of my hands. "So, show me around."

I tilted my head. "Was that a request or an order?"

"A bit of both." He smiled.

I laughed. "All right then, just this once."

We walked slowly down the street. The town consisted of two main streets: the one we strolled down, and a shorter one that intersected it like a T. The street we were on pointed north, and consisted of the main stores that outsiders stopping by our planet would use—like Charlie's store and the Pub—while the other street catered mostly to the locals, with a dressmaker, and storefronts for electricians, plumbers, and so forth. A small courthouse and park were located at the eastern most end, tucked away and almost forgotten. Law enforcement was almost non-existent on Mish, as the only sheriff spent most of his time at the pub. So, in general, we all took care of our own business, rendering the courthouse unnecessary.

I told Allard all this as we turned onto this other street heading for the courthouse. I liked the courthouse, and thought maybe he might be interested in it too. But as we made our way toward it, a group of men— about my age and dressed in brown cotton pants and filthy shirts with guns strapped to their hips—appeared from an alleyway by the mechanic.

I grabbed Allard's arm. "Let's go back."

"I thought you wanted to show me the courthouse?" He frowned down at me, his gaze darting to the men.

"There's a... ah... haunted house down the other end. I'm sure you'd find that way more interesting."

A throaty chuckle came from behind us. "Ahh, Apolline."

I cringed at Joshua's voice. "Allard, let's go."

"It's good to see you still around."

I tugged Allard away, heading back toward Charlie's store.

"Apolline?" Allard kept glancing back.

"Just keep moving."

"Apolline, come on." Joshua's voice sounded closer. "You are such a prude. We just want to chat."

I called back to him, "Leave me alone. You know I'm a better shot than you."

I kept walking, trying to ignore him as he kept after me.

"Apolline, Apolline, the girl who disappears in the woods. She lives with her crazy aunts, and thinks she's so goods." The group following him laughed at his pathetic attempt at rhyming. My eye roll came on its own.

Allard clasped my arm. "They can't speak to you like that."

I grabbed his hand and quickened my pace. "They always have. It's no big deal."

Joshua's voice interrupted us. "You are so *hot,* Apolline. Seriously, I know you're a virgin. Let me teach you a thing or two so your precious betrothed can really enjoy you. I bet you're a real tiger in the sack."

Allard's eyes flashed with indignity. He moved to turn on them, but I held him tightly. "Keep walking. We're almost back at the store and they won't dare mess with Charlie. He has the best tobacco and meats in this sector."

But Allard's reaction to their taunts caught their attention, and Joshua became very interested in him. "Who is this? A rich boy? Could this be the betrothed, finally come to take you away?"

I tugged on Allard's hand so we would go faster.

"Who *are* these men?" Allard whispered.

"They used to live here," I answered.

Joshua grabbed my elbow, pulling me away from Allard. "Apolline, Apolline, I always fancied you. You have so much spunk. You would be so much more fun than the girls down at the brothel, and your betrothed here can watch if he would like—"

Allard tugged my gun from its holster, and pointed it in Joshua's face.

"I am her betrothed," Allard said smoothly. "So you better let her go, or I will make sure you are hunted down and hanged for piracy."

The others laughed sarcastically, but Joshua's gaze locked with Allard's. He blinked, inhaling sharply. Allard stared him down. Joshua didn't flinch as they glared, waiting for the other to make a move.

"Or," Allard said quietly. "I could shoot you now and save myself the trouble."

Allard clicked the gun, loading it.

Joshua let go of me. Allard pulled me behind him. Joshua snarled at Allard and glanced at me one last time before turning away. He followed his friends as they made their way back down the street.

I took my gun from Allard and disarmed it. "Thanks for saving me, but you need to go now."

"I need to go now?" Allard's voice raised a pitch as his eyes narrowed. "Why? I thought we were getting along fine."

"We were, until you lied."

"What did I lie about?"

"Us being betrothed."

He paused. I had to admit, I did hope he would say something along the lines of "oh yes, you got me, I am he," because I enjoyed our playful banter and easy conversation. But I was greatly disappointed.

"I thought it would help with getting them to leave you alone."

I couldn't help huffing at his response. "Well, this is starting to get too complicated for me, so maybe you shouldn't come back anymore."

"What?" His eyes widened.

"You heard me."

He pressed his hands against his hips, drumming his fingers. We stood for a few moments staring at each other. Then he said, "I'm sorry for saying that, since it upset you so much."

I bit my lip and ran my fingers over my belt. He was getting to me, in a feel-good way. He made me feel things I had never felt before. So I said, "Please don't. Just come back next week so I can give that thing back, okay?"

"Hmm." He handed me the cart. "I'll leave you be."

"Thanks."

He scowled, but lifted his pad and teleported himself away. I sighed, slumping. I liked Allard, the first and only friend I'd ever had, but my feelings for him were more than that. I couldn't let them grow or the pain of marrying someone else would be unbearable.

I shuffled along, heading home disheartened. What a crappy day.

"Apolline!"

My stomach tightened. I glanced over my shoulder as Joshua marched after me.

"Get back here, tramp. No one talks to me like that and gets away with it."

I broke into a run. As I reached the pub, a shot whizzed by me. I flinched and threw my cart up on its end to use as a shield, and just in time, as another shot embedded into the cart. Whipping out my gun, I prepared to fire back.

"Apolline, we know you're carrying a purse full of miroans because your cart is empty. So just do us a favor and hand them over," Joshua called out.

I peeked around the cart and fired a warning shot at one of his cronies. It hit the man in the knee. He fell, wailing. Only one man stopped to help him, the others opened fire.

The magical cart absorbed the laser shots, but the bullets and pellets embedded into the wood.

"Damn it," I said under my breath, slipping a bullet into my revolver. I would have to fix the damage they made on my cart. What a hassle.

I fired another couple of shots at them, hitting one in the shoulder and another in the hip. Then Joshua appeared beside me. He grabbed me by my ponytail, pulling me to my feet. I swung around and we pointed our guns at one another's temples, staring at each other defiantly.

"Really, Apolline? Is a few miroans worth dying for?"

"I'm not the one who will die if this goes awry, Josh."

His eyes narrowed. "You think you're better than me, your highness?"

I pushed my gun against his head. "I know I am."

A click of a gun came from behind us. A rifle pressed against the back of his head. The sheriff—scruffy, and slightly drunk—somehow stood firmly upright, his gun pointing at Joshua's head, as he stared fixedly at him. "Let her go, boy."

Joshua didn't flinch. "Come on, sheriff, we was just playing around."

Charlie appeared beside me and raised his shotgun. "It's *were*, you moron."

I looked toward the pub. All the men stood out on the porch, holding their weapons, ready to take out the group of men who had accosted me. I smiled and pushed the barrel of my gun harder into Joshua's temple.

He snarled before pulling away.

Sophronia appeared in the street. "Apolline."

Her mere presence caused all the men to recoil. Joshua's cronies let out a strange wail and scurried away, leaving Joshua stranded. He let me go, but couldn't escape with the sheriff and Charlie still holding him at gunpoint.

Sheer terror filled his eyes as Sophronia approached us. He fell to his knees in front of me. "Please forgive me. I didn't mean to frighten you. We go way back, remember? I let you play tag with us. I walked you home from school…"

He went on and on. I definitely didn't remember any of it the same way he did.

"Please don't let her hurt me!" His voice sounded chilling, like he would be murdered.

I shuddered. Could Sophronia be capable of that?

But Sophronia had no interest in him whatsoever. Instead, she grabbed my arm. "Apolline, enough of this roughhousing. We need to talk."

I pulled away from her. "Why?"

She glanced down at Joshua, who cowered back, then she looked at the sheriff and the group of onlookers. "Never mind. I guess it's not important after all."

She snatched Joshua's gun from his hand and gave it to Charlie. "I think this needs a new owner."

She motioned for me to follow. With a flick of her hand, the men hurried to right my cart. I nodded appreciatively to them, and followed her back toward the cottage.

As we left, Joshua collapsed and sobbed, probably relieved that she hadn't wiped his memories or something worse.

I glanced back, surprised by the group who came to defend me. The sheriff lifted Joshua and took him to lock him in the rarely used cell in the rarely open sheriff's office. I smiled, glad to see that I did have some friends—if that's what you could call them—that would come to my aid.

Then I thought of Allard and sighed sadly. He was one of them as well, but he had to be kept at bay. He couldn't be my friend, not with the feelings that had begun to surface, feelings I didn't want to have for him.

We entered the woods and Sophronia pulled out her wand. "Silence."

The sound of birds chirping ceased, and the trees swayed without sound. She'd made a privacy bubble around us. I watched her back, waiting to be ripped into.

"Apolline, tell me the story of the lost princess."

"Ah..." I scrunched my nose, confused. Fantine told me stories, not Sophronia.

"Articulate!"

I cleared my throat. "She is the daughter of King Hernan and Queen Cytheria who was taken away by the royal fairies and hidden to keep her safe from Bryanna's curse."

"Tell me about the curse."

"When the infant princess was born, the royal fairies gave her gifts, as is customary. The first fairy gave the baby the gift of intelligence, so she could learn quickly and have a clear and thoughtful mind. The second fairy gave the gift of inner strength, so the baby could grow into an independent and unwavering Queen. But the third fairy waited, because she felt like something was wrong."

I watched Sophronia's head as her auburn hair bobbed. Why was I reciting this?

"Why did you stop? Continue."

I cleared my throat. "And the third fairy was right. Bryanna appeared and placed a curse on the baby. She said that on her twenty-first birthday, the princess would prick her finger on a spinning wheel and die.

"The King and Queen begged her to take the curse back, but Bryanna laughed and disappeared, leaving them to mourn for their child.

"But the third fairy hadn't given her gift. So she touched the baby's lips with her wand, and said that the child would sleep, and rise again with true love's kiss.

"The king made every precaution to prevent the curse by destroying spinning wheels, etcetera, and the betrothal for the prince and princess was made.

"But Bryanna discovered the counter curse, so she set out to kill the baby. Queen Cytheria ordered the fairies to hide the child until she would be required to return and marry the prince."

"And why is the princess' survival so important?"

I let out a gush of air, confused by her history quiz. "So the kingdoms can be unified peacefully through her marriage to Prince Allard." Allard. There was no way he was as hot as my Allard. *My Allard? Who am I?*

"Who are the Whites?"

"Allies to the Oran throne. Knights and ladies sworn to uphold and protect the crown."

"And why is that important?"

"Because they know of the sorceress' magic. Their grandmother tasted her grandmother's wrath. They are honor bound to assist the royals in their fight to eradicate black magic and bring about peace and prosperity."

"Very good." She bowed her head, letting out a long breath. "Your ability to learn and retain knowledge is where I expect and I believe you will adjust quickly to married life, as long as you let go of your unruly behavior. I know it is partially my fault for teaching you how to hunt, but your bold heart causes trouble too. Learn to control it, Apolline."

I nodded, unable to speak.

She dug into the pocket of her tight, emerald green pants, and pulled out two metallic rods. "These are shifters. I made them long ago and they've just been sitting on my shelf for years. You might find them useful where you are going."

I stopped walking as she stretched them out for me. "Where am I going?"

She frowned. "I can't say. You will know when we get there."

"Nothing?" I slumped. "Not even a hint?"

"Apolline." She grabbed my wrist and forced the rods into my hand. "You know it's not up for discussion. You will know when the time comes."

"On my birthday."

"That's right."

I stared at the rods, each no longer than my index finger. "What do they do exactly?"

"Shift."

"Shift?"

"Think about something metallic that you might need."

"Like a probe so I can poke your brain and get information?"

"Apolline." She folded her arms.

"I know, I'm so immature." I huffed. "Maybe a key?"

One of the rods shifted and changed into the shape of an uncut key. "Huh."

"They can shift into anything that is metal and not too large." She closed my hand shut around them.

"You know, you've never given me a gift before."

She snorted and turned to walk on. "I have."

"No, you haven't."

"Don't argue with me, Apolline." She raised her hand and snapped her fingers shut.

My mouth closed, and I could no longer speak.

"That's better."

I gave her a throaty growl.

Back at the cottage, I closed my cart in the shed and hurried in for dinner. Fantine stood by the stove doing the finishing touches, while Ashlan danced around the table, setting down the knives and forks sporadically. She smiled and waved her wand at me. "Apolline, I want to play with your hair after dinner."

"Nope." I flopped into my chair.

"Wash your hands," Sophronia said in a firm tone.

I dashed to the sink.

"Oh! You're filthy!" Fantine elbowed me away. "Have you been rolling in the dirt?"

"Sort of."

"That Hicks boy shot at her again." Sophronia sat gracefully in her chair.

"Oh! Him." Ashlan pressed her hands against her hips. "Will he never learn? I think a spell is in order."

"No!" all of us yelled in unison.

She pouted. "But it worked so well last time."

"Turning a teenage boy into a pig is not an appropriate form of justice," Sophronia said, sticking her nose in the air.

Ashlan looked at me, wriggling her eyebrows. "But it worked. He left as soon as the next pirate ship arrived."

I bit my lip to hold back a smirk.

"I could place a potion in something for him," Fantine said distractedly. "He likes beer."

Sophronia huffed. "We are here to observe, not make spectacles of ourselves. I knew we shouldn't have taken in a human child. It's made both of you quite emotional."

Ashlan giggled and sat in her chair next to mine, facing Sophronia. "You know there is nothing more important than having emotions."

Sophronia grunted. "Is the food done yet? I've been put back an hour having to retrieve Apolline."

Fantine tapped the stove with her wand and it pinged. "Yes."

Like always when we sat down for dinner, Fantine asked me about my day, how Charlie was doing, how much I earned... basically she wanted to know every detail of my life. But when I accidentally said, "And my friend defended me when Joshua tried to accost me," she stopped me.

"What friend, dear?"

I chewed on my cheek. "Just a trader. But he's not coming back."

"He?" Sophronia raised an eyebrow.

"Yeah." I shoved a lump of rabbit into my mouth, wishing I'd kept my big mouth shut.

"Apolline." Ashlan touched my arm, grinning. "Have you been flirting?"

"Ha!" Fantine stood. "Apolline would never. She's a good girl who knows her duty."

"Exactly," I mumbled through my food.

"A he?" Sophronia stabbed her meat as her eyes blazed.

I groaned, knowing what was about to happen.

"Apolline, you are betrothed. We made the decision to do this for your own good. The man will keep you safe and take care of you. Humans are petty creatures, and all this love nonsense only hurts them. With an arranged marriage—"

"He will be loyal through obligation and we will learn to love each other, blah, blah, blah." I rested my cheek on my fist. "But what about all these fairytales you always tell me about true love conquering all?"

"All nonsense." Sophronia turned up her nose.

Fantine slapped her shoulder. "Not nonsense and you *know* that."

Ashlan leaped to her feet and hurried to the medicine cabinet.

"Apolline needs to believe in love," Fantine said to Sophronia. "It will give her light in dark places."

"She needs to believe in science and logic, not your fairytales."

Fantine puffed up, her fuzzy hair sticking out on its end. "Sophronia—"

Ashlan forced a spoonful of potion into my mouth. "Swallow."

Everyone stared at me as I swallowed. Awful stuff. I gagged. "You really need to make that stuff taste better. I've been asking you to fix it for years, Fantine."

"It won't work properly if I change it," Fantine responded.

"Why do I still have to drink that every night?"

"It will keep the ogres away."

I scoffed, folding my arms. "Ogres don't come here. I've *never* seen one."

"They are Bryanna's servants," Ashlan said, returning the potion to the cabinet. "So it's probably for the best."

"Hmm." I glared at the table. "I don't want to take the potion anymore."

"While you live with us, you will take it." Sophronia glared at me as she stood, lifting her plate.

Fantine's face reddened. "You must take it."

"Oh, she will." Sophronia sank back in to her chair. "She will obey."

"You cannot force her!" Fantine pointed at Sophronia's nose. "She must—"

Ashlan glided up behind me and stroked my hair. "Can I play with this? It's so long now, clear down to your waist. Why do you always wear it in that messy bun?"

"It's practical," I replied.

Fantine visibly deflated. "I'll try again with the flavor."

Sophronia's fingers drummed the table as she glared at me. "Apolline, no boys."

I raised an eyebrow, grasping my cup. "I know." I sipped, then thought about our conversation in the woods. I slowly lowered my cup. "Am I to marry a White?"

Fantine, who had just taken a sip, spat it all out. Ashlan's hand drew back from my hair.

Sophronia stood so slowly I thought I heard her bones creak. "What?"

"Well..." I glanced between them, seeing shock and possibly horror in their eyes. "The story of Snow White was one you told me regularly, and you remind me often how important the Whites are. So, I put two and two together and—"

"No." Sophronia's voice boomed around the room.

My mouth sealed shut.

"Never ask again."

I tried to speak, but couldn't.

Ashlan bent over my shoulder. "Why don't you go to bed? It's a little early, so you can read if you would like. I think Fantine bought some new books."

I nodded, still unable to speak, and stood. They watched me as I shuffled to the stairs, heading straight up. When I entered my room, my mouth released and I let out a puff of air.

I punched my pillow. Why couldn't I ask about my soon-to-be husband? I'd waited for years, patiently, never complaining, never once looking at boys even though I wanted to. The teen years were difficult for me... but luckily the boys I grew up with weren't particularly appealing.

I collapsed on my bed. The metal rods in my pocket poked my hip. I pulled them out and twirled them in my fingers. I couldn't believe Sophronia gave them to me. Rolling onto my belly, I opened my bedside drawer to place them inside. The globe rolled and knocked against the wood.

I stared at the globe, Allard's playful, dimpled smile coming to mind. Slowly, I placed the rods inside and lifted the globe out. I turned it around and around, admiring the delicate beauty, and seeing new things from every angle. Figures seemed to move inside, and I could almost hear footsteps on the cobblestone courtyard.

Rolling onto my side, I hit the sensor beside my bed to turn off the main light and switch to my reading lamp. The smaller light made the castle look like a sunset caressed it. *Wow.*

I curled up with the glass ball, thinking of Allard. I had to give the globe back, that wasn't even a question. By the way the fairies reacted, my feelings for him were dangerous. I set the globe back in my drawer, not wanting to become more attached to it either.

CHAPTER SEVEN

The serpent slithered through the mirror. Bryanna turned from staring at her own reflection, her hand on her chin. "What news?"

"The girl is betrothed."

"What?" Bryanna leaned over and lifted the snake.

It coiled around her arm and looked up at her. "Yes, there was a great deal of yelling over it, and the prince even claimed he was her betrothed to force the hooligans to leave her alone."

"He claimed it?" She chuckled, but then her face fell. "I didn't know Mish had a living noble bloodline. I thought the Herrschers had long died out. Look into it while I try to find her betrothed. He must be removed if we hope to lure the prince away from the precious, darling, princess."

She set the serpent down, and he slithered back through the mirror. Once he'd gone, she hurried out of her chamber and through the mansion. She entered a dark library, lit only by flaming torches. A goblin sat surrounded by holo-projectors and screens. Data streamed all around him as his gaze darted from one thing to another.

"No sign, my queen," he said in a scratchy voice.

"I need you to look at something else for me."

Slowly, his gazed turned to her. "Excuse me?"

"You heard me." The flames dimmed and the projections flickered.

He turned to face her directly. "Your wish is my command."

"I need you to access the betrothal archives and find who an Apolline from Mish is betrothed to. Then, I want you to send the ogres to kill him."

"Oh." He chuckled evilly. "We haven't had a good murder in a while. I'll get right on it."

Not since Miriam. Bryanna turned, her emotions swelling. But she couldn't let her subjects see. Bitter and full of grief, she headed out.

Allard pushed the yuckah meat around his plate. He wondered if Apolline killed the beast. He sniffed, frustrated. She'd told him to come back only to collect the globe. He had no intention of retrieving the gift, but he did intend to use the time to convince her to remain friends.

He glanced up at the clock: 6:33p.m. Minutes felt like hours. His father tilted his head toward the prime minister, deeply engaged in conversation. The week had dragged. Although filled with pre-wedding events and planning, and working with his father for the restructuring of government, he felt like every minute lasted an hour. He hated leaving Apolline on a sour note and hoped she hadn't blown their disagreement out of proportion.

He sighed and took a mouthful of yuckah as a question filled his mind. He stared at his father beside him, hoping he'd feel his need to talk to him.

It seemed to work.

Brencis wrapped up his conversation with the prime minister and turned to him. "You haven't eaten much."

Allard shrugged. "Neither have you."

Brencis smiled. "Touché."

Allard poked a lump of meat with his fork and lifted it. "Why is yuckah meat so expensive especially compared to a normal deer?"

"Because they are magical," Brencis said matter-of-factly.

"Yes, but the magic cooks out."

Brencis' eyes sparkled. "Have you ever tried to catch one?"

"I've never even seen a live one."

"Ahh." Brencis wiggled his eyebrows. "There's the key right there. Yuckah are wicked fast and avoid normal mortals like you or I. Only a human exposed to fairy magic for an extended period of time can see or hunt them. The fairy magic gets trapped in their skin, causing the yuckah to be drawn to them, and it slows them down because it's like a drug."

"Fairies?" Allard frowned. That meant Apolline knew fairies. Fairies were few and far between even before the war with Bryanna. Mish did have the tingling sensation of a planet with abundant magic, so maybe some fairies hid out there, waiting for the war to pass.

Brencis cut into his meat. "I've seen both Hernan and Cytheria kill the beasts. There are several large herds on Tyrone that few people know about. Cytheria is better because she grew up in very close contact with two fairies; her mother's and her father's, but the royal fairy was in and out, so Hernan's exposure was intermittent."

"But the three fairies took the princess," Allard said. "Wouldn't the magic wear off?"

Brencis shrugged. "A little, but unless magic is used to remove it, it never completely goes away."

"Why don't we have fairies?"

Brencis chuckled. "You don't hire fairies, they bond themselves to families. Our family has never been of interest to a fairy. They are drawn to troubled loves, hope in dark places, faith when all else fails. Their magic is strengthened when there is love, hope, and faith."

"But mother…" Allard's heart ached.

Brencis' face fell as pain filled his eyes. "The fairies were all in hiding when Bryanna attacked here. Very few can combat her dark powers. Maybe they would have come if circumstances had been different, but there's no point dwelling on that."

Allard sighed, glancing at the clock again. "Am I needed? It's been a long week and I'm tired."

Brencis scanned the guests around the table. "I don't think so. I'll wrap things up soon anyway. You go."

"Thank you." Allard discreetly stood and hurried out the door. But instead of heading to his room, he made a beeline for the shuttle bay.

The tapping of hammers came from all around. I waved at Old Man Timmell as I passed his cottage. He waved back and continued hammering at the board over his window.

Although usually an unnecessary precaution, everyone secured their property when the larger pirate ships came to Mish. I didn't have my cart with me for that reason. I just carried my revolver on my hip and my shotgun over my shoulder. When the pirates came, I assisted Charlie in the store.

This particular group stopped by regularly. Their captain, one Barnibos Black—which I doubted was his real name—loved Charlie's yuckah jerky and tobacco. So the crew was all familiar with me and left me alone. If they did try anything, Barnibos gave them rather unsavory forms of discipline. Once he even neutered a man for his inappropriate and suggestive conduct.

I entered Charlie's store as he secured the back room. He glanced over. "Ah, Apolline. Just in time."

I hurried over and grabbed the cashier counter. "Ready?"

He grabbed the other end and we slid it in front of the door. No one but the two of us would be allowed in the store. We both placed our shotguns on the shelf underneath, and he set the till on a table by the wall; close enough for us to use, but not close enough for the pirates to reach.

Charlie's holo-communicator beeped. He answered and Captain Barnibos' face appeared. "Charlie."

"Good to see you again," Charlie answered.

"Where's our girl?"

Charlie turned the communicator to face me. I waved. "Hey."

His dark face split open with a white toothed grin. "How is my favorite huntress?"

I chuckled. "Just dandy."

He'd always liked me. I first met him when I was fourteen. I'd come to town without knowing about the pirates' visit, and he tried to steal the yuckah straight from my cart. I hit him over the head with a stick and yelled at him to put it back. He tried to take it again, but I kept hitting him until he finally set it down and stepped back. He laughed merrily and said he wished his men had as much spunk as me.

"Your birthday is coming up," Barnibos said. "Any gifts in mind I could scrounge up for you?"

"You mean steal?" I teased. "No. You know me. I like to keep things simple. So a nice day to relax is all I want."

He let out a deep, belly laugh. "I'll make sure we don't swing by that day."

"I'd appreciate that." I smiled.

Charlie turned the communicator to face him. "All right. Barnibos, what shall it be today?"

Charlie made his way out the back as Barnibos rattled off his order. I turned around to pirates already making their way to different stores, but mostly they gathered by the pub and brothel.

The first few came by, barely paying any attention to me as I fulfilled their orders. Charlie laughed from the storage room, so I glanced back, smiling. To us, Barnibos was about as fearsome as a fluffy baby bunny.

"Could I get some yuckah jerky?"

I jumped at the sound of Allard's voice, my stomach fluttering. "Allard!"

He bowed his head with a smile. "Hello again, Apolline."

Why does he have to be so charming? "Jerky?"

"Please." He set a handful of coins on the counter.

I grabbed a paper bag and filled it. "I have something else for you as well."

"What's that?"

I hurried to the storage room and grabbed the globe from Charlie's desk. When I returned, I handed him the jerky and the globe. "You dropped this in my cart—"

"I didn't drop it, I put it there."

I paused, thrown off guard by his frankness. "I can't accept this."

"Why not?"

"Because I barely know you and it's worth so much."

"You like it, don't you?"

"Yes…"

"Then keep it." He pushed the globe back toward me as he plucked the jerky from my hand.

"No." I stretched back out again, but still clasped tightly to the globe.

"You're a stubborn thing, aren't you?" He pushed my hand back.

"Not half as stubborn as you." I out stretched my hand again.

He pushed it back, and was about to speak when another voice interrupted. "Hey there, little lady. Are you going to give us some help, or what?"

I glared at Allard and placed the globe under the counter, then turned to the large bearded man. "How may I help you?"

"Well, I'm looking for a good time."

"They offer that down at the pub. We are strictly supplies." I turned to move away from him but he leaned over the counter, caught my hair and squeezed my behind.

Before I could react, Allard stepped forward and stared up at the man, forcing his hands off of me. "Apologize to this lady immediately."

The pirate's face lit up as he laughed. "Move it, rich boy."

"You do not intimidate me, sir." Allard blocked the pirate from stepping around him. "Do as I say and apologize immediately."

Charlie pressed up behind me just before he whispered, "What does that fool think he's doing?"

The pirate sneered down at Allard. "Who do you think you are, the prince?"

The pirate reached for his weapon. I pulled out my revolver and shot the pirate in the wrist before he could pull the trigger of the laser gun he had pointed at Allard's head.

He bellowed and dropped the gun, grasping at his wrist. "You crazy witch!"

"You get out of here before I blow your brains out!" I raised my gun so his left eye stared straight down the barrel. "Get!"

He growled at me as he retreated back to a shuttle.

Allard looked at me with his jaw hanging and wide eyes. "You shot him!"

"He was about to shoot you." I climbed over the counter and picked up the laser gun. "It was set to kill, too."

I tossed it to Charlie who disarmed it to put it on display to sell.

Allard gaped at me, trying to find something to say, but upon failing, he stood up straight and cleared his throat.

"Well, you could say thank you for saving your life," I said, signaling for Charlie to toss me a cloth to wipe away the blood splatter on the counter.

"Yes..." Allard stared at me vaguely, then blinked, shaking it off. "Yes, thank you. I will forever be indebted to you. And will you not thank me, too?"

"For what?" I replaced the missing bullet in my gun and grabbed the cloth Charlie tossed down.

"For defending your honor and saving you from being... you know."

"I could have handled it."

"You could have..." He stopped and laughed sarcastically. "Okay, is there anything you can't do? You handle guns, hunt, barter, voice your views without being concerned who you might offend—"

"Charlie, I'm going on a lunch break." I tossed the cloth and turned to head down the street, trying to lose Allard. But he stayed hot on my heels.

"Apolline! Don't walk away from me."

"I will."

"Hey! I swear, you are more manly than half the men I know."

I swung around and pointed in his face. "You go defending my honor and almost get yourself killed, then you turn around and call me a man? What kind of confused person are you? One minute you're trying to be my friend, then the next you're insulting me? How am I supposed to react to that?"

He stared at me wide-eyed. I turned and began walking away, and he quickly pursued again. "You're right. I'm sorry."

I rounded on him again, and he almost ran into me. "Excuse me?"

"I said I'm sorry. I am rather confused, yes. I have a lot to be confused about."

I rolled my eyes and resumed walking. "I don't want to hear your sob stories."

He grabbed me by the wrist and pulled me into an alleyway between two buildings. He pinned me against the wall and his face drew close, his intense brown eyes staring into mine with an unbreakable gaze. My heart raced as we stood there, a strange sensation passing over me. I grabbed his shirt over his waist, unable to decide if I should push him back, or pull him closer.

"I want to tell you something." His soft voice reverberated through my body. "But I don't know if I should because it's confusing for me, because, well, because I like you, and I think you like me too, but we are both betrothed so you are pushing me away."

He touched my hair, sending a quiver down my body.

"Stop it," I said breathlessly, my gaze darting between his lips and eyes.

"Do you really want that?"

I whimpered, and he smiled, his face drawing nearer. My breath came in sharp bursts, as my gaze remained locked with his. "Allard."

His body pressed against mine, as he caressed my face. I wanted him to do it. My whole body screamed for him to kiss me. Then, our lips barely an inch apart, he whispered, "I'll see you again tomorrow."

He pushed off the wall and disappeared around the corner. Frozen to the spot, I felt like he'd sucked all the air from my lungs in his wake. The sensation of his breath against my lips lingered. I shut my eyes and all I could see were his eyes staring into mine. Opening them quickly, I forced my feelings aside. I couldn't have feelings for him, it was breaking a vow. A vow I didn't make, but a vow all the same. I stood up straight and composed myself, then headed back out to the street.

I stepped out of the alleyway—

"Apolline."

Wincing, I turned to face Sophronia's deep, scornful scowl. I sighed with annoyance at her incredible ability to show up right when I didn't want her.

"Don't worry, no vow has been broken," I muttered as I turned toward the store.

"Apolline, follow me."

My body turned as she compelled me to follow using magic. I couldn't complain because I didn't want to be transformed into a squirrel for a day like the last time I told her off for using magic on me in a public place. She had said, "Do not mention magic around non-magic folk. It endangers us and you."

By the time we'd arrived back at the cottage that day, I was furry and had an overwhelming urge to eat acorns.

As she strode down the street, she opened her hand to reveal a vial of Fantine's potion. "I believe you didn't take this last night."

"Yeah, well, given the choice, since no one mentioned it, I chose *not* to."

"Drink it now. It will keep the ogres away."

I pouted. "Do I have to?"

"You're such a child."

I glared at the back of her head, snatched the vial, and swallowed the potion in one gulp. "Happy?"

"My happiness isn't the issue."

She led me into the dressmaker shop—the only shop left completely alone by the pirates—and waved her wand discreetly. The staff hunched over the counters and racks, asleep. She sealed the shop closed with a magical field, then turned to me. "I do enjoy a little privacy."

I scoffed, folding my arms.

She swiveled to face me, her green eyes ablaze and her auburn hair glowing like fire. "Apolline, you have done very well at keeping the vow that we placed upon you. Never have you developed any crushes or interest in boys. I think now I need to stress to you how important keeping this vow is."

"I know." I raised my hands. "It's for my own good."

She pressed her hands against her hips. "Don't sass me!"

I glared at her, the tension between us fizzling as sparks spat from the end of her wand.

"Nothing happened," I said slowly.

Her eyes narrowed. "Once a promise is made, it must be kept or grave consequences will follow. This vow was made for your own good, whether you want to believe it or not, and for the good of many others who will be affected by it. Do not allow yourself distractions, no matter how handsome or charming they may be."

"He's not a distraction."

"Are you sure?" Her lip stiffened.

"Yes. I told him he needs to stop coming here."

She eyed me over as if trying to read me. "Good," she finally said. Waving her wand, the shop brightened and the staff stirred. "Now, go to Charlie."

I left the shop, feeling as if I had betrayed the world, but also enraged at Sophronia for interfering in things she knew nothing about. I made it back to the store and Charlie stared at me suspiciously.

"Don't worry, I lost him." I climbed back over the counter, and there sat the globe.

CHAPTER EIGHT

Bryanna laughed merrily at the serpent's report. **"That** is all much better than I had hoped! The prince's gallantry, the girl's fearlessness, an almost forbidden kiss, and a confession of affection! I could never have planned it better. What a fool of a prince. Only two months left and he cannot wait because some pretty little thing tickled his fancy." She stopped, frowning. "Strangely familiar actually."

Darkness filled her eyes as her mind wandered. The memories of laughter, stolen moments, soft kisses... Then, with a blink of an eye, she returned to normal and smiled. "Is there anything more?"

"Yes, my queen, there is." The serpent paused. "After the prince left, a woman stopped the girl and the girl said that she had broken no vow, and the pair went into a dress shop that I could not enter."

"The shop is probably pixie or elf owned and is of no consequence." She tapped her chin. "But I have yet to locate or even discover who her betrothed is. I need to encourage her to fall madly for the prince instead."

She ran her fingers down the gold trimmed frame of her mirror as it swirled a murky green. "I'll send a griffin. Do you think that will frighten them?"

The serpent hissed his laughter. "Most certainly, but be warned; the girl is a yuckah hunter so she knows how to kill magical creatures."

Bryanna twisted her lips. "Yes, that could be a problem. I'll fit it with a magical shield and tell it to keep its distance. I just want them scared into each other's arms, not dead, after all."

"You are cunning, my queen."

"The prince will return in a few hours. I'll send the griffin through the mirror and you will need to guide it from there."

"Yes, my queen."

"Allard!"

Allard shot up, dazed. "What?"

"This is the second Saturday in a row." His father stood at the foot of Allard's bed, his hands on his hips.

"I was tired."

Brencis pointed at him. "You went out partying, didn't you?"

"What? No."

"Yes, you did. It was that White boy, wasn't it? You've always been thick as thieves."

"Beau's stuck out on Calcus with the dwarves. That's about a week's flight from here."

"His brother then." Brencis paced the room.

"Nathaniel is studying for exams."

Brencis growled. "Get up."

Allard jumped out of bed. "I'll be ready in a flash."

As he showered and dressed, he decided to set an alarm next Saturday. It didn't matter on Sundays, that was his only day off, but he didn't want his father sending someone to tail him and discovering Apolline.

Apolline.

He closed his eyes to see her face again. Her fiery expression, her brief undeniable look of surprise and excitement when she saw him at the doorway, her beautiful eyes returning his gaze as he held her against the wall. Her breath had become shallow and sharp. She bit her lip, forcing self-control when he touched her hair. He'd moved in, ready to kiss her, but her whimper held him back. He knew she felt frightened and confused, and he didn't want to force her.

But he'd felt something odd. A pull. A tug that felt so familiar. When he looked into her eyes it was like life could end and he didn't care. He'd had the urge to cart her off and keep her all for himself, except her whimper kicked his senses back into gear.

He stared at himself in the mirror. If only he hadn't had so firm of an upbringing to make him so respectful and honorable. He would have kissed her, and held her, and refused to let her go.

But that pull reminded him of… Cytheria. He shook his head. That would mean Apolline had been exposed to fairy magic, confirming why she could hunt yuckah, but fairies had been in hiding for many years to protect humans from Bryanna. They wouldn't hang around a huntress from Mish and risk the galaxy's safety.

He glanced back at the bed, remembering his dream from which his father had woken him. He swallowed hard and fought back the image of Apolline being pricked by a spinning needle as the faceless sorceress, who could only be Bryanna, laughed. Maybe Apolline *was* the Princess Elpida. No. He brushed the thought aside. No princess would be a huntress and trader, nor would the daughter of King Hernan and Queen Cytheria be allowed to wander around in plain sight the way Apolline did.

But how he wished she was his betrothed.

I moved silently through the woods, my crossbow held loosely in my hand, ready for any movement. I had already missed five animals, and felt incredibly frustrated with myself. My thoughts of Allard distracted me. He was so brave and honorable, but at the same time, such an inner planet snob—which made me want to slap him in the face.

I missed another one.

I dropped my crossbow and flopped onto the ground. I had always been so controlled and proud of the fact that I never let my emotions get the better of me. But something about Allard brought out my fight, my opinions, my passion. The feeling made me infuriated and intoxicated.

He was so handsome too. His dark brown eyes, and that dimpled smile, it just made me go weak at the knees... I smiled simply thinking about it... but I couldn't, I was to marry another. Or maybe... The thought crossed my mind again that maybe he was my betrothed, and was testing my faithfulness before our wedding in two months. How I hoped that to be true, but terribly unlikely.

A huge buck yuckah appeared ahead of me. I froze, and carefully moved my hand toward my crossbow. In one swift movement, I launched onto my feet, my weapon poised for the kill. The yuckah turned and gazed at me. I halted, its big brown eyes staring into mine. Brown eyes, like Allard.

I grunted. "Go, you stupid animal!"

I tossed an arrow at its feet.

The buck leaped into the air as the arrow landed, and darted off. After watching him disappear, I picked up the arrow and trudged through the woods toward the cottage, all motivation to hunt sapped right out of me.

Ashlan knelt outside the cottage, spade in hand as she removed weeds from among the vegetables. She looked at my cart, wide-eyed with surprise. "No animals today?"

"I should go see Charlie," I muttered.

She followed me into the shed. "Sophronia took your dress to the dressmaker yesterday. Thank goodness she gave up on that 'experiment.'"

I couldn't help smirking. "I won't argue there."

Ashlan's hand shot to my forehead. "Warm."

"I've been running around." I pushed her hand back.

She dropped it down over my heart. "Mmm." She smiled. "You'll be married soon. Are you excited?"

"Not overly." I pushed her hand away and collected the few items I had to sell. "Did you need anything in town?"

"We do need some more milk."

"Done."

"Apolline." She grabbed my wrist. "Don't be afraid to love. It's hard, and sometimes you think it's not worth it, but it always is."

I gazed firmly into her eyes. "Who am I marrying?"

She sighed. "I can't say."

I pulled away, grabbing my cart. "Then there's no point discussing it."

"Apolline—"

"I'll get some milk."

I hurried out, pain gripping my heart. For the first time in my life, I resented being betrothed.

I made my way into town. As I approached the store, Allard teleported onto the street. I smiled, but then forced it away. "You're back."

He turned to me, grinning shamelessly, which almost made my smile return. "I am."

I glanced around. "I'll secure my cart in Charlie's dock."

He followed me around the back of the store, then grabbed my hand when we made our way down the alleyway. "We're friends now, right?"

I shrugged, remembering how close we'd come to kissing.

Allard released my hand with a long sigh. "I would like to apologize to you. It was wrong of me to push you to break your vow, and to consider doing so myself. Vows should always be kept once made, and I know that's what we should both be trying to do. But I want you to know that I do very much enjoy your company and still wish to be friends."

"Oh." I couldn't help the sinking feeling in my stomach. But he was right, and doing the right thing. "I understand. I still want to be friends as well."

"You do?"

"Yes, if you could call this a friendship. All I seem to do is snap at you."

"Yes, but usually with good reason."

"Usually…" I bit my tongue. "I will not argue," I muttered, reminding myself of Sophronia's constant scolding.

Allard watched me with a sparkle in his eyes as I swallowed back the fight. "You look as if you're choking."

"I think I am," I said in a strangled voice.

His whole demeanor lit up as he grinned, even more amused. "You, Apolline, are a strange, yet interesting, woman."

"I aim to impress."

He laughed. "So, what exactly is there to do around here?"

"Hmm." I tapped my cheek, feigning thoughtfulness. "We should check out the haunted house. I think you need a good spooking."

"I can take it. The question is, can you?"

"Pft." I slapped his shoulder. "You're so weird."

He laughed and I led him to the haunted house. The rickety, double story building didn't seem to have any ghosts in it as we made our way through, so instead, we moved out to the graveyard next door.

"Have you always lived here?" he asked as we strolled between weathered gravestones.

I nodded. "As long as I can remember. My aunts found me abandoned in the woods."

"Who could abandon you?" He grazed his fingers over mine.

Blushing, I pulled away. "Someone. My parents."

"So they aren't real aunts?"

I shook my head. "I just call them that. They're scientists studying the effects of magic. If you hadn't noticed, there's plenty of it around here."

He side glanced at me. "Almost like fairies live here."

The fairies made it very clear to never mention to anyone they were fairies. Since Bryanna's attacks began, all fairies had gone into hiding to reduce her chances of finding the fairies that protected the princess.

"Fairies? If they do, I've never seen one." I paused at a gravestone. "Gretel Heinz."

"Huh?" He stared at the gravestone.

"Haven't you heard the story of Hansel and Gretel? This is *that* Gretel. I believe they were the ones who brought Mish into the Oran Kingdom." I glanced around. "Hansel Herrscher shouldn't be too far away."

He shielded his eyes with his hand as he scanned the area. As I turned my back to him, looking for the grave as well, he grabbed my arm. "Apolline, run."

"What?"

He shoved me backward, smacking me against a statue. A griffin swooped right at us, its talons extended. Why was there a griffin on Mish?

Allard pushed me to the ground beside the angel statue, and held me down. The griffin hit the statue with a squawk. Then, with a heavy flap, it ascended back into the sky. Before I could react, Allard pulled me to my feet and we dashed for the haunted house.

"Where did it come from?" I yelled, my voice high and tense. "We don't have griffins here!"

"Maybe it escaped from a pirate ship!" He whipped his head around and his eyes widened. He pushed me to the left, just as a talon brushed by me and grabbed Allard. Reaching up, he yanked at its feathers as it lifted him into the sky.

"Allard!"

I reached for my revolver, but the griffin dropped him. Allard landed on his feet with a thud and ran for me. The griffin landed, rubbing with its beak where Allard had plucked its feathers. I lined up a shot to fire, but Allard grabbed my arm and yanked me into a sprint.

"Let me shoot it!"

"Are you insane? Griffins are one of the most dangerous..." We skidded to a halt.

The griffin landed in front of us, letting out a piercing squawk.

Allard snatched out his laser gun and fired.

I pushed his gun down. "Don't use that!"

His eyes widened as the griffin absorbed the energy from the laser, the dim reddish glow spreading like a wave over its feathers and fur, then seeping into its skin. The beast shook its wings and squawked again.

I raised my revolver and fired. I hit the griffin's shoulder. The beast let out a piercing screech, stumbling backward. It lifted off, and flew swiftly over the woods.

Allard and I stood rigid, catching our breath, still clutching our weapons.

"Are you all right?" I asked.

He nodded, but blood seeped through his shirt. He followed my gaze. "Ugh... I didn't feel that."

"Let's get inside."

We hurried into the house, Allard yanking off his shirt as we entered the kitchen. I hesitated, examining his lean, but fit, torso. *What am I doing*? I hurried to find something to cover the scratches from the talons.

"It stings," he said.

"Some magic probably got in you."

"Magic stings?"

I chuckled, opening a cupboard and finding, miraculously, bandages. "No, but your immune system fighting it off will. When it comes in direct contact with your blood like that, your body treats it like an infection."

I carried over several bandages and sat in front of him. "Magic can slowly seep into your skin and you won't feel a thing. The body becomes familiar with it, so doesn't fight it. But if it enters through a cut or graze, the white blood cells just see it as a foreign body and attack."

"You're really smart."

I let out an uncomfortable laugh. "Not really. Not like you anyway."

"Why? Because I have a Masters?"

I raised an eyebrow as I padded the wounds clean. "Say that again and see what you think."

He grinned, gazing into my face. "A Masters does sound impressive." He winced and lifted his arm for me. "But you can be smart and *not* have one. You know more about magic than me, and hunting, and—"

"That's just life experience." I wrapped my arms around him to grab the bandage.

His hands rested on my back. "Has anyone ever told you that you're beautiful?"

I looked into his eyes, holding my breath.

"You saved us out there."

I pulled back, dropping my gaze to my feet. "Maybe you should finish this."

He took the bandage from my hand, his fingers lingering over mine before he pulled away. I walked to the far end of the room, and kept my back to him.

"I made you uncomfortable," he said, the chair creaking as he stood.

"I feel like we're dancing on thin ice," I responded softly. "It's not long until my birthday when I am to be married. I can't do this."

"Do what?" He pulled on his shirt.

"This."

"Be friends? What's wrong with that?"

I looked up into his eyes. "Is that all this is?"

He nodded. "I respect your duty and the oaths made for you, just as I respect my own."

The question that had lingered in my mind all week bubbled up into my mouth and burst free. "Are you my betrothed trying to test me? I know you said no before, but... are you?"

He stepped back, frowning. "No. Do people do that?"

"I don't know."

"That seems pretty harsh." He folded his arms. "I know who I am to marry, don't you?"

I shook my head.

"Hmm, that's unusual." He slipped out his pad and teleported a vest to himself to hide the blood on his shirt. "Apolline, we are just friends, and I hope we can enjoy our friendship until our obligations get in the way. I'd like to come visit you and enjoy your company, but only if you agree."

I stared up at him. Could I resist my feelings for him until my birthday? I wasn't sure, but I did know I wanted to see and talk with him. Everyone else I knew constantly tried to protect me, or order me about, but not him. I felt comfortable with him, like I could be myself.

"I would like that."

His face lit up. "Then I will keep visiting until you no longer show, or…" He shook his head. "We will have fun."

He grasped my elbow and we headed back to the street.

As we strolled onto the main street, now bustling with activity, Allard's hand dropped from my elbow. Not a second later, Charlie appeared. "Apolline."

Allard stopped and bowed his head. "She was just showing me around."

Charlie grabbed my arm, pulling me away from Allard. "I thought you'd been abducted! Someone said they saw a griffin."

"There was one," Allard responded. "But she scared it off."

Charlie's gaze flashed between us. "What?"

Allard told him what happened. Charlie turned on me. "You were *alone* with him?"

My jaw fell. "We were attacked by a griffin and that's what you're worried about?"

Charlie pointed at Allard. "Go. I have plenty of guns and I know how to use all of them."

"Charlie!"

"It's all right," Allard said, looking at me. "I understand how he's feeling. He sees you like a daughter, right?"

We both stared at Allard.

"Yes," Charlie finally said. "A father who doesn't want inner planet scum like you around his girl. You think you can seduce her because she's ignorant of your charms?"

Allard's eyes widened as he raised his hands. "Whoa, no. That's not—"

"Just stay away." Charlie pulled me under his arm.

I resisted. "Charlie!"

"Apolline, this is for your own good."

"Everyone keeps saying that," I muttered. I glanced back at Allard. Our eyes met and I smiled, giving him a subtle wave. He smiled back, and teleported away.

CHAPTER NINE

As the shuttle shot through space, Allard peeled the bandages back to clean his wound. He winced as his skin stung worse than anything he'd felt before. He flushed out the gashes, moaning loudly as bubbling, greenish foam ran down his side.

"Gross." He wiped the foam and blood away, revealing three clean slices over his ribs. Using the first aid kit fitted in his shuttle, he closed the wounds and covered them. He then stepped into his changing cubicle and pulled out a silky pale blue shirt to sleep in for the three hour trip.

His communicator beeped, signaling an inbound call. He froze; worried his father had caught him. He rushed out of the cubicle and looked. Beaumont White.

He grinned. "Beau."

"Al, how's it going?" Beau's image popped up in front of him. His porcelain skin never looked girly on him, but like all the Whites, he always made girls swoon when he smiled.

"You know, busy."

Beaumont laughed. "That's the understatement of the century. Hey, I've got good news."

"What's that?"

Beau's pale blue eyes sparkled. "I'll be seeing you in a few weeks."

"You will?"

"Uh, yeah. Did you forget you're getting married?"

Allard stared. "No, of course not."

"Man, you're really distracted. What's going on?"

"I've been busy."

"No kidding." Beau glanced around. "Wait, why are we in your shuttle? It's gotta be around two in the morning there."

"I needed to clear my head." Allard pulled at his shirt, hoping he hadn't left anything incriminating in view.

"Clear your head? Allard, are you getting cold feet?"

Allard glared at him. "No."

"Why are you out? Come on, you can tell me. I swear I won't tell anyone."

Allard sighed, leaning back. "There's a lot going on right now. I just need a break from it, to be somewhere where no one knows who I am before everyone does. I need to feel normal."

"Ahh." Beau ruffled his raven hair. "Are you hiding out on Latveydos?"

"What?"

"Mate, we haven't been there since we were in university."

"I didn't go to Latveydos."

"What's going on then? You're not doing anything illegal are you?"

Allard paused. He and Beau had done plenty of harebrained and reckless things in their time. "My father contacted you."

Beau pursed his lips. "I didn't say that."

"He did." Allard stood and paced the cockpit. "I'm fine. I'm not doing anything I shouldn't, and he should stay out of my business. I'm a grown man—"

"And heir to ruling the soon-to-be joined kingdoms."

Allard slumped. "Thanks for reminding me."

"Allard." Beau ruffled his hair again. "I get that you're blowing off some steam before stepping into your kingly duties, just be careful okay? Bryanna has been eerily quiet lately, and she would love having you handed to her on a silver platter."

"I'm being careful."

"All right." Beau hit several buttons before looking up at Allard again. "Why don't we, the weekend before your nuptials, hit Latveydos?"

Allard's eyebrows shot up. "Do you really see my father being okay with that?"

Beau chuckled. "He's not okay with whatever you're doing now. Imagine my shock when he called and blamed me for you sneaking out at night."

Allard let out a breath. "Sorry. I told him it wasn't you."

"But from his experience, that usually means it is." Beau grinned. "Do you remember that time we got so wasted your father had to bail us out? Geez, those cops were beside themselves when they found out who we were. They thought we were lying until King Brencis barged in."

Allard laughed. "The tabloids had a field day."

Beau ran his hand through the air. "Crowned prince jailed. Is he up for the task of ruling the kingdoms?"

"We were nineteen." Allard leaned back, chuckling. "Everyone does stupid things when they are nineteen. I love how that went viral for weeks, but my bachelors and masters graduations fizzled after a day. It's like they want me to screw up."

"Speaking of which, have you see Nathaniel's latest and greatest?"

Beau clicked on a few things, then a file beeped up onto Allard's screen. He opened it and a news article opened. "Nathaniel White, second son of Rupert White, is at it again. Today, as he left the university campus, he had two young women under his arms and a cigarette in his mouth. When he saw the cameras, he flashed them."

The image changed to the stunningly handsome twenty-one year old opening his pants and the image blurring as he hollered, "You like that? *Beep* off!"

"Charming," Allard said, closing the holo-vid.

Beau laughed. "He's such a prick to the media. You'd never know he's a good guy."

"I saw."

Beau laughed merrily. "Hey, I talked to him and he wants to see you before the wedding too. Maybe we should do something, for real."

Allard sighed. He wanted to spend that time with Apolline. It would be his last chance to see her. But then, she said she'd never left Mish before. Maybe... "Hey, I have a friend who I met while touring. This friend hasn't really had a chance to get out and about much. Mind if I extend the invitation?"

Beau shrugged. "Any friend of yours is a friend of mine."

"Excellent."

"Let's book it then. The Saturday before the ball and wedding, we'll meet at Latveydos around the H hour. It's usually quiet then."

"Deal."

"All right, mate, I'll see ya then." He disconnected.

Allard headed over to his pull-out bed and settled in. He smiled when Apolline's face filled his mind as his eyes closed.

"You look positively lovely!" Ashlan exclaimed. "The dressmaker has done a fine job!"

I looked at myself in the mirror. "I look like a mushroom."

"Don't be silly, mushrooms aren't purple."

Sophronia frowned. "Apolline, you look splendid. You just aren't used to wearing dresses—"

"I look like a plum then," I muttered.

Ashlan zapped me fiercely with her wand.

I jumped and grasped at my rump. "Why do I have to wear this anyway? I'd stand out like a sore thumb on any planets near here."

Sophronia and Ashlan exchanged grins.

"Shall I tell her or you?" Ashlan said in a squeaky voice.

Fantine burst into the room. "There you all are! I've been trying to find you for fifteen minutes! Look what I made..." She stared at me as her jaw dropped. "Oh my, Apolline, you look fit to be a queen!"

Ashlan shot Fantine an icy glance.

Fantine shut her mouth quickly, but then blurted out, "She just looks so pretty."

"All right, that's enough!" I lifted the skirt in an attempt to pull it off. "When Fantine starts saying things like 'fit to be a queen' and 'so pretty' I know that things really have gone too far."

Sophronia folded her arms, scowling. "Fantine, tell her where we are taking her for her birthday."

"I thought it was a surprise," Fantine whispered.

"Just tell the girl, but leave out some details," Sophronia responded harshly.

"All right." Fantine placed her hands on my arms. "We are taking you to a royal ball!"

"A royal ball?" I blinked, thrown off guard.

"Yes, a royal ball at the capital planet of Tyrone! We thought that since your birthday is close to the princess', we'd give you a special treat."

The room fell into a tense silence as they waited for my response. They expected me to explode with indignation and start protesting and attacking the idea from every angle, but that wasn't how I felt. A royal ball excited me. All the glamorous people, the dancing, the music, the royal families, and all that food! And, what if Allard was there? Maybe he wouldn't recognize me at first because I'd cleaned up and wore a fashionable dress, but when he did, he would never leave my side, and he'd dance with me, and... but maybe I was to meet my betrothed at this ball. It would be nice to finally meet him.

I tugged at my dress. "A royal ball?"

"Yes," they answered in unison.

"A royal ball!" I leaped forward and, grabbing Fantine in a waltz position twirled her around the room. I stumbled on my petticoats and burst out laughing. "A royal ball! How wonderful!"

Ashlan laughed and clapped her hands. "How fabulous! She actually likes the idea!"

But Sophronia wasn't smiling. "Unfortunately she can't go if she's going to trip on her petticoats all night. Apolline, you seriously lack in elegance and grace, and I am appalled that we have neglected you so badly! But I think with a touch of magic, and a *lot* of hard work, you will be fine."

I wanted to strangle her, but was too happy. Instead, I pranced Fantine across the room exclaiming, "A ball, a ball! I am going to a royal ball!"

Dark green goblin blood covered Bryanna's arm. She pulled the goblin's head back, making him whimper. "What do you mean there's no record of Apolline of Mish? Did you check the Hansel and Gretel families?"

"Yes, my queen," the goblin answered weakly.

"Urgh!" She tossed him to the ground as she resumed pacing. "And you searched for just Apolline?"

"Yes." He shuffled up onto his knees, bowing before her. "I searched all the Apolline's in the galaxy."

She screamed in frustration, black lightning shooting from her fingers. "How is that possible? She can't be nobody. She can't..." She paused, seeing the newsfeed for the day and, as usual, Nathaniel White showing his cruder side. Bryanna's lips curved into a smile. "The White's."

She reached over and motioned for the image to enhance. "Nathaniel White's betrothed is kept secret and they are about the same age." She spun to the goblin. "Look into it."

He scrambled up onto his chair to hack into the kingdom archives.

Bryanna marched from the room, her black coat flaring behind her as she went. In the hallway, she paused as she passed a mirror. She examined her long hair, full lips, almond shaped green eyes, and clear olive skin.

"I'm beautiful," she whispered, touching a line in the corner of her mouth. Although in her forties, her hair remained a rich dark chocolate, and her green eyes vibrant. Many men had desired her, but only one captured her heart.

Then her mother ruined it. Cytheria ruined it. The traitors.

A soft squawk from her chambers caught her attention. She rushed in. The griffin limped through the mirror from Mish, blood pouring from its right shoulder. She hurried over, stroking its head. "What happened?"

The serpent slithered up beside her. "The girl shot him."

"I said to be careful." Bryanna rested her hand over the griffin's injury. A soft green glow came from the wound, and she raised her hand, a single bullet now resting in her palm. She examined the round closely.

"She only left a slight imprint on it. I feel fear." She pressed the bullet to her lips. "And a hint of love." She looked down at the serpent. "How did it go?"

"Their bond is growing stronger. The prince protected her, and she in turn protected him. Then she saw to his wounds."

Bryanna ran her hand over the griffin's shoulder. "Go be seen to."

The griffin limped into the hallway.

She looked down at the serpent. "Find out what fairies or elves live in the town. I want to know who has taught her about magic, and if I can use it to my advantage."

"Yes, my queen."

Once the serpent had gone, she turned to her mirror, its cloudy gray swirl barely reflecting her image. "I'm beautiful, aren't I?"

The mirror swirled and showed Cytheria's face. "Not as beautiful as she."

Bryanna clenched her fists. "I hate you."

My body ached from a week of dancing and etiquette lessons as I dragged my cart into town. But knowing Allard would be waiting lifted my spirits. Even in the rain, with the mud suctioning my wheels, I managed to keep a quick pace. I wondered if I could convert it to a hover-cart...

I rushed straight to the general store where Charlie met me with a smile. "Apolline! I haven't asked you what you would like for your birthday yet."

"To sleep for the entire day," I answered grumpily. "My aunts have run me ragged! But at least I can curtsy now without falling over, and I know three dances by heart. Ashlan says that they are the hardest dances to master and all the rest are simply variations of them, so as long as I follow my partner, I will be fine. But I am so tired!"

I rested my head on my arms over the counter.

Charlie laughed. "Very well. You catch up on some sleep while I sort out these supplies."

He tapped my head and pulled my cart out the back.

I didn't move; just shut my eyes to enjoy a moment's rest.

"Hey."

I jumped up at the whisper in my ear, and smacked Allard in the face with my head.

"Ouch!"

"I'm sorry; you startled me."

"Obviously." He rubbed his nose then looked at me seriously. "Shall we step out?"

"It's raining," I whispered, glancing toward the storage room.

"Yes, but..." He looked over as well.

I grinned. "We can finally check out the old courthouse." I bellowed through the store at Charlie, "I'll be back in a few minutes!"

"Hollering like that is not lady-like!" he yelled back.

Allard and I left the store and strolled down the street under the porches of each store. We darted between the gaps, him holding my hand to prevent me from slipping in the mud.

"I love this place," he said as we turned the corner. "It's so quiet, even when it's busy."

"I can't imagine how crazy it gets on those inner planets." I squeezed his hand.

"So you've never, not even once, left here?"

I shook my head. "Not that I know of."

"Wow."

"Yeah, I'm pretty pathetic." I pulled free of his hand and dashed across the street toward the courthouse, hidden by the rain.

He stayed with me, and as we caught our breath between the two pylons by the stone entrance, he said, "You're not pathetic."

I shrugged, looking up at the engraving over the doorway. *"Always look forward,"* I read. *"Because the past is already gone."*

"Like bread crumbs." Allard touched the doorframe. "This is very old."

"It's apparently heritage listed," I responded. "It's supposed to predate the Oran Kingdom's rule of this planet. Hansel and Gretel judged Mish from here."

We stared at the stone building for a moment. Then he spoke, "I like it. It suits this place. It's rustic and full of character."

"It hardly ever gets used," I muttered.

"So?" He glanced down at me. "It's still a fantastic building." He took my hand and tugged me inside.

White sheets and a layer of dust covered all the furniture. The marble floor had gathered leaves in the corners, and several pools formed where the roof leaked.

"I should fix this place up," Allard said.

"Huh?" I looked at him, tilting my head. "Geez, you must be seriously rich to say that in such a blasé manor."

His lip curled. "Ahh..."

"Come on, it's pretty obvious you're a rich boy." I walked by him, staring at the rain pouring down the window. "I'd say possibly aristocratic, especially since you're betrothed, and by the sound of your accent, definitely Oranian, most likely you even live on Oran."

"I'm that transparent?"

I turned back to him, seeing a hint of alarm in his wide eyes. "Yeah." I walked back and pulled at his expensive cotton shirt. "This looks so finely woven it could only be pixie made."

He huffed. "Really?"

"Then there's all the schools you went to, your military rank…" I shrugged. "Basically, you scream *I'm rich.*"

He winced. "I thought I hid it well."

I chuckled. "Nope."

"What about you, then?" He asked, resting his hand on my waist. "You're difficult to figure out. You're a huntress, orphan, but betrothed."

I stepped back from him, turning toward the stairs. "Do you want to look up there?"

"Only if you talk about yourself."

I laughed. "I guess not."

He rushed at me, backing me onto the stairs. As I took the first step, he smirked. "How long is your hair?"

I rolled my eyes and pulled it out of the tangled mess of chestnut locks on top of my head. My hair fell straight around my shoulders, resting just above my waist.

"Wow." He ran his fingers through it. "That's pretty long."

"I like it."

He stepped closer, forcing me up another step. "I want to ask you something."

My breath caught, my pulse racing. "Go ahead."

"I was talking to a friend about the yuckah the other day, and I was wondering; if only people who have been exposed to fairies can catch them, then…?"

I had rehearsed the answer to that many times with Sophronia, so the words popped out automatically. "I've told you, I'm an orphan. My aunts don't know anything about my life before they found me, so I was probably exposed then."

He leaned back, staring at me. Then his dark brown eyes narrowed and he leaned closer to whisper, "That was a lie, wasn't it?"

I pulled back, alarmed. "Let's change the subject."

"All right." He looked me over, forcing me up another step. "Tell me something I am allowed to know about you."

"I like cake."

He chuckled, taking another step. "What else?"

"I'm friends with a pirate named Barnibos."

His face lit up. "His name is really Barnibos?"

"Yes, well, probably not, but that's what he goes by."

We continued up the stairs, him asking me weird and random questions. He made me laugh over and over, and I hardly noticed each step we took upward. A few steps from the top, he brushed his fingers against the heel of my hand. My pulse quickened as I opened my hand and he slid his into it, weaving his fingers with mine. The slight smile, and twinkle in his eyes told me he felt like he'd accomplished something. My heart melted, and I didn't feel like I needed to be so tough around him.

He led me to a metal bench and we sat together, our hands entwined. We talked for several hours before the doors below banged open.

"Apolline?"

I jumped at the frantic sound of Charlie's voice. "I'm here."

He dashed up the stairs as I headed down. He grabbed my arms as we met. "I was so worried! You said you'd be a few minutes. It's been three hours!"

His gaze shifted over my shoulder and darkened. "You again!"

Allard remained indifferent. "Has it really been three hours?"

Charlie turned red. "Apolline, he's not supposed to be here. You shouldn't be with him like this."

"Charlie." I held his hands, meeting his gaze. "It's fine. We're just friends. We're both betrothed, so nothing is going to happen."

He let out a long sigh. "I was afraid someone had murdered or kidnapped you."

I patted my gun. "I wouldn't go without kicking up a fuss."

Charlie glared at Allard again. "Is he armed?"

Allard pulled a laser gun out and tossed it at Charlie. "Not anymore."

Charlie handed it to me. "Get rid of him and come see me."

Charlie marched away.

Allard walked down to me. "I should go anyway."

"Yeah." I handed him the gun.

"I wish, just for once, we could part because we want to, not because someone is making us."

I shrugged, unable to look at him.

He took my hand as we walked down the stairs. "What are you doing three Saturday nights from now?"

I counted quickly. The Saturday before my birthday. "Sleeping."

"Could I take you to some places I like to go, away from here?"

I looked at him apprehensively. "I'm not allowed out after dark."

He raised his eyebrows. "Then sneak out."

I stopped. I'd never considered sneaking out, but then again, I'd never had a reason. "My aunts should be asleep by eleven. I'll meet you at the edge of the woods then."

"I could meet you at your home?"

I laughed. "You could try, but like everyone else, you'd end up lost—even though there's a clear trail from the edge of town to the cottage. Just meet me at the edge of the woods."

He leaned closer. "Deal."

I grinned deviously. How fun it would be to sneak out from the fairies and enjoy the company of people my own age! I looked down at my muddy boots and browned shirt, and brushed uselessly at my clothing. I had nothing to wear except my dress, and that I wanted to save for the ball...

CHAPTER TEN

Allard returned the next day, and again we strolled down the street. Since the rain stopped during the night, we ended up in the park where we sat in the grass for hours. I made him laugh easily, so I often resorted to imitations and sarcasm. He could also be quite serious, and would gaze intensely at me as he spoke about things he cared about with conviction.

At one point, after he had rolled onto his back from laughing, he switched to his serious side and asked me, "Do you ever dream?"

"You mean at night? Of course; I'm sure everyone does at some point."

"Do you think they have meanings?"

"Sure they do." I shrugged. "My Aunt Fantine says *dreams are warnings of what's to come, or just your subconscious telling you to relax.*"

A puzzled look flashed across his face and he sat up and looked at me. "What was that?"

"What was what?" I grinned.

He squinted. "I've heard someone say that before."

"It's probably just one of those old sayings."

"Probably," he muttered and glanced at his watch, then leaped to his feet. "I need to go. Time is slipping by and I'm expected." He helped me to my feet. "Look at this. I think this is the first time we've parted on our terms."

I shrugged. "About time."

He kissed my cheek. "Until next week." After tapping the button of his teleport devise, Allard vanished.

I touched my cheek, my heart pitter-patting. "Until next week."

I made my way back to the cottage, my head in the clouds. Ashlan stared at me as I walked by her at the top of the stairs. "Apolline?"

"Mmm?" I didn't stop, but headed straight to my room. Allard had kissed my cheek. He probably regretted it since I was so filthy, but I didn't care.

"Dearest, are you all right?" Ashlan followed me in and shut the door.

"I'm fine." I looked at her, surprised to find her with me when I wanted to be alone. "Did you need something?"

She rested her left hand over my forehead and her right over my heart. "Warm."

"Um..." I pushed her off.

"Apolline, do you remember the story of the cinder girl?"

"Fairytales? Right now?"

She sat on the armchair by the window. "Tell me the story of the cinder girl."

I sighed and sat on my bed facing her. "Once upon a time—"

"Drop the attitude." She pouted.

"Fine, fine. Once upon a time, a lord and his lady had a daughter. But the lady fell sick from the childbirth and died not long after. The lord grieved for her as she'd been the love of his life, but seeing his daughter as a gift and emblem of their love, he doted on her and did all he could to raise her well.

"As time went by, he realized he didn't have all the skills required to raise a young lady, so he married a widow with a refined daughter of her own. At first, everything seemed wonderful. The two girls, although two years apart in age, became best friends and did everything together.

"But then the lord died. In his will he left everything to his young daughter, and with his last breath, he spoke his dead wife's name. His living wife, furious with jealousy, hid the girl away and soon turned her into a slave.

"Time passed, and the girl bore her burden with grace and humility. She grew into a beautiful young woman despite her adversity. Then one day, to celebrate the prince earning his bachelor's degree, the king held a grand ball. All noble families were invited. The girl being sixteen desperately wished to attend. But her step mother would never allow it.

"After her step mother and sister left, the girl retired to her room and found a beautiful ball gown, jewelry, and delicate glass fairy slippers waiting for her with a note that said; *Love, your fairy godmother.* A moment later, an orange shuttle pulled up out front.

"The household, eager to help their beloved departed master's daughter, helped her dress and prepare in a flash, and she left, bubbling with excitement.

"But she was no fool. She knew she would need to be discreet to avoid drawing the attention of her step mother. So she slipped in unannounced, and hid in the corner to observe. She delighted in the finery, the elegance, and the presence of royalty.

"Then, a young man approached her. She was breath taken by how handsome he was and his chivalry. But then she saw her step mother approaching. She dashed away so she wouldn't be discovered and sent home.

"But the young man followed her, and discovered her pacing in the gardens scolding herself. Amused, he approached her again, and swept her up in his arms to dance. They danced through the gardens for hours, talking like they'd always known each other, and the girl knew she was falling in love.

"But then, as the old clock tolled midnight, she knew her time was up. She dashed away, and headed back to her shuttle to return home. But once she was on her way, she discovered she'd lost one of her glass slippers in her flight.

"She hurried to remove all evidence of her escapades and retire to bed. During the night, she heard someone enter her room. She peeked through her lashes and saw her step sister moving toward her closet. But a maid interrupted her, and made her leave.

"The next morning, the girl awoke early to do all she could to hide her evening excursion. But as she dressed, a royal entourage landed in the courtyard. The whole household was called to gather in the lobby. As the girl ascended the stairs, she saw the man, but he wore the royal crest of a dragon, and when all were called to attention, he was announced as the prince!

"When silence had fallen, he called her name. She froze, afraid of her step mother, as well as him seeing her in her worn and tattered slave dress. But the maid beside her called out, 'She's here!'

"The prince's eyes fell on her and he smiled as he produced her missing glass slipper.

"'What is the meaning of this?' her step mother called out.

"The prince nodded to the step sister, thanking her, for she pointed out that the slipper was fairy-made. He had then searched the archives for young maidens with fairy godmothers.

"He took the girl's hand, guided her to a chair, and placed the slipper on her foot. 'No one has ever made me feel the way you do,' he'd said. 'In just a few hours, you stole my heart...'"

I paused, choked up as Allard flittered through my mind.

"Apolline?" Ashlan touched my hand. She smiled. "Warmer."

I raised an eyebrow at her odd comment, but forced myself to continue. "But the step mother had kept a secret; she was a dark sorceress and had taught her daughter of the dark magic. The pair had a heated argument, and all hid as dark magic filled the room. When it ended, the step mother lay dead on the ground, and the step sister turned to find the girl.

"That was when the girl's fairy godmother appeared—"

"Hooray!" Ashlan clapped her hands. "My favorite part."

I laughed. "The fairy banished the step sister, and with the help of the royal fairy, sealed her on a planet. The prince and girl soon married and they all lived happily ever after blah, blah, blah."

I waved my hand in the air and collapsed back onto the bed.

Ashlan shuffled over and lay beside me, her head propped up so she could look into my face. "It's a good story."

"Yes, everyone gets what they deserve in the end." I huffed. "Real life isn't like that."

She ran her hand over my forehead. "Real life can be better." She kissed my forehead and sat up. "Sophronia wants to work more on your finishing lessons, but I think you should have a day off."

She moved toward the door and I sat up. "Ashlan?"

She looked back at me.

"That story, it's about Queen Cytheria and King Hernan, isn't it?"

She smiled. "What makes you think that?"

"It fits, especially with the dark sorceress banished and bound to a planet. That could only be Mahkba."

"You're a smart girl, Apolline."

"But that means they didn't live happily ever after, and the sorceress found a way to break the bond."

Ashlan nodded. "Happily ever after is something you have to make yourself, it won't just be handed to you. I think the king and queen are happy, despite all their tragedy. So just imagine how much happier they will be when their daughter returns."

Twisting my hair free of the messy bun, I stroked the tangles out as I thought about Princess Elpida. How wonderful it would be to know that just your existence brings so much joy and hope to so many. To know you are destined to marry a prince, renowned for his charisma, chivalry, and for being incredibly handsome. What a charmed life.

I thought of the king and queen, along with King Brencis and Queen Miriam. They hadn't been betrothed, and I wondered... "Ashlan, when did betrothals become so popular?"

Ashlan opened her mouth to answer, but Sophronia's voice responded. "When the sorceress cursed the princess."

I looked up at Sophronia as she stepped into the room beside Ashlan. "Why?"

Sophronia sighed. "The sorceress almost married King Hernan, and many believe she'd put him under a spell which Cytheria broke with *true love*." She said the words with distain. "Many began to fear dark magic making its way into their families, but when the princess was cursed, and the fairies advised a betrothal to break the curse if it played out, many other nobles followed suit to protect their own children. They researched families closely, and made the contracts for their safety, riddling them with clauses regarding dark magic."

"So you made my contract for the same reason; to protect me from dark magic?"

She nodded.

"But I'm not noble born. You don't even know who my parents are."

Ashlan and Sophronia exchanged knowing looks.

I narrowed my eyes on them suspiciously. "Do you?"

"You cleared all security checks," Sophronia said.

"That's not answering my question."

Fantine poked her head in between them. "Are you hungry? I just finished my roast."

"Oh yes!" Ashlan clapped her hands and darted down the hallway.

"Wait, no," I protested, as Sophronia turned after her. "Don't avoid my question."

Fantine wrapped her arm around my shoulders. "Come, eat."

I groaned, knowing I'd hit a brick wall.

Allard sat in his father's office, watching Brencis pace, waiting to be scolded. Brencis paused and opened his mouth to speak several times, but continued pacing. Finally, Allard decided to break the ice. "Father, I'm doing nothing wrong."

Brencis waved his finger at him. "You've told me that before."

"When I was a teenager."

"Which was the last time you acted like this." He pressed his hands on his hips. "Why now? We are only weeks away from the wedding and the unifying of the kingdoms, and you decide *now* is the time to act out."

"I'm not acting out." Allard folded his arms. "I'm just enjoying my last few weeks of anonymity."

Brencis growled. "Then go kick a football around, go to the racetrack and break your arm."

"You want me to break my arm?"

"No, I meant..." He let out a puff of air. "This sneaking around looks bad."

"At least I'm not flashing the media."

Brencis rolled his eyes. "That Nathaniel White. Yes, thankfully you have some sense."

"Then trust my sense," Allard said, standing. "I won't do anything to jeopardize the future of the kingdoms."

Brencis sighed, slumping. He reached up and touched Allard's cheek. "You are so like your mother. Such spirit." He shook his head, turning to his desk. "Go, do whatever it is you're doing, but just be careful. Bryanna's spies are everywhere. Don't let me regret trusting you."

Allard's heart soared. He had permission to visit Apolline! No more sneaking around. "You won't regret it, Father. In fact, I'm learning about normal people so I can better lead them with understanding."

Brencis swung around, his eyebrows right up. "Why did you hide that? That's very noble. It makes me wonder what you think of me."

Allard grinned. "I should have known you'd understand."

Brencis pointed at him. "Keep it between us. The media will have a field day if they find out."

Allard thought of Apolline being flashed around everywhere and exploited. "I won't let that happen."

Allard and I sat by the courthouse again and conjured up my escape plan. I felt like a giddy school girl, but I didn't care. It would be the weekend before my birthday, so I deserved a little fun.

As I performed my lessons one evening with the three fairies watching me, Sophronia spoke up. "Charlie informs me you have been spending time with that man again."

"So? He's my friend."

"He cannot be your friend, Apolline."

Fantine froze and averted her eyes, while Ashlan turned her back to me. I stood stiff and gritted my teeth. "He is, and will continue to be, my friend. You cannot deny me that!"

"Yes I can."

"No, you can't! I have no friends my own age because the girls are all whores or are afraid of me, and the boys tease me or are off pillaging. I'm tired of being on my own. I just want this one friend, this one person who doesn't treat me like a freak or a child."

"I'm sorry to upset you, but it's impossible."

I looked down at my feet, tears welling up in my eyes. "But you're not sorry. You love torturing me. You love denying me things I like. You've always only tolerated me being here."

Sophronia pointed her wand at me. "Enough."

"No. Fairies are supposed to be good, but you're cruel."

"Apolline." Fantine frowned. "Enough."

I looked into her eyes, my emotions bubbling over. "I just want a friend."

"Not with a man." Sophronia folded her arms, her gaze boring holes in me.

I looked to Ashlan. She kept her back to me as she hummed. *Useless.* "Very well," I whispered, and briskly left the room.

Ashlan caught my arm at the door, but I pulled away without looking at her.

"It will be all right, Apolline," she whispered after me.

I marched to my room and slammed the door shut behind me. How dare they? We were doing nothing wrong! I marched over to my bed, picked up the pillow, and pounded my bed with it. My tears streamed down from the pain in my heart. I sat and sobbed into my pillow. As my tears faded, my mind kicked into gear. I would be married soon anyway, so Allard could be my friend then, and I was not going to back out on the trip. I looked at my door with defiance. I didn't care what they said.

CHAPTER ELEVEN

Allard stood by the store waiting for me. Our eyes met, and I tilted my head to signal for him to move. He nodded, and headed to the courthouse.

I pulled my cart out of sight, and we went inside.

"I'm excited for you to meet my friends," he said. "You've probably heard of Beaumont White."

I nodded, knowing I had to tell him he needed to stop visiting, but I did still intend on doing our trip.

"I've known Beau for years."

"Wait." I raised my hand. "Isn't he the prince's best friend?"

Allard tensed. "Yeah."

"So, you know the prince?"

Allard drew a sharp breath. "Yeah."

"That's crazy." I walked by, staring in the doorways. "I've never met anyone who knows royalty before, well, except Charlie, but he doesn't count."

"Charlie?"

"Yeah. He used to be a lord or something like that, until that big attack on Oran when his family was killed. He came out here to escape it all then."

"Huh." Allard rested his arm around my waist. "So you're not going to ask me about the prince?"

I scoffed. "Why? I can just look up everything I want to know about him. Isn't he a drunk or something like that?"

Allard's eyes darkened. "No."

"Well, as you once said, the media does make things worse than what they are." I sighed; this would be the best time to bring up my problem. "Allard, I have to tell you something."

"What's that?" He pulled me closer.

"Charlie told my aunts about you and, like the media, they kind of blew it out of proportion. If I get caught with you again, they'll probably neuter you."

He stopped walking and pulled back. "I'm not sure if you are being figurative or completely serious."

I shrugged.

He tensed and his hands fell over his crotch. "Geez, you're serious."

"But I want to do our trip, so much." I grabbed his arm. "Maybe, just for the next couple of weeks, you shouldn't come here. Then I'll be able to slip away without them watching me so closely. If you keep coming, they may lock me up or something drastic like that."

He clasped my face as desperation filled his eyes. "I want to see you. I make it through my weeks because I know I'll see you at the end. I've never known anyone like you."

I grasped his wrists, pulling his hands away from my face. "Don't talk like that."

"You've become my best friend. I've never felt like I could be myself with anyone else quite like I do with you."

"Stop it." I turned away as tears formed. "I want to ask you something else."

"Anything," he said so tenderly it just about ripped my heart out.

My voice trembled as I asked, "Do you know who the Whites are betrothed to?"

"Beau yes, but Nathan..." He trailed off, so I turned to him. His eyes were wide with alarm. "No."

"What?" My stomach tightened.

He stepped back. "No one knows who Nathaniel's betrothed is."

I swallowed, unable to meet his gaze. "Do you think...?"

Allard turned away, running his hand through his hair. "No."

"You don't?"

Allard groaned. "I didn't mean that."

"My aunts tell me about the Whites a great deal."

He winced and stared into my eyes. "I have to go."

"Allard." I grabbed his arm as he turned away. "Are you upset?"

He let out a long breath. "I have no right to be. I'm betrothed." He looked down at me. "You're right. Our trip shouldn't be jeopardized by our contact. It's only two weekends away. I'll send you messages at the email office under the code name Edgar Rage."

"What should I reply with?"

"Jane Smith." He pulled away from me, heading to the door.

"Allard, please don't be angry at me."

He looked at me, his jaw tight, but with clear sadness in his eyes. "I'm not angry at you." He hit his teleport and vanished.

Allard immediately called Nathaniel. As he waited for him to answer, he drummed his fingers on his elbow. The thought of Apolline with Nathaniel made his blood boil. She deserved better than that chronic flirt.

"Allard!" Nathaniel's grinning face—that looked nearly identical to Beau's—appeared in front of him. "How's it going, buddy?"

"You need to stop being such a prick."

"Wow." Nathaniel's hands rose. "Where is this coming from?"

"Flashing the cameras, really?"

Nathaniel laughed. "They blurred it out. I knew they would."

Allard snarled, his irritation growing. "Do you take anything seriously?"

Nathaniel's grin vanished. "Hey, you know all that is just for show. What's going on?"

Allard ruffled his hair. He couldn't tell Nathaniel about Apolline, especially how he felt. "Do you know anything about who you're betrothed to?"

"Nope."

Allard tensed. It had to be Apolline. Why Apolline? "Nothing at all?"

"Nope. Why?"

Allard had to avoid leading him to know the truth. "It's frustrating, isn't it? I mean, I at least have a name, but nothing else."

Nathaniel snorted. "Yeah. I watch girls walk by every day and wonder, is that her?"

"Then why do you act like such an idiot?"

Nathaniel's jaw dropped. "I don't know, why are you out exploring the outer planets? To let off steam, right?"

"Touché." Allard flopped back onto his chair. "But aren't you afraid she'll look at you when the time comes and think, 'Oh great, *him*,' because she's heard all about you? What if she's already in love with someone else and the betrothal will do more harm than good?"

"Allard." Nathaniel's pale blue eyes stared steadily at him. "The princess will love you. If it comes to it, you will give her that 'true love's kiss' and save the day. I'd say every girl in the two kingdoms would die to be your elusive princess."

He tried not to cringe as he thought of his dream where Bryanna killed Apolline.

"Hey, Beau told me about our night out. I'll be there, we'll chill, let go a bit, and everything will be fine for the wedding. Plus, I'm excited to meet this friend Beau said you're bringing. A normal person, huh? Should be fun."

"Yeah." He didn't want to bring Apolline to meet Nathaniel anymore. What if they got along better? Or worse, what if they didn't, and they were betrothed and didn't know it? "I better go."

"All right. It's late there. I'll catch ya later."

Allard disconnected and leaned back. He couldn't bear the thought of Apolline marrying Nathaniel. She would be so close he would find it hard to resist her, to forget her and love Elpida instead. Also, what if Nathaniel didn't make her happy and he watched her live in misery? The thought made him sick.

He pressed the heels of his hands into his eye sockets. If he could just convince Apolline to be with him, to find a way out of their contracts... Yes, there had to be a way. But the princess, what if the sorceress' curse played out and she needed him to kiss her to set her free? Maybe he could kiss her and convince her they weren't meant to be together.

He snorted. He felt like such a jerk.

I shoved the data chip into my pocket and hurried across the street to Charlie's. Although eager to read Allard's message, I needed to keep my feelings hidden. If anyone found out about our secret communications, I'd be in trouble.

I dumped my bag on the counter and hollered, "Charlie!"

His footsteps approached and he appeared through the doorway. "I thought your aunts had been working on your manners."

I leaned over the counter. "I know how to do the tricks, doesn't mean I'll always do them."

"You're obnoxious."

"And you're an old fuddy duddy."

He smirked. "Mature."

"I don't care." I opened my bag. "Not much today. Yuckah are hard to find right now, so Fantine gave me some extra medicines."

He raised an eyebrow. "Really?"

"Mmm hmm."

He grabbed the bag. "What kind of medicines?"

"They're all labeled."

He looked inside and let out a long whistle. "She's given me a good stash. Some of the farmers on the islands would pay good money for these. I'll give you five hundred for them."

"Five hundred?" I looked into the bag. "Geez, I should be making medicines, not hunting. There's only about twenty bottles in here."

"These are exceptional medicines." He lifted the bag over his shoulder with a wink.

I smiled back. Fantine's "medicines" were definitely exceptional.

The news report flashed up on the projector, and the name *Nathaniel White* caught my attention. The image of what appeared to be a lecture hall at the university filled the projection. Flames lapped at the windows as smoke billowed out. I shot over and turned up the volume to listen.

"...Fortunately White wasn't in the building at the time of the explosion, but five are confirmed dead, and many more injured. Reports are saying ogres appeared out of the bathrooms and set the place on fire, trapping many inside..."

I gasped. "Charlie, have you seen this?"

"What?"

"Oran University was attacked."

Charlie appeared at my side. "What?"

"Yeah. I guess Nathaniel White was supposed to be there."

Charlie grabbed my arm. "Had to be Bryanna. She must be striking out at those close to the royal family in an attempt to flush out the princess."

I stared at the projector. Nathaniel White appeared surrounded by reporters firing questions at him. Wow, he was gorgeous. Tall, dark and handsome, with the expected White family pale skin and blue eyes... I'd be fine with marrying him.

"I feel terrible that this has happened," he said in a rich, silky voice. "I'm trying to find out who was hurt. They were my classmates."

"Why weren't you there, Mr. White?"

Nathaniel glanced around, then answered. "I slept in, pure and simple. I'm pretty glad I did. Now, if you'll excuse me, I want to find out how my friends are."

He pushed through as the reporters tailed after him.

"Vultures," Charlie said with a growl. He handed me a sack of coins.

"Charlie?" I said, looking at him. "Am I to marry Nathaniel White?"

Charlie roared with laughter. "What could have possibly led you to that conclusion?"

"So *you* know who I'm to marry?"

Charlie cut his laughing short. "No more questions."

"Charlie—"

"Apolline, it's not my place. Your aunts will reveal it if they feel it's appropriate."

I groaned. "I have two weeks, *two weeks,* until I have to marry the guy. Can't I get just a small clue? Can you at least tell me if he's handsome, or old, or even if I'll like him?"

"You should like him," Charlie answered dismissively. "But that's all I'm saying."

I pouted. I wouldn't get a good answer from him, so I changed the subject. "I'm going to sell you my cart."

His head snapped up. "But that was a gift from Fantine."

"I know, but I doubt I'll need it wherever I'm going."

"Mmm." His gaze fell onto the counter. "I won't buy it until after you're gone."

"All right." I tied the pouch to my belt, feeling the chip in my pocket. "Well, I'm going to head home. I've got nothing else to do around here today."

"Bye. Be safe."

I hurried down the street, waving to the tipsy sheriff when he called to me from the pub. Once off the main street, I pulled out the chip and inserted it into my pad. The message popped up on my screen. I smiled as Allard told me jokes and answered questions I'd asked him. His messages were always so cheerful.

At the bottom, he'd attached a file. I opened it and saw; *Application for an Annulment of Betrothal.* Was he completely mad? I glanced around, hoping no one was looking over my shoulder, and deleted the file.

CHAPTER TWELVE

Allard brought his shuttle into orbit around Mish, the main continent shrouded in darkness. His time to meet Apolline drew near.

He hurried to check the shuttle again and made sure no evidence of his royalty sat out in view. He checked his change cubicle, and smiled at the red dress that hung there. He hoped Apolline would like it. When he saw it, he thought of her.

He took a deep breath. She hadn't mentioned anything about the annulment form he'd sent, so he wasn't sure if he should bring it up. But every day that passed without seeing her, he knew more and more that he loved her. He felt guilty about ending his betrothal, but he'd determined to make a relationship with Apolline happen.

That night... day... was his chance to convince her. He didn't doubt she would protest, but he had to try.

He grabbed a second teleporter, shoving it in his pocket, then teleported to the surface of Mish. He headed to the edge of the woods where they'd agreed to meet.

Silence had filled the cottage for half an hour. I glanced at the clock by my bedside: 10:53 p.m. I fiddled nervously, suddenly afraid to follow through. I'd never deceived the fairies before, and I had a twinge of guilt for it. Then I remembered our argument and my guilt vanished. I pushed my window open; the cool night air wafted in. Taking a deep breath, I smelled the fresh scent before I climbed out. I moved silently through the woods toward town, glancing around nervously as I went. The familiar route looked eerie with its dark moonlit shadows and the sounds of the night creatures on the prowl.

A yuckah appeared in my path and I jumped, letting out a quick screech. "Stupid beast," I growled at it as I ran by.

I had slept during the day in the woods. With yuckah mating season in full swing, they were harder to find, so not catching any didn't seem suspicious. I had set up traps for other animals to make it look like I'd at least done something, and gone to sleep for several hours in preparation for that night.

As I approached the edge of the woods, the little farmhouse at the end of the road leading into town came into view. I glanced around for some sign of Allard. He leaned against a tree.

"Allard?" I spoke in a hushed voice.

He straightened and peered into the woods. "Apolline? I can't see you."

With the confirmation it was him, I approached quickly, unable to stop from smiling.

He smiled too, and attached a teleport device to my shirt. "I have something for you in my shuttle."

"Oh?"

He activated our devices and the woods faded before my eyes. My whole body tingled, then a small room with only a door formed and the tingling stopped.

Allard chuckled. "Never been teleported before?"

"I told you, I've never left Mish before."

He walked toward the door and it opened before him, but he turned back to me, frowning. "It's unusual. Everyone travels between planets."

"My aunts don't have a shuttle, so..." I shrugged. "I like Mish anyway."

"I do too."

He led me to the cockpit and we looked down at Mish. My eyes widened with amazement. A huge ocean faced the sun, and the other half of the planet had broken islands scattered across it and lay in darkness. On the sides, the light faded into the darkness with a bluish glow from the ocean. The planet looked enormous. I hadn't realized how large Mish was.

"Your town is just over there." He pointed to a large island to the southwest of the cluster of islands. "It's the biggest town in the planet. In fact, most of the islands are single farms, except the bigger ones of course, like Gelb in the north."

I didn't answer, I already knew that, but seeing it clearly like that mesmerized me. I moved forward and pressed my face against the glass.

Allard chuckled behind me. "This is going to be an interesting day."

He moved something, then he touched my shoulder. As I turned, he placed a red dress in my arms, then handed me a pair of flat, slip-on shoes. "I thought you might like these. If they aren't the right size, there's a re-fitter back there in the change room."

I stared blankly at the dress. Did he really want me to wear it? I ran my hand over the heavy satin, having never owned something so pretty.

"It's not very fancy," he said. "But it's fashionable, so you won't get any odd stares."

I looked up at him. He smiled hesitantly. I wanted to grab him and kiss him for his thoughtfulness, but instead just whispered, "thank you" and gave him a hug.

I darted into the tight change room. Inside, a small closet sat opposite the door, a full length mirror on one side, and a cushioned ledge on the other. I sat and yanked off my boots and unclasped my belt. Within seconds I had changed, and stood admiring myself in the mirror. I found the knee length dress and flat shoes surprisingly comfortable, and also found the transformation fascinating. I couldn't believe that I actually looked like a regular girl. Although I had to adjust the dress in places—letting it out slightly here, or bringing it in a little there—it felt strange to look at myself in the mirror and see someone

I wasn't used to seeing. My long hair looked too wild to be left hanging, so I quickly decided to put it up in a ponytail.

Then I looked again at the closet. Curious of what could be inside, I fingered the handle, contemplating the pros and cons of looking at Allard's personal possessions.

A rapping on the door made me jump. "Are you all right in there?"

"Yes," I answered, flicking my hair back. "I'm coming out now."

Allard moved to the pilot's seat as I opened the door and stepped into the main cabin. In front of him, the sky now appeared black with tiny dots shooting by.

"We have two destinations today." He swiveled around on his chair, and slowly looked me over with a smile. "You look great."

I brushed the skirt and shrugged as my cheeks warmed. "Thanks."

His chest puffed out as his smile turns into a wide grin, his eyes sparkling. "The first stop will be the planet of Latveydos. It's a small planet that is so far from its sun that it's permanently night, so it became a planet covered in night clubs, casinos, theaters, and so forth. It's also in the same solar system as my university, so we should see some of my old friends there."

"I've heard of Latveydos. It's full of the rich and famous," I responded as I sat beside him.

"Yes, I guess that's true," he said without looking at me. "We will meet my friend Beau there. You should like him."

"Beau White." My mind whirred with thoughts of my conversation with Charlie. If Nathaniel White wasn't my betrothed, then who could it be?

"He said he might bring some friends too, if that's okay with you?"

I looked into his eyes, my stomach doing summersaults. "Like the prince?"

Allard's eyebrow twitched. "Doubtful. He's supposed to get married in about a week."

"To be a princess!" I stretched my arms. "Could you imagine knowing your whole life you are going to marry the Prince of Oran who is supposed to be the most handsome man in the galaxy?"

Allard's face lit up as he smirked. "Most handsome huh?"

"Don't take it personally." I slapped his shoulder. "He's a prince. Everyone wants their own prince charming."

He let out a short laugh. "Anyway, after that, we will go to the capital planet of Oran. It's a pleasant place; tall buildings, busy streets, large green gardens, and of course, everyone's favorite attraction, the royal palace." He looked at me with a coy smile.

"Does the palace look like the Tyronian one?" I asked, thinking of the globe in my nightstand drawer.

He shook his head. "Quite different, actually. It's built out of metals and glass instead of stone. It's still beautiful, just in a different way."

I smiled excitedly and sat back in the seat. I stared up at the screen, watching the stars shoot by with anticipation.

The console beeped loud and rapidly, like an alarm.

"What is it?" I asked.

"A pirate ship must be nearby."

"Oh! Which one?" I leaned forward to see.

He gave me an odd look. "Does it matter? We should get moving."

Something bumped the ship and we came to a halt. In front of us, a huge, dented and scarred silver ship appeared. Allard glanced at me nervously. "Don't let them see or hear you. They'll let us go if they think we aren't worth their time."

The monitor let out a different beep, signaling a communication connection request. Allard pressed a button which brought up a screen.

A dark skinned pirate appeared. "I don't feel like killing you, just give us your valuables."

"I am without any valuables. I am returning from an errand," Allard answered.

"You look like a rich boy."

I looked at the screen. "Captain Barnibos?" I leaped in front of Allard.

Allard tried to push me back, but Barnibos saw me. "Apolline? What are you doing off Mish?"

"I'm rebelling," I answered.

He frowned. "Apolline, if Charlie hears about this, he will be very angry—"

"Then don't tell him."

His frown deepened. "I'm taking you back—"

"No! Please don't. If you let us go, I won't say anything to Charlie and I'll even add some extra jerky to your next order."

"No, Apolline, you need to go back. It's too dangerous for you out here, and your aunts will have my head."

"Captain Barnibos," I pleaded with the most pathetic expression I could muster. "Haven't I always been good to you, and given you good deals, and taken care of your men? Don't I provide the best yuckah you have ever tasted?"

"Yes, but—"

"Please let us go, just this once."

He hesitated, then said, "Who is that scoundrel with you? What are his intentions?"

"He is my long lost brother—"

"Apolline..."

"A cousin then?"

"Apolline! You are betrothed."

"I know, I know. He's just a friend who wants to let me see what it's like to be a young person out in the kingdom."

"Where are you taking her, boy?"

"To the capital of Oran to see the palace," Allard replied quickly.

"Hmm." Barnibos stroked his goatee. "Apolline, you watch yourself. I'm sending you my contact code if you need me. And boy, if you lay a single hand on her, I'll cut it off and gouge your eyes out."

"Sounds fair," I answered as Allard rubbed at his wrists.

Barnibos pursed his lips. "All right, you can go. But don't tell Charlie I did this, and I expect that extra jerky in my next purchase."

"Deal."

The image on the screen vanished and the ship pulled away.

Allard shuffled. "Who are you?" A smile slowly grew on his face. "I can't believe you spoke to a pirate like that."

I sat back on my seat, grinning. "We go way back, ol' Barney and me. He tried to steal one of my yuckah out of my old cart once, so I smacked him with my spear. He thought it was so amusing to have a little teenage girl trying to fight him that he paid me enough for two."

Allard laughed. "You're nuts."

We soon arrived at Latveydos, and landed on the roof of one of the larger hotels. As we walked toward the roof entrance, the shuttle moved into a parking place on conveyer belts. I stared, mouth hanging. Allard tugged on my hand, smiling with an amused twinkle in his eye.

I grunted and trotted after him.

In the elevator, he turned to me. "This is the club where my friends and I would always come after exams and a long week in school. It's nice because everyone is trying so hard to be respectable and honorable that there are no drugs and hardly any alcohol, so it stays pretty tame."

The elevator doors opened and music exploded in our ears. He walked toward the door where a tall, muscular man greeted him. "Allard! It's been a while, my friend."

Allard shook the man's hand. "It has. I've been on tour."

"I heard. But who is this? Is this—?"

"No, this is my friend, Apolline. She's from little Mish. I met her while touring."

I stuck out my hand; he gripped it tentatively, his lip curling as looked at me like I carried some kind of disease.

He looked to Allard. "What about—?"

"Apolline here is betrothed as well, but she has no idea who it is," Allard said.

"Oh." The man's disgusted look faded and he smiled at me. "It's a pleasure to meet you, Apolline."

I nodded, not really feeling like responding to the man. He stepped back and motioned for us to enter.

The music blared and holograms projected a video clip all around the room. Colored lights flashed, and smoke clung onto the floor, sending my senses into overload.

Allard touched my back, guiding me over to a table in the corner where we had a perfect view of everything. He sat close to me and leaned into my ear so I could hear him. "See those glass windows up there? They are one way. On the other side, the really rich people hold private parties. This planet, because of its pull for the upper class, has a strict no-media policy. If you get found posting pictures or anything for the public to see from this planet, you can get fined thousands of miroans. So, there's a very good chance those rooms are all being used right now."

I glanced up at the four windows. "I wonder who they could be?"

He grinned. "Who knows?"

A waiter approached us, so we ordered our food and drinks, and he disappeared again. Then Allard pointed out different people. A singer and his groupies dominated the space on the dance floor. By the right wall, a son of a duke hovered, watching the twin daughters and heiresses to the largest casino chain in the Oran Kingdom. Allard continued pointing out more as we waited for our food.

We ate, and I watched everything with excitement. The place gave me a buzz, and felt so lively compared to Mish. Everything looked new and modern. The people were glamorous and stylish.

Allard grabbed my arm, smiling. "Ah, here we are. Looks like Beau brought all his siblings."

My stomach tightened at the prospect of meeting the Whites. After years of stories about them, to meet the real Whites in person seemed surreal. I shielded my face with my hand and looked up at Allard. "All of them?"

Allard leaned closer to me so our faces were barely inches apart. "You see the four people who just walked in the door?"

I nodded. There were two young men and two young women, all bearing a striking resemblance to one another. But what struck me most was how incredibly attractive they looked. They all had thick, dark hair, and clear, porcelain skin, with pale blue eyes and red lips.

"Meet the Whites, Snow White's grandchildren." Allard gestured toward them.

"No!" I gasped. "I can't meet them."

"Yes, you can. They're expecting you." He stood and waved at them.

They all waved back as they redirected their path toward us.

I ducked a little lower. "I can't meet them."

"Why not?"

"Because they're practically royalty! Everyone knows about their family. The oldest daughter is to marry the prince's cousin after the return of Princess Elpida, Beau is to marry some courtier, and Nathaniel, well, Nathaniel is a nutcase."

"So?"

"Well, I'm, I'm..." I shifted uncomfortably. I'd never felt lowly in station before, but being away from Mish, all my bravado sucked out of me.

"You're what?" He smiled.

"I'm—"

"Allard!" A male voice interrupted.

Allard stood and grasped Beau's hand. "Beau! It's been a while."

"Well, you were off doing your military thing. How was it?"

"It was definitely a learning experience." Allard motioned to me. "This is Apolline, the friend I told you about. I met her on my way back from Tyrone."

I felt self-conscious again as they looked me over.

Beau stretched out his hand. "It's nice to meet you, Apolline. How did you meet Allard?"

I struggled to answer calmly. "He stopped in on my planet to get supplies."

Allard grasped my shoulder. "Apolline here is a yuckah huntress, and a very good one, too."

The sisters scowled as they eyed me over again. To them, I must have looked a frightful mess.

"Love yuckah," Beau said, drawing my attention back to him. "They have the sweetest meat you will ever taste."

Nathaniel grinned at me, a grin that, despite his unsavory reputation, made me feel weak at the knees. He stretched out his hand. "Interested in taking a spin, Apolline?"

I glanced nervously at Allard who nodded encouragingly, so I took Nathaniel's hand. "Sure."

Nathaniel pulled me eagerly onto the dance floor.

Bryanna scanned the line of ogres preparing to go through to Latveydos. "Don't shoot anyone," she said sternly. "I don't want another incident like at the university. I want it clean, and precise, and most importantly, the huntress from Mish cannot be harmed."

"Yes, my queen," the ogres said in unison.

"You all have DNA scanners, so only kill the Whites, especially Nathaniel. He is your primary target."

"What if we get hold of the prince?" one asked.

She wheeled on him, glaring. "The prince must live. I want Cytheria to taste the bitter flavor of betrayal. I want her hopes to be dashed by the boy she thought would save her precious daughter."

She waved for them to go. The time for her revenge drew nigh, and she needed all her cards in place. But even if Nathaniel wasn't the huntress' betrothed, at least there would be one less White running around.

CHAPTER THIRTEEN

Allard watched with envy as Nathaniel led Apolline onto the dance floor. They matched well, and he resented it. But she hadn't mentioned the form he'd sent, so he tried to distract himself, afraid she would refuse, or that she didn't return his feelings.

He turned to Beau. "Don't say anything about me being the prince."

"She doesn't know?" Beau raised his eyebrows.

"No."

"Allard, what's up with you? You're supposed to marry Princess Elpida in a week, and you are running around with some huntress? I'm sure she's lovely, but—"

"It's not like that, Beau. She's betrothed, too." Allard sighed as he watched Apolline dancing.

The two sisters turned to him and the oldest one, Jamila, spoke. "Allard, you can't be in love with her."

Allard frowned. "It's not like that."

"Hmm." She examined Apolline. "She's pretty, but no princess."

Beau grasped his sister's shoulder. "Leave it alone, Jamila."

"Just don't mention that I'm the prince. It will probably freak her out," Allard said, then turned to Beau again. "Can we talk?"

Beau nodded and they walked away from the sisters and out of earshot of any possible eavesdroppers.

"So," Beau began. "Who is she, really?"

Allard raised his eyebrows. "She's who I said she is."

"Then she's not secretly the princess?"

"No." Allard straightened. "Why would you say that?"

Beau raised his hands. "Hey, I believe you, but doesn't she kind of remind you of King Hernan?"

Allard watched Apolline as Nathaniel twirled her around the dance floor, examining her features in the dim light. "Maybe a little, but that's not what I want to talk to you about."

"All right. What is it?"

Allard leaned in closer. "I want to find out who she's betrothed to."

"You think I know?" Beau laughed.

"Well, you went on that blitz our second year at university trying to discover who your betrothed was, and you found the documents listing every betrothal."

"Doesn't mean I memorized it."

"But is she, maybe…" He paused. "Yours or Nathaniel's?"

Beau shook his head. "No, I'm marrying some girl who's still only fifteen. I'm going to be just like my father; almost thirty and marrying a teenager." He glanced at Apolline. "I'd much prefer her." He looked back to Allard. "I'll access the archives again and have a look, eh?"

He pulled out his pocket-pad and quickly hacked into the royal archives. Then, within a few moments, he scanned through the betrothal records. "Where is she from?"

"Mish."

Beau paused and looked up at him. "Mish? Seriously?" Allard scowled, and Beau continued. "I can't seem to find her. Does she go by another name at all? Was she born on Mish?"

"Not that I know of, and she said she's an orphan."

Beau sighed. "Well, she's a mystery to me. I can't find her anywhere. There isn't even someone from Mish listed. It could be an unregistered betrothal."

"What about Nathaniel?"

Beau exited out of the archives and put his pocket-pad away. "Nathaniel is to marry a girl he knows, but can't stand, one Lucy of Gerusha."

"King Hernan's niece. Yeah, he can't stand her."

"That's why he doesn't know it's her. Our parents and hers are negotiating a betrothal annulment."

Allard let out a long breath of relief. That had to be the best news he'd heard in weeks.

"Allard?"

Allard focused on Beau, realizing he'd been staring at Apolline. "Sorry, I'm just worried about her. She's kind of sheltered. She comes across as tough, and is definitely well informed, but everyone on Mish kind of keeps her on a tight reign. Every time anyone saw me with her, I was chased away, and all we did was talk! I'm worried her betrothed will take advantage of her."

Beau punched his shoulder. "You idiot. You're in love with her."

"Ouch." Allard rubbed his shoulder. "No, I'm not."

"Are you trying to bring the kingdoms down? Do you want to hand it all over to Bryanna?"

"Of course not."

"Then you need to stop. She needs to go home right now and you must never see her again." Beau rubbed his eyes. "I don't mean to sound harsh; she's sweet, so I get it. But Elpida needs to be your true love. You remember what happened with my grandparents."

"Who doesn't?"

Beau scowled. "Allard, it will be over soon. Once you're married, you don't want to look back and regret anything."

Allard watched Apolline as Nathaniel led her over to his sisters. He felt a twinge of pain, his feelings for her stronger than ever, but his honor and sensibilities told him Beau was right.

I enjoyed dancing with Nathaniel. He didn't make me feel uneasy in his presence, or below him. He was charming and funny, and to my relief, he wasn't the crude, vulgar creature the media set him up to be. In fact, I found myself a little disappointed that he wasn't my betrothed.

As Nathaniel walked me back over to his sisters, they barely acknowledged me. Luckily, Nathaniel made up for their lack of interest. "You were crazy out there! Where did you learn to dance like that?"

I shrugged. "I watch holo-clips."

He laughed. "That explains everything."

"Nathaniel," the oldest sister interrupted. "I think you should let Apolline come with us for a moment."

His smile faded. "Why?"

"Just so we can have some girl talk. Plus, Allard needs to tell you something important."

Nathaniel looked over at Allard. "Oh... okay." He leaned in and whispered in my ear, "Don't let them get the better of you. I love my sisters, but they can be a tad over-protective." He squeezed my hand then made his way over to Allard.

Once he'd gone, the oldest sister spoke to me. "I'm Jamila, by the way."

I nodded, uncertain whether she was being rude, or trying to be polite through her snobbery.

"So, Apolline, correct? Where are you from?"

"Mish."

"Mish? That tiny agricultural planet on the lower perimeter?"

"That's the one." I smiled.

She raised her eyebrows, giving me the once over. "So, you're betrothed? May I ask to whom, and why, since you are so obviously not an aristocrat?"

Her blatant snobbery irritated me. "I don't know, actually." I wrapped my arm around her shoulders and pointed to different men around the room. "It could be him, or him, or... oh, I hope *not* him, or..."

My finger slowed and I pointed to Nathaniel's back. "Maybe him? That would mean we would be sisters."

She glared at me as the younger sister giggled. Jamila turned on her.

The younger sister pulled away. "What? She's funny."

Jamila narrowed her eyes, then turned back to me. "You cannot hang around Allard. He is above you in every way. He's most likely taking pity on you for your lowly state, or finds your crude outer planet ways amusing and will tire of you soon. I'd recommend leaving now before you humiliate yourself more than you already have."

I straightened, holding her gaze. "Don't you speak to me like that. I may not have blood status, but I work hard for my living, and do very well for myself. Allard and I are friends, and whether that lasts or not, is none of your concern."

She scowled. "Do you think that it would be right for him to been seen with a huntress who most likely consorts with pirates? How would that look to the kingdom?"

I placed my hand on my hip and tilted my head. "What is that supposed to mean?"

The younger sister nudged Jamila and shook her head.

"Who *is* Allard exactly?" I asked.

A hand wrapped around my elbow. "Ladies," Allard interrupted. "Shall we all dance?"

Jamila's scowl deepened. I ignored it and smiled at Allard. "Sure."

She moved away from us, dismissing me with a wave of her hand. "I'm going to get a drink."

The rest of us made our way out onto the dance floor. I loved spending time with them. They were such fun and easy-going. I loved feeling normal with them and not the freaky orphan who was adopted by fairies.

After several songs, Allard grabbed my wrist. "Come with me for a second." He tugged me away, then stood by the bar, ordering us drinks. "So do you remember asking me if you might be betrothed to Nathaniel?"

I nodded, feeling a hint of pain from the memory. He left so upset.

"Well, it turns out you're not."

"I know."

He took a double take and stared at me. "You know?"

"Yeah, Charlie let that particular detail slip."

He turned to face me directly, stepping closer. "Did he tell you…?"

I huffed, looking away. "No."

"Did you get the form I sent you?"

I took a sharp breath. I glanced up to his eyes, but couldn't look for more than a second. Too much feeling poured out of them. "Allard—"

Beau rushed at us, dragging his youngest sister behind him. "We have to go."

Allard glanced around and his eyes widened. "Quick." He slid his hand into mine and pulled me toward the door as Nathaniel rushed after us with Jamila.

"What's going on?" I asked.

In the far corner, the emergency exit hung open, broken, and several ogres forced their way inside. All the people in the club scattered as Allard tugged me out the door.

"Ogres?" I yelled to him over the noise. "Why are ogres this far into the kingdom?"

Allard didn't answer until we were in the elevator. "They periodically search the aristocrats for the princess. They use bio-scans and such."

"Why doesn't anyone stand up to them?"

"They're not like pirates, Apolline. They could rip you limb from limb with their bare hands."

The elevator door opened. On the roof, six ogres snatched up people, scanning them. Allard grasped my hand and pulled me into a sprint across the parking lot. He pushed me into the shuttle and rushed into the cockpit. As Allard fired up the engines, I reached to my hip—

My belt.

I rushed into the change room and lunged for my gun, yanking it from the holster. Ogres had a small amount of magic in them, but not enough to stop a bullet.

I flung the door open and ran back out.

"Apolline, stop!" Allard yelled as I shut the door behind me.

Allard tried to open the door, but Apolline had somehow jammed it shut. "Apolline!" he called in vain.

He rushed back to the cockpit and dialed in Beau's code. As he waited for a response, Apolline stepped out onto the empty lot, holding her gun at her side. Why did her red dress, long hair, and a revolver held loosely at her side look so incredibly sexy? He watched as she took a deep breath, and opened the barrel to check her bullets.

He heard Beau's voice. "Allard! Is that your friend out there?"

"Yes, she locked me in my shuttle—"

"Is she crazy?"

"Most likely." He watched through the windshield as Apolline strode toward the ogres. "I need you to help me get her back in here."

"Oh geez, Allard!"

"Come on! She said, 'Why doesn't anyone stand up to them?' Then off she goes! How was I supposed to know she meant *she* needed to?"

"She's ballsy, I'll give her that." Beau grunted. "I'll be over in a minute."

Checking my rounds, I strode toward the ogres as they chased the last few people into a small ship. One of the ogres lifted his head, locking his gaze on me. He stared at me, frozen on the spot as I rushed toward him. He tapped on the shoulder of the ogre next to him. They all swung around, my apparently unusual behavior rendering them immobile, like deer in headlights.

"You volunteering to be scanned, girlie?" the first ogre called out.

"I think you should all go back where you belong," I shouted, stopping to stand my ground.

They laughed deep, throaty laughs. Then the ogre asked, "What cha' gonna do about it?"

Huh. Ogres really aren't as scary as the fairies made out. I raised my gun and capped him. He fell to the ground with a thud. The other five ogres stared at his body. I cocked an eyebrow as I turned the barrel.

"That's no laser gun!" one of them hissed with an edge of fear.

"Kill her!" another called.

They charged screaming at me.

I had five bullets left, so I needed to make them count. One of the ogres shot a laser at me. I swung to my left dodging it, then fired at him. He fell as the bullet hit him in the heart. The next ogre came at me the fastest, so I shot his femoral artery. He fell grasping at it desperately to stop the bleeding. The next picked up the laser gun and tried to fire, but I shot him in the eye. Then, one grabbed me by the hair and pulled me to my knees. I swung around and shot him point blank in the chest. As he fell, I turned to face the last ogre, my gun pointed between his eyes. His gaze locked with mine, then turned and ran.

I looked at my gun and smiled. "One left."

I flicked the barrel out, and dropped the round onto my palm. The bleeding ogre rolled on the rooftop as he moaned, clinging to his leg. That was easier than I expected. For such brutes, they went down really easily.

Allard ran at me, grabbed me by the arm, and hauled me back toward the ship. He shut the door and locked it, then met my gaze, his eyes alight and wide. "You're insane, you know that!"

"Hey, I just got rid of those ogres for you."

"They will send more now! We better get out of here."

He rushed over to the controls, tugging me behind him and sitting me down to keep an eye on me. We lifted off and soon a beeping came through for a call. Allard answered to Beau and Nathaniel's laughter. They both leaned into view, eyes wide and smiles even wider.

"Apolline," Beau began, "*that* was awesome!"

"Yeah, no one has ever just blown them up like that before!" Nathaniel laughed, holding his belly.

Allard sighed, forcing a straight face. His lip twitched. "You shouldn't encourage her, she doesn't need it."

"Oh, Allard," came the youngest sister's voice. "You're just bitter because she locked you in."

The brothers laughed harder. Allard looked at me, frowning, though his eyes sparkled with his restrained amusement.

I smiled innocently.

He shook his head, his grin finally breaking free. "It was very bold."

Nathaniel pushed in to take up the whole screen. "Apolline, if you weren't already taken, I'd beg you to marry me right now!"

I laughed.

Allard frowned. "Nathaniel..."

Beau pushed into view. "We better go. Apolline, it was fantastic to meet you, you crazy, mad girl."

The call ended with a beep, and I looked at Allard as he charted in our course.

He tried to ignore me as he spoke. "Promise me you will behave on Oran."

I didn't answer but waited for him to look at me, then I grinned.

He laughed and shook his head.

"All right, I'll behave. I'll be the epitome of discretion." I handed him my gun. "Lock it away so I'm not even tempted."

He took the weapon from me. "Really?"

"Yes, take it away."

He disappeared into the change room, returning almost immediately, empty handed. He sat back down beside me.

"Are you upset with me?" I asked.

He shook his head, smiling. "No, you just scared me."

"I'm sorry."

He looked me over and sighed. "Don't worry about it. I should have known you could handle it. I've just seen so many people hurt by them, while they do the sorceress' bidding... I didn't want to see you get hurt either."

I touched his arm. "You're a good friend, Allard."

He grasped my hand, then cringed. "Gross. Go wash up. You've got blood on you."

"Really?" I turned my hand over. "Ogre blood is—ironically—good for the skin. It's supposed to make it soft and youthful."

He scrunched his nose, horrified. "Go wash it off."

I waved it in his face and he shoved me away. I laughed. "You're a prude." I headed to a small bathroom. "Allard?"

"Mmm?"

"I had fun," I said, washing my hands. "Although the combination of dancing and an ogre massacre wasn't what I originally had in mind, I enjoyed myself."

"You seem so... unaffected."

I shrugged. "It wasn't much different to killing a yuckah. Ogres don't think much; they're followers. But their body parts are great ingredients for magical potions and remedies."

"And how do you know that?"

I stiffened. I'd said too much. "Oh, you know, people passing through."

"Uh huh." His chair squeaked and he walked toward me.

I didn't dare look around, but focused on scrubbing my hands clean.

"I was genuinely scared for you." His voice was directly behind me.

I scrubbed harder at my hands, focused on them rather than Allard standing so close. "I know, and I'm sorry. But I'm quite capable of taking care of myself."

"Are you sure?"

He rested his hands on my waist; my breath caught.

"Apolline." He brushed my hair away from my neck, and pressed his lips against my skin.

I shuddered, my whole body tingling at his touch. "Oh my..."

He slid his hands over my belly, wrapping his arms around my waist and pulling me closer to him. "I'm glad you're not marrying Nathaniel. I think it would drive me mad."

I focused on our reflection in the mirror. He buried his face into my hair, kissing my head. I couldn't believe how good he looked there, with me in his arms. Resting my hands over his, I leaned back against him, and I closed my eyes. "We can't do this."

"You're not protesting."

I took a deep breath and looked into the mirror again. For years I'd resisted feeling anything for any man, knowing all it would do was cause me heartache, and Allard, well, he proved that pain to be real.

I couldn't have him.

Biting my lip hard, I peeled his arms back and stepped out of his grasp. "You're confused. The stress of the moment has gotten the better of both of us." I pushed out of the bathroom and returned to my chair. "Tell me about Oran."

He stood behind his chair, resting his hands on the back of it. "Oran? Well, the cities glisten in the sunlight, but the rest of the planet is so green." He stared ahead, his mind elsewhere. "I love it. It's my home, and I'd die for it if I had to."

I stared at him, wondering at the melancholy which swept over him. "I can't wait to see it."

He snapped out of his trance and smiled at me, revealing his dimple. "You'll love it."

CHAPTER FOURTEEN

n ogre lunged through the mirror into Bryanna's lair. She turned to him, startled. "What are you doing here?" He gasped for air, struggling to catch his breath from running. "My queen, we must send reinforcements. There was a girl... she shot the others."

Bryanna whirled to face her mirror. "Who is the girl who can defeat ogres?"

An image of Apolline shooting the ogres appeared. Bryanna watched as they each fell, while the ogre whimpered behind her, mortified by having to relive the moment. She turned to him, smiling. "It is good you showed me this. That girl is the one I warned you about. She is to be left alone. She is distracting the prince perfectly."

"But, my queen, she killed—"

Bryanna waved him off. "Just give me the scans and retrieve your companion you left bleeding on the roof."

He placed a handheld scanning device on her desk, then bowed and stepped back through the mirror.

"Mirror, show me again." Bryanna watched Apolline as she wielded the gun with ease. Apolline had such strength, such confidence, just like herself at that age. Nothing could stop Bryanna in her youth, but although her powers had grown much stronger, her passion had died. A broken and heavy heart would do that to a person.

She watched Allard as he scrambled from the shuttle. Miriam. A male version of Miriam. Bryanna's already shattered heart crumbled as a single tear fell. Cytheria had caused this, all of this.

She paused the image on Allard grabbing Apolline and pulling her back to his shuttle. She leaned closer, smirking at the protective look she saw in Allard's eyes. Yes, now it was Cytheria's turn to suffer from a broken heart.

We entered orbit around the Oran capital planet. Shuttles buzzed everywhere, large cargo ships waited in queues to dock, and even bigger battleships locked into their station. The planet itself appeared to easily be more than twice the size of Mish, and large cities covered over half of its land masses. They looked as Allard said; glimmering surfaces in the sunlight, separated by the deepest green I'd ever laid eyes on.

"It's incredible!" I said breathlessly, my gaze darting everywhere.

Allard attached an earphone over his ear. "It is rather impressive."

He fell silent as he listened, then typed in a code on the console. A brief pause followed, then he looked over at me. "We're clear to land. You should put on your seatbelt. It can be a little rough going through the atmosphere."

I clicked my seatbelt into place.

We landed in the biggest city, the capital, which stretched westward from the ocean. Allard shut down the shuttle and stood, grinning. "Are you ready to go sightseeing?"

He led me out to the hanger where people busily worked. As we moved away from the shuttle, a crew rushed over to it. I watched them shoot by with fascination, but Allard paid no attention to them. Hoping he hadn't noticed my foolish gawking, I scurried after him.

I followed him to a counter where a man sat behind a laser-proof shield. He looked up casually, then leaped to his feet. But before he could say anything, Allard spoke. "Just take it to its usual place, good sir. I will be back in a few hours."

Allard swiped his card, smiled at the man, and walked away.

I rushed after him, confused, but he simply grabbed my hand and wrapped it around his elbow.

We arrived at the exit and, with one swift push, the city unraveled before me. I couldn't help stopping to stare at the skyscrapers, the hovercrafts buzzing by, and shuttles weaving their way between buildings which glistened in the sunlight, with their walls made of glass and metal. People from all walks of life, from traders to aristocrats, filled the pristine streets as they rushed by on their business.

But I didn't pause for very long to take all of it in, as Allard tugged me onward. As we walked, I continued to marvel at the city. Huge holo-decks advertising all kinds of products loomed everywhere. Life-like robots in shop windows sang jingles as we went by, and as we walked past the universal exchange building, it had a display of all the planets in the two kingdoms, and a stream of numbers and strange names constantly changing around the entire display.

Allard noticed my wide eyes gazing around and asked, "So, do you like it?"

I nodded eagerly. "Very much."

"Allard!" someone called out, but he ignored it.

I looked up at him. "Did someone just call to you?"

"Unlikely," he muttered.

"Allard!" the voice came again.

He quickened our pace without looking around. "You know, I think we should go in there." He nodded toward a three story building.

"But I definitely heard someone call your name." I spun around to find the source of the voice.

"Don't look around! It's a second cousin. She's terribly annoying, and I would rather enjoy this time with you and deal with her tomorrow." He yanked me through the door.

Inside, the building was so unlike anything I'd ever seen before that it took my breath away. Ahead of me, the building stretched out beyond my view and appeared to be made entirely of marble and gold. It stood three stories high, with the center of the second and third levels open so that the glass roof was visible from where I stood on the bottom floor. Along the sides of each level lay little shops with their goods on display in the windows. There seemed to be everything imaginable for sale: from clothes to jewelry, holo-cameras to souvenirs, and in the air, the smell of food cooking.

"It's called a shopping complex," Allard said as we walked down one side. "But some of the young ladies call it a mall."

We walked along, me buying a few items from shops using the money I'd saved up, while Allard offered to pay every time. Then, in a window, I saw a small globe. I rushed over and gazed at the tiny castle inside. It looked just like mine, and beside it in another globe was the Oran castle, just as Allard had described it—made of metal and glass—but inside its walls lay a vast garden with a small lake on one side, and beside it, a maze. I grinned at Allard eagerly. He laughed as I squeezed his wrist and ran inside.

Royal merchandise filled the shop; clocks, spoons, mugs, everything imaginable, and it all had the royal emblems or one of the kings embedded on them somewhere. Very few items had Queen Miriam because she had died years ago, but the most beautiful objects in the shop had Queen Cytheria on them. To the back of the shop up on the wall, I found a collection of portraits of both the royal families. Only one depicted Princess Elpida as a baby in her mother's arms and her father standing behind them, and none of Prince Allard any older than five years.

"I wonder what they look like now?" I whispered to myself.

Allard overheard me and answered. "A handful of people know what the prince looks like, the aristocrats and such, but Princess Elpida remains a mystery. Many believe she looks just like her mother."

I stared up at Queen Cytheria. I found it hard to fathom that someone could be so beautiful. She was more beautiful than the Whites by far, and even Ashlan with her fairy beauty.

"She's stunning," I said. "What a lucky girl to inherit that appearance."

I glanced over at Allard. He stared up at the painting as well, but he stared at King Hernan instead.

"King Hernan is a great king," I said, trying to get a glimpse into his thoughts.

Allard looked quickly back at me, then his gaze flicked back up to the painting, then back down to me. "Yes, he's a wise and compassionate ruler, and also very courageous in the face of danger." He paused, then added, "A lot like you."

I laughed. "Yes, those pirates and ogres really bring out the worst in me." I headed for the door. "Come on, there's nothing I want to buy here."

We continued walking along the shopping complex. About halfway along the second floor, Allard quickened his pace, then a voice called his name again. The people around us stared. He grabbed my hand and darted into an elevator. As we shot to the roof, I spoke quickly, "What was that about?"

He dodged my gaze. "That cousin again. She always makes a scene."

"But why did everyone stare?"

The doors opened and he rushed me into a taxi. "The palace, please."

During the brief ride, I stared at him suspiciously. He had to be someone important. I even wondered for a brief moment if he was, in fact, Prince Allard. He did resemble Queen Miriam a little... I pushed the thought aside. After seeing Queen Cytheria, the prince would never look at me with the promise of a younger version of that. I stared at my hands in my lap, rough and dry from use. No prince could possibly be drawn to someone like me.

But the question still remained: who was Allard?

We arrived at the gate where two guards stood at attention on either side. On the western side of the gate stood a booth with a sign that read, *Palace Tours*. A group of about ten people gathered beside it, waiting.

Our taxi pulled up, and Allard led me over to join the group. The gate opened soon after, and Allard swiped his card as payment for entry. He smiled at me, looping his arm for me to take it. I did so, and he led me to the group as it waited to pass through security.

The tour began in the grand foyer, a wide open area with smooth curving lines of steel and glass. The floor appeared to be polished granite, and in the center, a fountain sprang up from a glass cube. I gazed around, awestruck by its striking magnificence.

"Do you like it?" Allard whispered.

I leaned closer. "It's very shiny."

He chuckled and pressed his hand against my back, encouraging me to follow the group. We moved through the palace as I gazed around, amazed. Never had I seen such architecture or even comprehended it. The whole palace was built of metal and thick glass. Leather and black furniture adorned the rooms. The guide explained it to be, "the most modern and technologically advanced building in the two kingdoms."

Allard whispered to me that it was, "the ultimate man-pad," which made me snort as I held back my laughter.

We reached a huge wall of glass, and outside stretched the gardens. Right outside the window was a pond with a family of ducks on it. Bushes and trees lined its shore, along with several stone benches spread out evenly. Beyond this area, a tall hedge could be seen.

"The hedge you see is the maze Queen Miriam designed. The original maze had been so well trodden that everyone knew the route to the middle," the guide explained. The group gave a polite laugh and she continued, "At the center of the maze is a classic fountain that has remained unchanged for centuries. It is believed that the prince himself and Queen Cytheria race to it and spend hours conversing there."

I moved over to the window and pressed against it. "Wow."

I felt Allard behind me before he touched my hair, moving it away from my ear so he could whisper, "Let's go race to the center."

Goose bumps rippled over my skin from his breath on my ear, and I again fought to suppress my attraction and feelings for him. I glanced at the guide who led the group to the next room. "I don't think we're supposed to leave."

"Since when has that ever stopped you?"

I smiled and turned, looking up into his eyes. "And how do you propose we get out there unnoticed?"

He pointed to a door off in the corner of the room that exited out behind some bushes. Then he motioned at a path that led to the maze, obscured by a string of trees and more bushes.

"Excellent observation," I muttered, surprised.

He grasped my hand and tugged. We reached the entrance to the maze and he began taking off his shoes.

"Why are you doing that?" I laughed.

"Habit," he muttered, then quickly glanced at me. "I mean, I have been to other mazes before."

"Whatever, it just gives me a head start!" I ran off into the maze. I darted through—turning, hitting dead ends, turning back.

Every now and then Allard called, "Are you there yet?" and I answered, "No!"

Allard sat on the edge of the fountain listening to Apolline as she dodged and weaved through the maze. He could tell she loved the sport, and that she believed she could beat him. He listened carefully so he could move off and dart in just before she made it to the center. He smiled, enjoying the moment with this amazing young woman. She huffed as she hit a dead end and his heart flipped.

He knew without a doubt he loved her. That moment in the shuttle with her in his arms felt right. She'd given in to him for a moment and allowed him to be close to her. He rubbed his arms, still feeling the smooth satin and the warmth of her body. Her hair smelled like vanilla, and her skin felt surprisingly soft considering her rough and hardworking nature.

He needed to be with her instead of the princess, but that thought, that feeling, broke his heart when he came to the same conclusion as he always did: it was impossible. Too much was at stake. He focused on the here and now, this time with Apolline.

He heard her make the right turn, so he darted to the opposite entrance.

Bryanna stroked the crystal, melancholy overcoming her as she watched the prince and the huntress in the maze. No one had ever really loved her, not like that. She frowned, and shook it off. King Hernan may have.

They first met at Miriam's wedding, but she avoided him like the plague. He was a prince after all. Then, they met again several months later at a social, held by the duke of the neighboring planet. Her mother did everything in her power, and spent every spare kep, to make her the most beautiful young lady in the room.

"Nothing is more important than beauty," she told her. "Beauty catches wealthy dukes, brains scare them away. So mind your tongue and don't act too clever." She then paced the estate, muttering something about how her stepsister had ruined her life.

Every man at the social had eyes for Bryanna. Her long, wavy, chocolate brown hair gleamed, her green eyes were bright. She looked dazzling, and she found their attention flattering, but none could captivate her. As smart as she was, everyone else seemed stupid in her eyes, until a tall, handsome man approached her, Prince Hernan.

He ran his fingers through his thick, light brown hair apprehensively. But his dark eyed gaze locked with hers and he asked her to dance. He was far from stupid. Politics, literature, everything she could throw at him he knew at least something about. She didn't even notice the eyes watching them as time slipped by.

When they parted and she headed home, her mother muttered, "Beauty is the key, my dear. You caught a prince tonight, now you must keep him. So I will show you something that is very secret, that has been passed down from mother to daughter."

She climbed out of the hovercraft, and Bryanna darted after her into the house. "Mother, what...?"

Her mother's arm pressed against her chest. She looked at her, then followed her fierce gaze to her fifteen-year-old stepsister, Cytheria.

"Beauty will steal away men's hearts," Mother whispered.

Cytheria heard them and turned, smiling. "Hello, Mother, Bree."

Darkness filled her mother's eyes. "Come here, dear."

Cytheria skipped over, her blonde curls bouncing. "I know I should be in bed, but I wanted so much to hear how the evening went. Bryanna, did you meet anyone lovely or royal?" Her eyes glowed up at Bryanna who was two years her senior.

"Well..." Bryanna began with a smile.

Her mother cut her off. "Cytheria, you know you shouldn't be up this late, you are grounded."

Cytheria's face fell. "I'm sorry, mother, really, I just—"

"Silence! I don't want to hear your whining. Bed, now!"

Bryanna remembered that as the last night she could be close to her sister. That was the last night Cytheria had slept in her own bedroom before being moved to the servant's cottage, demoted from a Lord's daughter to servant by her jealous stepmother. But it was also the first night her mother had shown her sorcery, and she had felt the intoxication of its power.

Something else happened that night she'd long forgotten, but whenever she tried to retrieve it, it buried deeper. Just a feeling remained. A sense of loss and if-only. She'd given up trying to remember, but it still niggled at the back of her mind.

Bryanna breathed in deeply through her nose. Her powers had grown since then. Even the royal fairy would struggle to defeat her now. But true love's kiss conquered all. That needed to be headed off, and, like all men, a pretty face distracted the prince from his heroic cause.

I ran into the center of the maze, but Allard barely beat me there. "No!" I groaned and playfully punched his shoulder.

"It was a fair win," he said, huffing to catch his breath.

I collapsed onto the edge of the fountain and looked around. "It's strange to think royalty sat in this very place."

He looked down at me. "Yes, but the whole palace is like that."

"Not really. This has been the same for generations, and this is where they came and still come to have privacy, informality, and a moment to just be normal like you and me. Plus, isn't this fountain supposed to be magical?"

I reached to touch the surface.

Allard caught my hand, pulling it away from the water as he sat beside me. His head hung as he looked at our joined hands. "This may be our last moment together."

My stomach filled with a sick sensation, dreading the prospect. "No, we will still be friends no matter what."

"No, I mean..." He paused, hesitating. "Are you fine with marrying a stranger?"

I looked away, pulling my hand free. His question plagued my mind. The more time I spent with Allard, the more I had fallen for him and wanted to be with him, but I struggled to fight my feelings. As a result, his words tugged at my heart. "I have to be, don't I? Everything was arranged for me when I was a baby for my own good. I'm a simple commoner, after all."

"You're not common. Or simple." Allard sat quietly for a moment. "Even if someone offered love?"

Butterflies filled my belly and I became lightheaded. No, I had to keep fighting my feelings for him. They couldn't overcome me and blind me from the reality that we were both betrothed. He wasn't mine to love. "Who would ever love me?"

His head snapped up at my words but I turned away. "Anyway, I'm going to the royal ball where the princess is being introduced to the kingdoms. Am I right to assume you will be there?"

He stared at me pleadingly, but I gazed back firmly. So he simply replied, "Yes."

I relaxed, smiling. "Then would it be too much to expect one dance from a friend?"

He smiled back. "Not at all." He stood and grasped my hands. "Apolline, I—" His pad beeped, interrupting him. He let me go, reaching into his pocket. "I have to get you home right now!"

He pulled me to my feet and we ran through the maze. I held back tears the entire way, my heart breaking at what I'd just done. He'd been on the verge of asking me to be with him, but I pushed him away. Being so deep in my thoughts, I barely noticed how easily he led us out of the maze.

CHAPTER FIFTEEN

In the shuttle, I changed back into my clothes. I sat beside Allard, and an awkward silence fell between us. I sighed. "I left the dress in there."

"You can keep it."

I looked at him. He kept his gaze fixed ahead, and his jaw clenched.

"Allard—"

"How can I go on feeling like this?"

I turned away, fighting back my tears. "We're just friends. You have to remember that."

He scoffed and stood. "There's a pull out bed back there. You'll probably need some sleep."

"Allard—"

"I don't want to talk to you right now. I can't..." He clenched his jaw. "Get some rest, Apolline."

He marched into the bathroom and locked the door behind him.

Fighting the urge to cry, I entered the alcove where a bed slid out from the wall. I fell asleep quickly, apparently more tired than I realized.

Allard woke me when we arrived at Mish, and we teleported to the edge of the woods. As I handed him the teleport devise, an odd braying sound drifted across on the early morning air. We both looked into the woods at a small herd of yuckah staring at us.

"That's strange even for them," I muttered.

They walked toward me and the braying stopped. A doe approached, sniffed me, snorted, then grunted to the others. They all turned and headed back into the woods.

I looked up at Allard. He shrugged, just as shocked as me.

Before the doe followed the others, it looked at Allard then bit him. "Ouch!"

I slapped its neck. "Hey! Get!"

It jumped, startled at being struck, and trotted into the woods.

Allard turned to me. "Are you a fairy?"

I laughed. "No. Fairies don't marry." I nodded to the yuckah. "Obnoxious creatures they are."

"What?"

"It bit you."

"No, you said, 'Fairies don't marry.' How do you know?"

Again, I'd said too much. "Well, you know, they don't have males. They regenerate."

"What?"

"Huh?"

"How do you know so much about fairies?"

I scoffed. *Stupid big mouth.* "Everyone knows that."

"No they don't."

"I'm going."

He grabbed my arm. "You live with them, don't you? Enchanted woods, yuckah are drawn to you, you know about magical things. Everything says you have fairy contact."

A dark figure appeared from the woods behind Allard and pointed a shotgun at him. I gasped. Allard spun and pulled out his laser gun, pushing me behind him. As the figure moved closer, I recognized him. "Charlie? What are you doing?"

"Protecting you."

"I don't *need* protecting!"

"Yes, you do." He focused on Allard. "Go home and never come back. I told you I'd use this if I saw you again. She's not yours to have, boy."

Allard glanced at me.

"Don't even look at her!" Charlie snarled. "Just hit your teleporter and leave!"

Allard kept his gaze on Charlie as he slowly raised his hand to the button. "Goodbye, Apolline."

He vanished.

Charlie and I rushed at each other. We grabbed each other by the arms, but with Charlie being stronger than me, he swung me around and began us both marching into the woods. I wriggled and squirmed, trying to break free.

"What do you think you're doing?" I demanded. "You have no right!"

"I have every right."

"No, you don't! All you are to me is a trader! I'm not your daughter, and you're not my father!"

He winced. A twinge of guilt hit me for saying it. He turned on me. "No, but I speak for your father. I am his eyes and ears, his only link to you."

I froze dead in my tracks. "Wha... What?"

His sharp tug pulled my momentum onward.

"But I'm an orphan."

"There's a great deal that has been kept from you for your safety, which will all be revealed at the right moment."

I tried to shake him off. "Like what, Charlie? Like *what*?"

He pulled me into the clearing out front of the cottage. I glanced around, surprised that he'd found his way there. "What's going on?"

He banged on the cottage's door. Fantine appeared, frazzled, then startled, with her hair wild from sleep. "Charlie, what is this?"

Sophronia pushed in beside her. "Apolline!"

"Her little highness took the liberty upon herself to sneak out with that young man," Charlie snarled.

"She what?" both fairies exclaimed in unison and burst out the door at me, both giving me swift slaps on each cheek. I glanced in the doorway at Ashlan standing heavy-eyed by the stairs.

"You're betrothed!" Sophronia snapped. "Have you forgotten that? Is your virtue still intact?"

"Excuse me?" I looked at her, horrified. "Of course it is! Do I look stupid?"

"Sometimes," Sophronia snarled. She spun on her heals and sat on a log nearby.

Fantine looked at me, frowning. "What were you thinking?"

I fumbled at her look of disappointment. "I just wanted to have some..." I paused, glancing at her heartbroken expression. "Fun."

Ashlan darted over and grasped my elbow. "Everyone inside."

We rushed in. They sat me down, turning their backs on me as they went about performing menial tasks; Fantine washed some dishes, Ashlan swept, Sophronia moved books back into alphabetical order on the shelf, and Charlie unloaded his gun and began cleaning it.

I rubbed my dirty pants, thinking through what Charlie had revealed to me. I had a father who was still alive! Then why wasn't I with him, and why didn't he come see me? I looked at Charlie in a new way. Who was he really? He noticed me staring at him and glanced over at Sophronia, chewing his lip.

I stood and rushed at him. "Who is my father? Where is he?"

Sophronia whirled on Charlie. "You told her she has a father?"

He leaned back, intimidated by her advance. "I had to!"

"No, you never *have* to do anything! We'll have to change our plans now, as dangerous as that will be."

I turned to her. "What plans? Why will they be dangerous? Tell me!"

Fantine rushed over, pushed between Sophronia and me, and grabbed me by the shoulders. "In due time, dear. Let's just say you are to marry someone very important."

Ringing resounded from Charlie's pocket, making us jump. He grasped a communicator, quickly turning it off. Reacting without thought, I snatched it from him, then ran upstairs to my room, dialing back the caller.

"Apolline!" Charlie called after me.

As I jammed the door shut, a male voice came through. "Charles—"

"Who is this?" I asked.

He paused. "Who is this?"

"You should never answer a question with a question," I snapped. "And I asked first."

"Apolline?" the voice responded.

"How do you know that?"

Another pause. "Where's Charlie?"

"Indisposed," I answered, as they made loud thumps and cracks while trying to break through the door. "Are you my father?" I waited in anticipation, wondering who this man could be. How could I have a father, and the fairies and Charlie *knew*, but didn't feel it necessary to tell me? Why didn't he want me with him? I fiddled with the buttons on the communicator, trying to pull up an image, but Charlie had it locked.

"Didn't you want me?"

The man let out a long breath. He cleared his throat. "Apolline, you are my daughter, but that's all you can know for now. Listen to Charlie and the fairies; they will guide and protect you until I meet you before the ball in Tyrone."

I smiled, my heart fluttering. "Really?"

"Yes."

"But why—?"

The door burst open. Charlie snatched the communicator out of my hand and cut off the connection. He glared at me, with Sophronia and Fantine behind him wearing the same expression. I held their stares stubbornly until Ashlan's humming coming up the stairs broke the trance. Charlie shook his head and pushed out of the room.

Sophronia stepped forward, her eyes glowing bright green. She lifted her wand and the whole room boarded up tightly. I looked at her, horrified as she spoke in a voice that echoed throughout my body. "You will not leave this room until we are to head to the Tyrone Palace."

She and Fantine turned and walked through the closed door.

I ran after them and slammed my body against the door. I wailed in frustration. "This isn't fair! Why won't anyone tell me what's going on?"

I slammed my body against the door over and over in vain. I collapsed on the ground, tugging at my hair. I didn't know what to make of it all. I had a father? My father lived? Then why did I live with the fairies?

Their voices drifted up from downstairs. I pressed my ear against the floorboards, but I couldn't hear. Glancing around the room, the magic rods Sophronia gave me caught my attention. If anything could break a magic lock, it would be a magic key. The second I grabbed one, it shifted into a key.

I shoved it into the lock and my door opened. Ha! I tiptoed to the top of the stairs to listen, and peered around the corner.

Sophronia and Fantine stood in the kitchen facing Charlie. Ashlan stood by the stairs with her arms folded.

Sophronia spoke softly. "There has been a snake from Mahkba drifting around the woods recently. Fantine, it's time you ended his snooping."

"But won't that make Bryanna suspicious?" Fantine protested.

"Make it look like he was trampled by yuckah. It's better he dies before tales of tonight are passed on to her."

Fantine nodded and left the cottage, grabbing a spear as she disappeared into the woods.

Why did it matter if Bryanna knew about me? Maybe I was to be a decoy princess! That would be why I needed to be at the ball, and as payment, I'd been given an aristocratic marriage. My birthday was so close to the princess' it made sense. My time hiding also fit in with it too. I wondered if several girls my age faced the same fate.

Charlie's communicator buzzed again. He looked down at the screen, then back to Sophronia.

"Answer it," she said.

"Yes, sir," Charlie said, then paused. "Yes, I am here with the fairies also, sire."

Sire? One of the kings? I had to be a decoy, I couldn't think of any other explanation. I definitely couldn't be the princess; I'd know, and I looked nothing like Queen Cytheria.

"Apolline?" Charlie said, cutting into my thoughts. "I'm sorry about before, sire, she has gotten herself into some trouble, sneaking out, I'm afraid." Charlie paused again, and I held my breath— "Well, she can be somewhat reckless."

Reckless? Bite me, Charlie.

"Yes. Our plans may be at risk." Charlie frowned. "That's not good news at all."

"What?" Sophronia said in a strained tone. "Let me talk to him."

Charlie shook his head, but Sophronia snatched it from him. "Sire, it's me. What's happening?" Pause. "With another woman? Is he mad? Do you need me to curse him?" Pause, then she sighed. "Yes, King Brencis does have a strong influence over him."

I shuffled closer, eager to discover the royal scandal, but my movement made the floorboards creak.

Ashlan turned around, looking up the stairs, and smiled. She winked at me, then said too loudly, "I don't think the princess will mind."

"What?" Sophronia shoved the communicator into Charlie's hands. "Ashlan, you're still a young fairy, so your bond is still... weak."

Ashlan batted her eyelids. "Weak?"

Sophronia straightened, folding her arms. "That wasn't what I meant. I've been bonded with this family for generations without regenerating. I know what—"

Her gaze shot up the stairs and locked on me. "You!"

"Ah crap." I scampered to my room. She caught me as I entered, and pinned me onto my bed.

"Give... me... the... Ah!" She pulled the rod free of my hand and snatched the other one. "What did you hear?"

"Get off me!" I hadn't realized her strength, but I felt it as she held me down with one hand.

"What else do you have hidden in here?"

"That wasn't hidden! You gave them to me."

She glanced around at a set of yuckah hooves on a shelf. "What about those?"

"I've had them for years. Fantine gave them to me. They're from my first yuckah kill."

She marched over and snatched them. "No more magical items."

I sat up as she marched out the door. Several large locks materialized, and with clicks and clunks, bolted me in.

I slammed the door with my fist. "Let. Me. Out!"

"Shut up, Apolline."

I screamed. "Charlie! Ashlan!"

Fantine's sobbing drifted softly through the door a moment before she materialized in the room. I ran at her, grabbing her arms. "Fantine! Please, you understand me better than anyone. Please, tell me what's going on."

She shook her head, stroking my cheek. "Not yet." She sobbed, her cheeks stained with tears. "But we need to leave. That serpent was a spy."

"What?" I remembered the serpent I found in the woods and gasped. "Why would it come here?"

Fantine pulled out her wand. "Sit down."

"Why?" I backed away from her.

"Please, sit."

"No! Tell me what's going on."

With a flick of her wrist, she took control of my body. She made me lie on the bed and pulled out a bottle of sleeping potion. "I'm sorry."

"No!" I pursed my lips.

Ashlan burst in and glanced around. "Apolline, where's the globe?"

Fantine paused and looked at her. "The what?"

"Globe, come."

My drawer flew open and the globe shot across into her hand. She opened a pink box, trimmed with lace, and winked at me. "I'll keep it safe."

"What?" I tried to sit up, but when I opened my mouth, Fantine forced the potion into my mouth. Immediately it took effect and I passed out.

CHAPTER SIXTEEN

King Brencis burst into Prince Allard's room. Allard swung around from staring out the window, longing for Apolline. Brencis marched toward him, red faced, teeth clenched.

Allard raised his hands. "Father—"

"Silence!" King Brencis boomed. He slammed a projector down and the headline erupted in a female voice.

"...Who is this maiden seen earlier today with our prince? No-one can confirm anything about this mystery woman who appears to have perhaps stolen the prince's heart. Some sources are saying she was sent by Bryanna to tempt the prince and prevent the union with Princess Elpida..."

Allard rushed toward the hologram as Apolline's face flashed up in an image of him and her running away.

"Son." Brencis turned to him, his hands on his hips as he forced control. "What are you doing running around with this girl within a week from Princess Elpida's arrival?"

"It's nothing—"

"It doesn't look like nothing! Who is she? Where did you meet her?"

"I met her on one of the lower perimeter planets on my way back from Tyrone. She had never seen Oran before, so I thought I'd give her the chance before... but she's just a friend—"

"A friend, Allard?" He pulled the image up of the two of them and shook it in front of him. "This doesn't look like *a friend* to me or anyone else. What were you thinking? How could you bring an anonymous female *friend* to Oran this close to your wedding?"

"She..." He stared at his father's red face and changed his course of defense. "She's betrothed to someone else. She's not some girl I have lined up to be my mistress; she *is* my friend."

"So this is where you have been disappearing to at night the last few weeks." Brencis placed the hologram projector back down.

Allard nodded.

"I knew something more was going on that you weren't telling me."

Allard frowned, averting his gaze.

Brencis stared at his son, examining the expression on his face. "Does she love you too?"

Allard's head shot up. "She does not love me."

"But you do love her."

Pain filled Allard's heart. He turned away from his father. "Elpida is to be my bride."

"Don't turn your back on me!" Brencis bellowed. "Who is she? She better be worthwhile if—"

Allard swung around and stood over his father. "She's more than worthwhile! She's the most incredible girl I have ever..." He trailed off, realizing what his father had just done. He sank onto the couch.

Brencis took a deep breath and sat in front of him. "Son, more than anything I want you to be happy, and that's what your mother wanted too. If this young woman is who you want to be with, then I will make arrangements to dissolve the betrothal."

"No, Father. She's betrothed as well; didn't you hear me? She has made her choice. She's admirable to keep a promise made for her despite... despite..." He sighed. "She didn't realize that I knew she was fighting back the tears. I think she might love me, but she has more honor than I do to keep faithful to someone she has never met."

Standing, he ran his hands over his face, then straightened. "Everything stands as it always has, Father."

Brencis stood as well. "My son, if we—"

Allard wheeled on his father and stared him down. "Father, I cannot hear it. It hurts too much."

"Very well." Brencis bowed his head. "I shall inform the media and King Hernan that everything is as it was." He moved to turn, then stopped. "Allard, you will make a great king."

After Brencis left, Allard stood motionless. He stared down at the hand held projector. Apolline would no longer be part of his life, and it hurt as much as his mother's death years earlier. He reached down and turned on the projector, pausing the image on Apolline's face. He stared at her, his heart pounding, then he bit his lip and turned off the projection. He wrapped his hand around the projector and marched over to his window. He pulled it open roughly, then, with all his strength, he flung the devise as far as he could.

Bryanna paced, irritated. She had lost contact with her serpent on Mish, so she'd sent another to find it. When the second returned, it brought her the news that the serpent had been trampled by yuckah. The timing was too close to the princess' return to be a coincidence.

She stared at Apolline's face in the crystal ball, trying to piece things together. She smiled at the uproar caused by this girl, who, only two days earlier, caused such scandal with the prince. Yet, there was something off about her.

Several things then crossed her mind simultaneously. Apolline was a yuckah huntress who lived somewhere within an enchanted woodland, which meant she lived with fairies. It dawned on her that the man, Charlie, she once saw in the courts of Oran, but most significantly, she noticed Apolline's eyes, those deep, stunning, mesmerizing, blue eyes.

"Who is the fairest one of all?" she asked her mirror. Cytheria appeared. "Their eyes…"

She leaned forward, examining Cytheria's eyes. She grabbed her crystal and brought up the huntress' image. "She looks nothing like her except…" She let out a long breath. "Who is the handsomest one of all?"

Beaumont White's image appeared.

She growled. "Hernan! I need…" She paused, realizing she needed a different approach. She tapped her chin, thinking. "Who is the handsomest king of all?"

King Hernan's image appeared.

She lifted the crystal and compared the huntress' image to his. Similar cheekbones, same smile, same hair… she couldn't believe she hadn't seen it earlier. The huntress looked like a feminine version of him. Except her eyes.

Then the question that had eluded her all those years came into her mind. She clenched the crystal, dreading the truth. "Mirror, who is the fairest princess of them all?"

Bryanna's eyebrows lowered as the reflection swirled and formed the face of a young woman. "No!"

A low hum filled my ears. Forcing my eyes open, I squinted in the bright light of the cockpit. I moved, but my hands and feet were tied.

I resented the fairies in a way I didn't even know was possible. I glanced around at their backs, watching them as I struggled against my bonds. I managed to pull my feet loose, when Ashlan turned, smiling. I stopped struggling and glared at her.

Her smile widened, and she came over to me. She reached out to touch me, but I pulled away. She continued toward me, unflinching, until she grasped my face.

I wriggled, trying to escape, when images shot through my mind. Women, war, birth, death. I flung myself backward, smacking my head against the wall. Tears watered in my eyes from the pain and I groaned. But not from my head, from the emotions Ashlan planted in me.

I shuffled away from her. This power that I had never known about terrified me. She reached for me again. I pulled away, whimpering. No-one else seemed to notice.

Despite my best efforts to escape her grasp, she caught me again. Her voice whispered in my head. "Do you know what my name means?"

"No," I heard myself reply.

"It means 'dreamer'. Watch as I give you dreams of things past."

She pushed my head back so I looked directly into her eyes. Then I felt as if I had been teleported to another place and time. Ashlan appeared as a little girl entering a small manor where another little girl stood smiling. They were instant friends, and played and learned together, completely inseparable.

As they grew, Ashlan's aging slowed when they hit sixteen, but the girl kept aging. Then a young man appeared, and the girl, now a young woman, married him. Ashlan moved into their home with them, then the woman suddenly had a newborn baby in her arms.

Again I watched the baby grow, while Ashlan's friend grew even older until the baby was a young woman with another baby in her arms. Then soon after, Ashlan's first friend, elderly and frail, passed away.

I felt Ashlan's grief as she buried her childhood friend, and my heart cried out as well. But, there was still love to be shared with her daughter and granddaughter, so the grief faded.

The cycle continued. Generations passed by in what felt like seconds, until it slowed and a blond man held a tiny baby in his arms, as he wept over his wife who died from childbirth. The tiny girl grew into the most beautiful young girl I'd ever seen. Her face blurred, and soon a baby girl lay in her arms as she gently lifted the child out of a crib and handed her to Ashlan.

Fantine stood at Ashlan's side, and soon Sophronia stepped up and led them away. They hid the baby in a city, but soon the city burned to the ground, so they fled to a different planet. A few months passed, and that planet was evacuated just moments before it exploded. The path of destruction followed them as they fled, until they finally arrived at Mish and set up the strongest defenses they had to hide their location.

She dragged my consciousness back to the cockpit where I remained staring up into Ashlan's eyes. Her voice spoke in my head again. "I have been with you since before you were born, and will still be with you long after you have passed from this mortal realm. I have shown you a glimpse of the secrets that have been kept from you, dear Apolline, and as the next few days pass, many more will be revealed. Be wise with the choices you make, for they will decide your fate. All these things have been done for your own good, don't ever forget that."

Ashlan let go of me. I fell to the ground, sapped of energy. I recoiled from her, but it didn't matter because she returned to her seat.

Fantine then stood and headed to me. I looked up at her in horror, afraid of what surprise she would give me, but she simply reached down to remove my gag and gently gave me some potion.

"It will restore your strength," she whispered.

A few minutes later, I sat back up, feeling better than I had in days. I gazed out the window at a planet further up ahead. By the lush green continents and the purplish rings around it, it had to be Tyrone. I looked at the time. We were less than an hour away! It seemed impossible. How long had I been unconscious? How long did Ashlan take? The journey to Tyrone from Mish usually took just shy of a week. I stared at the tiny dot of a planet up ahead.

Soon, I would meet my father. Soon, I would know my lineage and true identity.

Allard stared out at the stars. With a day's journey left until they arrived, he felt worse than ever. Two days until he married the princess, while the woman he loved watched it from somewhere, probably the arms of her betrothed.

He needed to break something.

He marched out of his cabin, heading toward the gym. A punching bag would do. As he entered the elevator, a crewman stopped him. "Sire, the queen wishes to speak with you."

Allard stuck his hand out to stop the elevator doors closing. "Now?"

"Yes, sire."

He sighed. "Patch it through to my cabin."

He hurried back. As the door opened, a beeping sounded, informing him of the waiting call. He answered. "Cytheria?"

"Allard!" Her image appeared in front of him like a ghostly figure. "Allard, I feel like I have no one else to talk to who would understand. I'm sorry if I'm bothering you."

"Not at all." He lied, but he needed a distraction.

Queen Cytheria paced uneasily. "Elpida will be here this evening, but I won't be able to see her until tomorrow, right before the ball. But what if she hates me?"

"No one could hate you," Allard said.

She let out a terse laugh. "Bryanna does."

Allard looked away.

"It breaks my heart," Cytheria continued. "Bryanna and I were so close once. Then she just turned on me, and all this…" She waved her hand in the air, chewing on her lip. "My stepmother hated me too. She locked me away when guests came, and stood and watched as I dug out the gardens like a robot, or whatever filthy, horrible chore she could dream up. She bought horses just so I could muck out their stalls."

"You were lucky to escape," Allard said.

Cytheria sighed. "I know, and I've moved on from all that. But my Elpida, my precious daughter… I can't help thinking she will hate me for abandoning her, or blame me for her life in exile. What if all she ever wanted was me, her mother, but I wasn't there?"

"I'm sure the fairies reassured her that the separation was for her protection."

Cytheria burst into tears. Allard stood tense, not sure how to react. She sunk into a chair and spoke through her sobs. "Allard, I was so afraid when the scandal with that girl came up."

Allard's gut tightened.

"I thought you'd finally grown tired of waiting."

"No." What could he say to that?

"I would have understood, really. Sometimes I think it's harder on you than anyone else. But you have so much faith in us, faith in the future, that it gives me hope. I know my daughter will be well taken care of by you."

Allard chewed on the inside of his cheek trying to force his guilt into submission. He had to focus on Elpida. Apolline made her choice, a choice that made her the stronger and better person than him. "I will do everything in my power to keep her safe. Bryanna will never come near her."

She nodded, delicately wiping her tears away. "Thank you, Allard. For everything. And I'm sorry for this. I bet you think I'm a fool for crying like a baby."

"No. You're her mother. I understand where you're coming from."

She smiled that dazzling smile which made men stop breathing. Allard included.

A voice filtered through in the background and she looked over her shoulder. She gasped and stood, then paused, looking to Allard. "I better go. Hernan received word that... well... I have to go."

"Everything will be all right."

She pressed her fingertips to her lips and stretched out her hand. Her holographic fingers touched his cheek. "We'll see you soon."

Her image vanished and Allard released a puff of air, then drew a deep breath. He needed to forget Apolline. Seeing Cytheria like that set his resolve. But how could he forget? The overwhelming urge to hit something returned, so he marched out the door and straight to the gym where the punching bag awaited to take the brunt of his emotional release.

CHAPTER SEVENTEEN

Bryanna slipped unnoticed through the planet's defense systems and quickly approached the palace. She knew exactly where to go. Years of rats searching the castle had revealed a secret passageway to an old isolated tower from very primitive times of plague. She stroked her spinning wheel with satisfaction. Soon, so soon.

Darkness hid our arrival at the Tyronian Palace. I watched out the window as we landed, marveling at how it looked exactly like the globe depicted.

As security rushed at our small ship, Fantine tossed a cape around my shoulders and covered my head. I didn't argue. Decoys need to be discreet, and a royal decoy was the only explanation I came up with for everything that had transpired.

Being the princess was absurd.

The guards stared at me as I alighted from the ship, Fantine and

Ashlan on each arm, and Sophronia striding out in front. The captain saluted her and she nodded. "Where to?"

"The east wing."

"The east..." She clenched her fists. "Come along."

Fantine and Ashlan coaxed me onward. The party of guards followed.

"Wow, this is intense," I whispered.

"Hush." Fantine glanced around. "We don't want to draw attention."

And sneaking around the palace with an armed guard won't draw attention? But I didn't dare argue. It all seemed beyond me and my humble understanding.

They led me into a room where men in black suits nodded to the captain and Sophronia. They muttered about the room being secure, then left.

Sophronia turned to all of us. "You and you," she pointed to two guards. "Stand by the door. Ashlan and the rest of you, follow me. Fantine—"

"I won't leave her for a moment." Fantine's arm tightened around mine.

Sophronia sighed and nodded. "I know." Her firm tone returned. "Let's go."

They bustled out of the room, leaving me alone with Fantine. The door clicked closed. She slipped the hood off my head. "You should get some sleep, dear."

I did feel tired, and didn't feel like yelling for answers when I would only hit a wall of silence. So I moved to the bed and sat on the edge to pull off my boots.

"Oh, you grew much too quickly."

I glared up at Fantine as I removed my boots. "After everything I've seen and heard over the last few days, I don't know what to think of you."

She slumped. "Apolline, please don't be like that. It's for the best, you know."

I slid up on the bed and lay facing her. She sat in a wooden chair by the door, closing her eyes as she sighed. Lines and wrinkles around her eyes gave her the appearance of tired and old for the very first time. My heart cried out to her. I stood, moved over to her, and wrapped my arms around her.

"Oh!" She gasped, surprised, but she rested her head against me and wrapped her arms around my waist. We held each other, neither of us saying a word, simply understanding, exchanging our feelings, and cherishing the moment.

I let go first and returned to the bed, yawning. As I lay back I asked, "Nothing will ever be the same again, will it?"

She drew a deep breath. "No, dear."

I rolled over as my heart sank. Memories of my life flashed through my mind while I drifted off to sleep.

When I awoke, the early rays of sunlight beamed through the gaps in the curtains. I rolled over. Fantine slept on the chair, her chin resting on her bosom. Refreshed and daring, I carefully slipped on my boots and snuck out of the room.

Peering through the cracked door, I glanced around. Two guards faced away from me as they patrolled the hallway. I ran as soft footed as possible in the opposite direction. I made it to the end of the hallway when the door to the room opened.

"Apolline?" Fantine's tense voice echoed down to me.

I turned. Fantine and the guards stared at me, stunned. Without hesitation, I darted around the corner.

"Apolline! Get back here!"

Fantine's familiar tone made me smile as I ran, but my smile soon disappeared as the sound of two sets of feet came after me much faster than I fled from them. I ran harder to the end of the hallway where it opened into a wider corridor heading to my left and right. I sped around the corner, hoping they hadn't seen which way I turned, and took a sharp turn up another narrow hallway.

A dark doorway caught my attention so I darted into it, pressing up against the wall. A few seconds later, one set of footsteps slowed and stopped. I held my breath, hoping the guard wouldn't notice me.

Soon, the footsteps grew faint as the guard trotted away. I released my breath. Cautiously, I peeked out to find myself completely alone. I grinned.

Exploration time.

I walked around for a while, finding nothing special, just basking in the freedom after a week of captivity.

Through a door, came Sophronia's voice. I moved toward it and slowly turned the doorknob. I paused to make sure she hadn't noticed. She continued speaking, so I carefully pushed the door open a crack. Her words flooded out clearly and I listened, curious to discover why I could be so important.

"...she's wild and free-spirited, dear Cytheria, but you would be proud of who she has become. Those attributes will fade in time as they are youthful follies, but she is smart and strong."

"My dear Sophronia, is she beautiful?" another woman pleaded.

"Oh, she's pretty enough, but not like you. She's the female replicate of her father."

"Thank heavens." The woman sighed.

"Yes, Fantine's potions did the trick at countering the effects of excessive fairy exposure."

They had to be talking about me, and I dared to push the door ever so slightly more ajar.

"Did you hear that, Hernan?" the woman said. "Dear Fantine. That's all I ever wished for."

"Indeed," a male voice answered. "Surely that made it so she was easier to be kept hidden."

I straightened, alarmed. Hernan? Cytheria? The king and queen? Why were they talking about me? I shook off the impossible thought that came into my mind. I couldn't be the princess!

"Can we see her?" the queen urged. "I am desperate with anxiety."

"Of course," Ashlan said. "Your daughter is standing on the other side of the door."

I flung myself backward.

The door flew open and Sophronia gaped at me. "Where's Fantine?"

"I out ran her," I muttered, backing away.

She looked like she wanted to rip my heart out. "You, you..." Her eyes narrowed.

Then, the most dazzling woman I had ever laid eyes on pushed passed her. Her gaze fixed on me and she smiled excitedly. "My Elpida."

I backed into the wall. "Excuse me, your majesty, but you must be mistaken. My name is Apolline."

Her smile faltered, but she stood firm. "You look just like Hernan, except you have my eyes."

I glanced quickly at her eyes and recognized them instantly as my own. "No."

Then the king appeared. I *was* his image on a female. "Come in, Apolline," he said gently.

He sounded like the man on the communicator, the man who called himself my father. Sort of. My pulse quickened. Impossible. *I* couldn't be the princess! I glanced at Sophronia, anger flaring up in me. "Is this some kind of sick joke?"

She pursed her lips, like she always did when her patience wore thin. "No. Stop being a brat and get in here."

"Don't talk to her like that," the queen said softly.

"I'm sorry, my queen." Sophronia bowed her head. "As I said, she's wild and still needs chastising. I recommend some intense finishing lessons—"

"Shut up!" I yelled, my voice much too high. I glanced at the king and queen again. My heart raced violently, growing faster by the second. I grabbed my head in an attempt to ease the dizziness that swept over me. "I'm not a princess! I'm just me, a huntress from Mish."

King Hernan stepped forward. "Apolline, please, I know this is a shock for you. Why don't you come in so we can talk about it properly?"

I backed down the hallway. "No. This is all... this is... impossible."

A rush of thoughts ran through my mind. I *was* the princess. There was no way they *couldn't* be my parents, the resemblances were too apparent. That meant my betrothed was to the Prince of Oran. The very palace I walked through with Allard would become one of my homes.

The king, queen, and Sophronia crept toward me, so I backed off some more…

That also meant that Bryanna hunted *me*, she wanted *my* life. That very night she had set a deadline for my death. I unconsciously rubbed my hands on my pants at the thought of pricking one of my fingers on the spinning needle. I looked at Sophronia. Surely she had to be the fairy who cast the counter spell to have me sleep rather than die. I bet she regretted it now.

Then again, how had I never realized before? The stories were legendary throughout the kingdoms; the three fairies had taken the child and hidden from Bryanna. It all seemed so obvious now I knew. But then, people on Mish had realized, or even known. I always thought them calling me 'princess' and 'highness' to be some kind of sarcastic quip, but they had known, just as they had known what the fairies were. *I* was the planet's best kept secret.

I met King Hernan's gaze. "I spoke to you on the communicator?"

His eyes lit up with hope. "Yes."

"Where's Charlie?"

"He's meeting the Oran royal family's fleet."

"How does he fit into this?" I snarled the words, trying to find some kind of diversion.

"He was a general in the Oran Army. I needed a contact on Mish, and his wife and daughter were killed in one of Bryanna's raids. He wanted to do everything he could to make their deaths worth something and not in vain, so King Brencis agreed to send him to watch over you and be my liaison."

My eyes widened, my heart now pounding so hard I thought it might jump out of my throat. "My whole life, hasn't anything been true?"

Queen Cytheria stepped forward. "Please understand. We wanted to protect you."

"You wanted to protect me? I could have handled it!"

"We couldn't risk it," Sophronia said calmly.

I turned on her. "Shut up, just shut up! I hate you! You never cared about me, just your plans and spells. Get away from me!"

I spun to run away, but found myself face to face with one of the guards. He grabbed my shoulders to restrain me.

"Let me go!" I screamed and began crying. *I can't believe I'm crying!* Struggling to compose myself, I fought back the tears. "No, take me back actually, back to the room with Fantine."

He hesitated, then guided me back the way I came.

The door to the room shut behind me, but Fantine wasn't there. She must have gone searching for me. I leaped onto the bed curling up in a tight ball. I didn't know how to feel. It all seemed so impossible but yet, it really *was* happening to me. But how could *I* be the princess? I still had a picture in my mind of what Elpida should be; beautiful, docile, and doe-eyed. Far from what I could ever be. My nose tingled and my cheeks grew hot as tears welled up again.

I sat up abruptly, trying to shake it off, then thoughts of Allard came to me. An uncontrollable sob wrenched itself out of my chest. I had saved him from great public humiliation. He would have been labeled a servant of the sorceress and a traitor of the kingdoms for leading me astray. Yet, a small niggling thought came through. He never said he wasn't the prince. Everything about him screamed noble born, and his friendship with the White's reinforced that... plus, everyone knew Beaumont White and Prince Allard were best friends. Allard *did* seem to know his way around the Oran capital city and the palace gardens almost too well. He knew a lot more than he should, and the media... that woman who he said was his cousin had a holo-camera.

I slapped my forehead refusing to let myself believe it, only to be disappointed. But he could be. He really could be. Rolling over, I grabbed the room's pad and opened the royal archives. Although public archives couldn't show Prince Allard's face, maybe internal ones could.

A gentle tap came on the door. It opened a crack to reveal a gentle looking, middle aged woman. She wore an emerald gown, setting off the green in her eyes. Her chocolate brown hair swept back from her face, then hung loosely over her shoulder in an elegant, soft curl.

"Elpida?" Her voice sounded soothing.

I sighed, clicking on the pad's screen. "Apparently."

A stunning smile swept across her face. "May I?"

I didn't have a chance to refuse her as she slipped gracefully into the room. I watched her as she moved to the end of the bed. "I'm sorry to startle you, dear, but I couldn't wait any longer to meet you. You see, I am your aunt."

I rolled my eyes and scowled. "Great, more unknown relatives."

Her smile fell and she gave me a sympathetic look. "Yes, everything must be very shocking for you right now. I just want to help you prepare for the ball tonight. It will preoccupy your mind."

I sat up on the bed. "Thanks for trying, but I would prefer it if you just left." I glanced at the door.

"Oh no, you mustn't be alone," she said, shaking her head with a frown.

Dumping the pad on the bed, I stood, glaring at her. "Please, just leave."

Her face darkened. "I will not be dismissed like a common servant."

"Look, I don't understand the whole social decorum thing, so don't get offended. I just want to be left alone."

I tensed, transfixed by the woman's sudden change in her countenance. In fact, I couldn't move at all. Her face became fierce and dangerous.

"What are you doing?" I gasped, fighting to regain control of my body.

"Were you ever told what the connection was between the queen and the sorceress?" Her voice echoed around the room.

"The sorceress loved the king." My voice came out strangled.

"No, it was more than that! The queen is the betrayer of her own sister."

I gasped, realizing what that meant. "Bryanna!"

"Oh yes, that's me. Not as stupid as you look, are you?"

Panic tore through me. She wanted to kill me! I could die with a flick of her wrist. "Let me go. I didn't even know until—"

"Of course you didn't know." She looked at me with a fake

sympathetic pout. "Couldn't have a little girl accidently telling everyone she was the princess, could they? No, not after a year of my relentless pursuit. I almost had you at least five times. If only Sophronia wasn't such a bloody good soldier."

Her magic felt like Sophronia's, except it tightened as I struggled, like a rope around my neck.

"Elpida, you should have been mine." She ran her finger down my cheek. "Let's see what Mother and Father are doing, shall we?"

She turned to a mirror. She brushed her fingers over its surface, and the reflection swirled until the king and queen appeared in their room with Ashlan and Sophronia.

Cytheria sat staring blankly ahead. Silence filled the room as the others watched her, waiting for her to respond.

"I knew her the moment I laid eyes on her," Cytheria said softly. Her face fell into her hands. "But she doesn't want this. She was devastated by the revelation of her identity." Tears ran down her cheeks as she glanced up at Sophronia. "Take her back where she's happy."

Sophronia stepped toward her. "Dear Cytheria—"

Cytheria stood, her emotions pouring down her cheeks as tears. "Please, I cannot bear to be the cause of her unhappiness."

Hernan turned her toward him. "My dear, her reaction to what was revealed is understandable. It will pass, and she will accept who she truly is."

Cytheria looked up at her husband with wide, glistening eyes. "I cannot bear to have her hate me."

My heart twinged with pain. She loved me. My mother—not dead, but very much alive—loved me. She gave me up to protect me, and I hurt her by throwing it in her face and denying my birth.

"Cytheria." Ashlan's voice cut through the room causing everyone to turn to her with surprise. "Everything has aligned. The players in the game are prepared for what is to come, and are where they need to be. Do not worry about sending your daughter away."

Hernan and Sophronia stood dumbfounded, but Cytheria's face darkened. "Where is Bryanna?"

The door opened with a bang, causing all in the room to jump. Fantine gazed around, frazzled. "Apolline, she ran and I, I…"

Sophronia gasped. "She's alone! Quickly, to her room!"

Bryanna laughed. "Oh my, what an uproar." She waved her hand over the surface and the image vanished. "Now, I believe you know what happens next. Follow me."

She ran her finger over the frame of the mirror and it opened to a narrow spiral staircase.

I struggled with all my might against the magical bonds that held me. Terror tore through me and I fought to avoid the inevitable. Despite this, my legs began to move of their own accord and, to my despair, I began climbing step by step up the stairway.

CHAPTER EIGHTEEN

A shuttle approached the lead ship of the royal fleet where Allard and his father stood on the bridge. Allard held himself composed, despite his heart pounding and his feelings surging. The shuttle carried the liaison his father sent to watch over Princess Elpida for King Hernan.

As the shuttle docked on the lower decks, a message beeped up on the control panel.

King Brencis ordered it opened. The royal chief guard of Tyrone appeared on the screen. "Prince Allard, we have reason to believe that the sorceress Bryanna has infiltrated the castle. We warn you *not* to approach the capital. Repeat, do *not* approach the capital until further notice."

The message ended. Allard looked at Brencis who issued the order for the fleet to halt.

Brencis turned to his son, frowning. "This is bad news. Bryanna is a cunning woman, always has been."

Allard tilted his head. "You knew her?"

King Brencis raised his eyebrows. "Oh yes, she was lovely once. She and Miriam..." He stared ahead, his chest heaving. "They grew up together. Miriam said she first noticed changes after she gave birth to you. She thought..." Brencis rubbed his eyes. "She thought Bryanna's feelings for Hernan made her distant. To this day, I can't understand why Bryanna would allow her wolves to kill Miriam."

Allard's jaw fell. His mother and Bryanna were friends? "Father, why didn't...? You never..."

Brencis looked into his eyes. "There are things I wish I could have done differently, things I should have seen. But you and Elpida can pave the way to a brighter future. Don't allow the mistakes of the generation before prevent you from making things better for future generations."

Allard's heart swelled. "Father, I—"

The door onto the bridge opened and a tiny woman entered. Allard and Brencis turned.

Brencis rushed opened armed to her and kissed her on the cheek. "Ashlan! It has been too long!"

Allard spun back around, his back to the pair, shocked. He breathed deeply, trying to hold his composure as he fought to think clearly. He thought the liaison had been a man, but this was a fairy, *the* royal fairy, Cytheria's family fairy. His mother had shown him pictures from the family's private archives. Her name was also familiar. He had a vague recollection of it being mentioned to him recently, but he couldn't remember where.

A gentle hand rested on his arm. He looked down into her dark eyes. "My prince, you must come immediately."

He hesitated, then fumbled to say, "Why are you here?"

She smiled gently. "Moments ago, I sensed Bryanna's presence in the castle, so I came to collect you."

"Moments ago?" He paused. "But we're still hours away."

She smiled, nodding. "I *am* a fairy, my prince."

"Yes..."

She tugged his arm. "Come. Let us get you into position."

She led him down the hallway. He didn't say a word as he stared at the back of her blonde head, wishing he knew more about magic. If only

Apolline... he needed to stop thinking about Apolline. With Bryanna in the palace, he needed to focus on protecting Elpida.

The fairy glanced back at him, grinning. "You're hot."

"Excuse me?" His eyebrows shot right up.

"Hot. Yes, very hot."

"Ah, I'm betrothed."

She chuckled. "Not that hot. Hot."

She pulled him into a closet and shut the door. She rested her hand over his heart. He leaned away from her, but her hand remained on his chest. "Mmm, it's so strong. I can feel its power."

"Ahh—"

"Shh." A faint pink glow emitted from her skin. "Mmm, rejuvenating."

Allard gazed around, bewildered at the fairy as she stood, eyes shut, next to him in the closet, her fingers caressing his chest. He opened his mouth to say something, then shut it again. He shuffled uncomfortably and glanced around before he tried to speak again. "What are we doing?"

She raised her finger. "Just listen."

He listened to the sounds of the ship; people walking by, the soft hum of the life support moving the air around. "What am I listening for?"

Ashlan opened her eyes to gaze up at him. "Anything new."

He went quiet again, and soon he heard a voice. A male voice that was familiar, but from where? He felt as if he should know, like he had earlier when he heard Ashlan's name. He looked at Ashlan who stared at him.

"Think, Prince."

As he listened, the man addressed his father. "My king."

"Charles."

Charles. Allard ran the name over and over in his mind.

"It's good to have you back."

"It's good to be back, sire. May I ask to see the prince? I wish to tell him about the princess."

"He's gone. The royal fairy just came and took him."

"Ashlan? Why?"

Brencis sighed. "Bryanna is in the palace."

"Impossible!"

"It's true."

"We must get to the palace as quickly as possible."

"Agreed. But Sophronia told me *not* to dock, but remain in orbit."

"But..." Charles hesitated. "Ashlan always knows best."

A long pause followed, punctuated by beeping.

"Charles, what...?" Brencis trailed off.

"*That's* the prince?" he said with a gasp.

Allard leaned toward the door. That voice. That voice reminded him of Mish and Apolline.

"Yes," Brencis answered.

"Impossible."

"What is it?"

"Ashlan must have done it. She was there the first day he came to the store..." A crazy laugh echoed in the corridor. "That fairy! True love's kiss! Of course they had to actually *fall* in love first!"

Allard had a glimpse of recollection. "Wait, it can't be." He reached for the door.

The fairy's hand wrapped firmly around his. He turned to her as a smile swept across her face. "Hold tight."

A pulling sensation rippled up through his arm. Her hand tightened around his and suddenly he shot through space and into the Tyrone solar system.

I reached the top of the stairs, heaving from the struggle against climbing them. I entered a dome shaped room with a four poster bed in the center. The bed had the curtains drawn, except the one facing me, which allowed me to see the turned down linens waiting to be slept in. For me to sleep in. Permanently.

I looked away, trying to find hopeful objects. A large window overlooked the palace and surrounding city, and mirrors hung on every wall. Nothing hopeful there, unless I jumped out the window to my death—which I hoped to avoid.

Then, Bryanna moved and stepped behind one last object: A spinning wheel with a large needle that seemed out of proportion to me—probably because I couldn't look away from it.

"Come into the room, Apolline," she said soothingly.

My legs moved involuntarily. "No! Stop moving!"

But they kept going. I stopped in the middle of the room.

She moved smoothly toward me, looking me over. "It's hard to hate you when you look so much like Hernan." Then her eyes met mine. "But there *she* is."

She stepped back and looked me up and down. "We can't have you looking like that now, can we? An eternal sleep needs grace and style, not this drab peasant attire. I think I saw a dress in your room which will do."

Instantly the corset wrapped around my waist and the heavier fabric of the dress rested over me.

"Purple is no good though." She tapped her lips. "It needs to be blue, to remind everyone of those treacherous eyes." The dress changed color to a deep blue. "Perfect." She moved back to the spinning wheel.

"Please don't do this," I said, the desperation in my tone frightening me.

"Don't beg, Apolline. You're better than that. Now, come here."

My left foot moved. "No!" I screeched, managing to pull it back.

She frowned, and with a wave of her hand the spinning wheel slid across the room and stopped right in front of me. "Stop fighting."

"I won't!"

She stepped up beside me and moved my hair back from my ear. "Did you know this is the tower Rapunzel locked herself in to keep from catching the plague? The girl went mad in here with no contact to the outside world, no one able to reach her and tell her the plague had ended. There's no hope for you now. No one knows how to get up here, and I have already arranged for that boy you fancy to be eliminated. He will never come, and the prince is useless to you now. You need love's kiss."

"You're lying."

"Raise your hand," she commanded.

She stepped back and watched me as I fought to keep my arm down. My strength held against her magic until she grabbed my face and tilted it to look in the mirror. "Who else could love you? You aren't even that pretty. Stop fighting and lift your hand!"

All my muscles writhed in pain as my right arm raised itself. I wailed in frustration and fear. "Stop it! Stop!"

She smiled and stepped behind the spinning wheel again. "Touch the needle."

"No!"

I screamed, but to my horror, my index finger lowered itself onto the needle point, drawing a tiny drop of blood. A great surge of exhaustion ran up my arm and spread through me. My body gave out. As I hit the ground, my eyes heavy, her laughter echoed into my ears. I tried to fight the sleep, but it consumed me.

CHAPTER NINETEEN

Allard hit the stone floor hard, stumbling back into the wall. Ashlan stood by one of the stone arch windows that ran along that part of the palace. She glanced around before turning to him. "I need to contact Sophronia and Fantine."

She dug into his pocket.

This fairy couldn't get any more awkward.

She pulled out his communicator and examined it. "Hmm. They're a bit different to what I remember." She turned it around in her hands for a moment, then whipped out her wand.

"Hey, whoa!" Allard reached for it but she pulled it away.

She tapped it with her wand and a holographic image of a plump, fuzzy haired woman appeared. She smiled. "Ah! It works! Fantine, look at me."

The woman looked up. "Ashlan? What's happening?"

"I have the prince."

The image vanished, and a slender red head appeared. "Bryanna has her. We came as fast as we could, but the mirror closed just as we arrived."

The little fairy shrugged. "Oh."

Allard raised an eyebrow. "Oh? Didn't she just tell you the princess has been taken by Bryanna, you know, the sorceress?"

"Allard!" Cytheria's face appeared. "Are you all right? Has she done anything to you?"

Allard looked at the fairy who seemed too calm. "She said I was hot."

"Not Ashlan," Cytheria said in a scolding tone. "Bryanna."

"No."

Cytheria let out a long breath. "As long as you're safe. The fairies can—"

"My dear Cytheria," Ashlan said with a sweet smile. "It's not up to us to finish the journey that has been undertaken. The foundations have been laid, so the players must be set in motion. There are things in this universe far more powerful than magic."

The red head appeared again. "Ashlan, I will watch over the king and queen. But..." She glanced around. "Will the prince suffice after...?"

Ashlan giggled. "Oh my, yes. Everyone loves a prince."

Fantine reappeared. "Will he be harmed? This is very dangerous."

Ashlan tilted her head. "He's smart, and I will provide him with some assistance."

"You've always been tricky, so I will trust you. Goodbye, old friend."

Ashlan disconnected and tossed the communicator out the window.

"Hey!" Allard darted to the window just in time to see it smash on the cobblestone below.

"You won't need it," she said. With strength far greater than a woman her size should hold, she turned him to face her, her expression now stern. "To defeat the sorceress you must destroy what humans avoid breaking for fear of misfortune."

"What?" Allard hissed. The disjointing and startling journey, her odd behavior, and all the strange and bizarre surprises, had overwhelmed him. But he also wondered if the voice he heard back on the ship had been Charlie's.

A screech echoed across the courtyard. Ashlan darted back to the window, closely followed by Allard. She turned her gaze up to the tallest tower where a great darkness poured out of its window like oil in the air.

In the courtyard below, a handful of courtiers gazed up in alarm. Allard knew all eyes across the city would be doing the same thing. He turned to Ashlan who had her eyes shut. She hummed quietly what sounded like a lullaby. Allard looked back down to the courtyard as the courtiers made themselves comfortable on the cobblestone, before drifting into a sleep. Then, Ashlan sang softly;

"Sleep tiny world,

To keep your secrets safe.

While the Princess slumbers,

Destinies will awake.

Your silence will bring,

The good a chance to win.

You will wake when the task is completed,

And Bryanna will finally be defeated."

The tune and lyrics weren't beautiful or memorable in anyway, but it did its job. The whole world seemed to fall asleep. Allard heard the clatter of guards collapsing, the hum of the city outside the castle ceased, even the atmosphere dimmed the sunlight as if to aid the sleep along.

Once she finished, Ashlan turned to Allard. "Hurry, get up there."

She pointed to the tower.

"How? I've never seen a way into that tower."

She smiled. "Seek. All your tools are in place."

She vanished. He stared where she had stood, then grunted. He looked at the tower, bewildered. No one knew how to get up there. It had been sealed off centuries earlier. He huffed and decided to try to find a way in, so began running.

He reached the end of the open corridor and turned into the next wing, then ran down into the Grand Ballroom. King Hernan had first seen Queen Cytheria in that ballroom, and Allard would meet and dance with Princess Elpida for the first time, and marry her there.

He scanned the ballroom, easily the most spectacular room in the whole palace after the throne room. Gold trimmings lined everything, and a painted vault ceiling depicted the history and magical creatures.

He hurried along, seeing his own reflection all around him in the mirrors that ran all along the sides.

As he ran, he noticed something odd in one of the mirrors. He stopped abruptly and back tracked. The mirror, instead of reflecting the other side of the room like the others, showed a different room entirely. In the mirror he saw a dome room, with the walls covered in mirrors and a four post bed near the center, with all its curtains drawn. It had to be the room at the top of the tower as he'd never seen it before. He stepped over to it and tried to touch its surface, but he felt nothing there. He put his hand through. The mirror had become a doorway. He smiled and muttered to himself, "Fairy portal," as he stepped through.

The air changed around him as he entered the room. He shuddered in the ice cold. He glanced around for Bryanna, but saw no-one. Instead, by the window sat the spinning wheel. He approached it, noticing a tiny drop of blood on the needle. Chills ran down his spine, and he turned to face the closed off bed.

Light breathing came from behind the curtains. His heart sank. Everything that had been done to prevent the princess from falling under Bryanna's curse had been a waste. He turned to the spinning wheel. Anger swelled up inside him as he pushed the window open and kicked out the wheel. It fell and splintered into pieces as it hit the cobblestone below. He stared down at it, not as satisfied as he wanted to be.

He turned back toward the bed. He slowly approached it, his stomach doing somersaults as, for the first time, he would see the princess—his soon to be wife.

He reached the bed and fingered at the curtains as he tried to squash the tiny hope for it to be Apolline. He listened to her breathing as he pulled the curtain open a crack at the foot of the bed. Blankets covered her feet. He took a deep breath. Then, with one movement, he pulled the curtains back.

A force launched him backward onto the floor. He moved to jump up, but found himself pinned to the ground. He struggled, but his body refused to obey him.

A beautiful dark haired woman leaned over him. "You thought it would be that simple?"

Her voice sounded so calm it gave Allard chills, but he felt the need to answer her, defy her. "Well, I was hoping."

She scowled. "You are as obnoxious as your father."

Allard smiled. "Thank you." He fought to move again.

Bryanna watched him struggle against her magical bonds. She knelt, looking into his eyes. "You are a handsome boy."

He looked up at her, disgusted.

She waved him off and scoffed. "No, I didn't mean it that way. I just hoped you'd grow up to be ugly. But you inherited your mother's looks. If you'd been ugly, it would have made my life easier and more satisfying."

"Sorry to disappoint." He glared at her. "Does it make torturing me harder to look into the face of your old friend?"

She drew a sharp breath. "I didn't intend for your mother to die, if that's what you mean." She squeezed his jaw. "I liked her, but she had to go all noble and protect you. I only wanted *you* that day, but the wolves picked up your scent on her and went mad."

"You're disgusting."

She grimaced. "You're spoiled and ignorant." She bashed his head against the floor.

He groaned, his head spinning.

She glanced over at the bed. "I bet you would like to see her face before I whisk you away."

Allard looked to the bed. He did, desperately, but Bryanna must have seen the longing and curiosity in his eyes.

She smiled. "Too bad."

With a wave of her hand, the curtains pulled shut.

Allard looked up at her. "What are you going to do with me? Do you plan to kill me?"

She laughed. "I love your sense of humor! No, I just want to destroy Cytheria, not you. Plus, you're a better bargaining chip alive." She turned to the window. "Come now."

Allard's body stood and followed her. Every step he took he fought to break free of her magic bonds. As they approached the window, a cloaked shuttle opened its door.

"Hop in and go into the closet right there." She pointed to a door.

Allard's body obeyed. He stepped into the closet, turned and glared at her.

She smiled again. "Plead for mercy."

"Princes don't plead," he snarled.

"Oh?" Her smile grew wider. "But you made an exception for that tramp Apolline."

Allard's heart skipped a beat.

"That hit a nerve, didn't it?" She touched his face, but he flinched away. "The best part is; she's nobody, so I can do what I like with her and no-one will care."

"Don't touch her—" The door slammed in his face. Once the door shut, he regained control of his body and slammed his fists against it. "Leave her! She's innocent of all this!"

The closet jolted as it moved. It seemed to travel a short distance, then its door flung open and he found himself locked in a cell. Two ogres and a rat stared at him through the bars with smirks on their faces.

The rat, being the most startling with its smirk, spoke. "Oh your royal prince-ness, all those plans and years of waiting, and you will never even know who she is."

The trio laughed and walked away, leaving him alone.

Allard sunk to his knees. He'd failed.

Bryanna had caught the prince easier than she expected, so felt satisfied. She closed the shuttle door and a rat appeared beside her. She bent over and lifted him. "Go with the prince and make sure the ogres lock him in my dungeons. I need to visit with my dear little sister for a while."

She walked across to the mirror in the shuttle. It changed its reflection into a portal to her dungeons. She placed the rat back on the floor. He darted through, and stood waiting for her to send the prince.

The closet lifted out and drifted through the portal. She watched it, frowning. Too close. He'd come much to close. How did he find his way in so quickly?

The portal closed and she saw herself in the reflection. "I'm not disgusting." She opened a drawer and pulled out her crystal. "Show me Cytheria."

The green fog inside the crystal swirled and formed the image of the fairies, king, and queen inside Apolline's room. Fantine turned to Ashlan as she entered, while Cytheria sobbed on the bed. Fantine pulled Ashlan aside and spoke quietly. "How is it?"

Ashlan nodded. "All is going well."

"And Apolline? Is she alive?"

"Of course she's alive."

Fantine sighed. "That was my greatest fear, that Bryanna would kill her once she was asleep."

Ashlan shook her head. "She has been planning this for far too long to simply kill her. Plus, she couldn't kill the face of Hernan."

King Hernan glanced up from his wife upon hearing his name. Bryanna stared at him. He looked old. Apolline looked more like the man she remembered.

"She *does* look like him, doesn't she?" Fantine sighed again. "I wonder how we never seemed to notice?"

Bryanna waved her hand over the crystal, blotting out the image. The time had come to confront Cytheria and lay out ultimatums. Her fairy magic had bewitched Hernan for long enough.

Bryanna climbed out of the shuttle and made her way to the mirror connected with Apolline's room. With a wave of her hand, it turned into a portal.

As she stepped through, the three fairies whipped out their wands and turned to face it. Hernan clasped Cytheria closer to him as Bryanna stepped down from the dresser, staring fixedly at Cytheria. "Sister."

Cytheria leaped to her feet. "Bryanna—"

Bryanna turned away from her. "You still look just as I remember."

"I cannot help that, Bree."

Bryanna spun, her eyes blazing. "Don't try to be affectionate with me! You took everything from me because you are so beautiful and remain beautiful now, as time has barely touched you!"

"You are beautiful too," Cytheria whispered.

Bryanna snarled at her. "I don't want to go through this argument again." She glanced at Hernan who stood stiff and stale faced. She turned away. "I have your daughter and that pathetic excuse for a prince."

Hernan rushed toward her. "What have you done with them? Where are they?"

She kept her back to him. "The princess remains in the castle. The prince I have sent elsewhere."

"Let them go, Bryanna. They have no part in this—"

"Oh, but they do." She glared down at Cytheria. "I will tell you where they are if you accept my conditions."

Cytheria gazed up at her. "What are they?"

"No!" Hernan pulled Cytheria away. "She will trick you, Cy."

"I just want our daughter to be free." Cytheria clasped tightly to his arms. "And now Allard, too. What will we tell Brencis? His heart will break if he loses Allard like he did Miriam. Miriam died to save Allard."

Bryanna scowled. "It was unfortunate. I liked Miriam. She shouldn't have gotten in the way."

Hernan turned on her. "Have you no conscience?"

She stepped back from him, but glared at Cytheria. "No more or less than she does."

Cytheria's gaze flashed to Bryanna. "What are your conditions?"

"Your majesty." Sophronia stepped beside Hernan, but spoke to Cytheria. "I am with the king and advise you against hearing her terms."

Bryanna grinned at the three fairies. "Oh Sophronia, the royal family's trusted fairy adviser. I just bet you loved lowering yourself to babysitter all these years. You probably thought it was below you, caring for a child and hidden away like an outcast. It's a far cry from your glory days of conquest in the name of Tyrone. Tell me, how do you feel about the girl? I doubt you love her in anyway."

Sophronia's eyebrow twitched as she looked away, her guilt written all over her.

"No, I didn't think so, but you fulfilled your duty, didn't you?"

Fantine stepped between them. "That's enough, Bryanna. This is not a game."

"Sweet Fantine." Bryanna turned with a fake smile to Fantine. "*You* probably loved her though. You always enjoyed spoiling the neighborhood brats and strays. This was probably your thing. You were the one who woke for her at night when she felt sick or had nightmares. You probably loved giving her tonic with her breakfast to keep her strong and to shield her from absorbing too much fairy magic. You probably even sat and did all her schoolwork with her. Yes, I bet you loved her like she was your own child. You probably pretended she was too. You forgot Cytheria, your master's sweet little angel, and made believe you could keep Apolline as yours forever."

Fantine's wand fizzled.

"Oh come now!" Bryanna stuck out her lower lip in a pout. "You know you are not more powerful than me." She glanced at Ashlan. "You maybe, but Sophronia and Fantine..."

She waved her hand. Sophronia and Fantine flew back, landing in a chair each. The chairs came to life, wrapping their armrests around their arms, binding the fairies down.

Bryanna then turned her attention back to Cytheria. "You see, even your fairies aren't loyal to you, because without your beauty, you are nothing." She stepped into the mirror. "I will return in three hours. These are my conditions: I will set Allard and possibly the princess free if you simply disappear, dear Cytheria. For good. Without the fairies, or your... husband." Her lip curled, disgusted. "Think about my offer while you wait, and I'll enjoy my time with the handsome, yet useless, prince."

She vanished as the mirror returned to its reflective state.

She hurried to pull out her crystal to see their reaction to her appearance. Their images appeared.

Cytheria clung to Hernan, crying. "Now Allard's in trouble too and it's my fault."

"No it isn't," Hernan responded. "This is all *her*, Cytheria. She doesn't have to be this way. She could have forgiven and moved on years ago."

He turned to Sophronia who struggled to free herself. "Go to Brencis and make sure he is protected."

She nodded. Ashlan waved her wand, setting Sophronia free. Sophronia stood, saluted, and vanished.

Cytheria rushed to Ashlan and held her in her arms. "Tell me what I need to do. Will Allard be safe? Will she torture him?"

Ashlan smiled, reaching up to touch her face. "Oh no, the prince is safe."

Bryanna waved her hand over the crystal. She needed to force Hernan away from Cytheria. Brencis. She'd go to him.

She turned to a mirror and made the connection, then stepped through to a bathroom. She rolled her eyes. Of course it had to be a bathroom. She clicked her fingers and appeared in swirls of black onto the bridge.

Laser guns activated around her as the crew turned on her.

"Oh stand down." She waved her hand and the guns powered down. "Better." She looked to the captain's seat where Brencis stood. He glared at her, his fists clenched.

"Brencis, it's been a while. You've definitely seen better days."

"Get off my ship."

"Is that how you talk to an old friend?"

"You killed my wife, your best friend," he said in a low voice.

The pain seared her heart, but she refused to let it show. "That was fourteen years ago."

Brencis' face turned red. He roared and grasped for his gun. She raised her hand and he froze. A soft gagging escaped his throat.

"Brencis, I have no desire to rehash old disagreements. I came to tell you Cytheria gave up your son for her daughter. Not that I'm complaining. The prince is far more interesting than that dull little airhead."

"Let... him... go..."

Bryanna strode toward Brencis. "I made a fair trade. Hernan didn't want to of course. He stood by you, but Cytheria.... Well, what she wants, she gets."

"You won't win."

Bryanna chuckled. Movement caught her attention. She raised her other hand, halting Charlie in his advance. "Charles Quinton. You haven't aged well. Mish made you leathery and skinny."

He flew back against the consoles. Gasps filled the room, but he forced himself to his feet. "You won't win, Bryanna. They're already in love. Ashlan—"

Bryanna laughed. "Ashlan?" But the name struck fear in her heart. "Ashlan has no power over any of this."

A bright green flash filled the room. Sophronia appeared with several armed soldiers. She pressed her hands against her hips. "Bryanna."

"Sophronia." Bryanna tilted her head.

"You can either come quietly, or I'll restrain you."

Bryanna laughed. "Restrain me? You know I'm more powerful than you."

Sophronia raised her wand.

"Anyway, if you *restrain* me, you'll never get the prince back. If I don't check in, the ogres will rip him limb from limb. Or worse, the wolves will devour him."

"You witch!" Brencis fought against his magical bonds. "I will have your head—"

"My head? How graphic." She touched her throat but smiled. "But don't blame me, dear Brencis. This is entirely Cytheria's doing. She offered him up, and my servants are simply trained to protect me. No word from me, and they attack."

"You would allow Miriam's son to follow the same brutal fate as her?"

Bryanna flinched. "Stop talking about her."

"She was my wife. He's her son."

"And she betrayed me!" Bryanna yelled. The lights flickered and dimmed. "She betrothed her son to the daughter of that thieving backstabber."

"You are the thief. You stole those years that they should have spent with their daughter. You took my wife's life. And what for? You chose the darkness. You tricked us all with it. You blinded King Absolon and tricked Hernan into pursuing you, but Hernan never loved you."

The lights flickered out as Bryanna's rage erupted.

"But someone did love you," Brencis yelled. "But you let the darkness overpower you."

She screamed. Something burned the back of her mind, a dead memory; not retrievable. A fireball erupted from her fingers.

Sophronia leaped in front of Brencis, deflecting it back at Bryanna. Bryanna caught it, absorbing the energy back into her arm. "Your son will die in three hours."

She snapped her fingers and returned to the bathroom. She stared into the mirror, her heart aching. Her mother had manipulated—possibly even killed—King Absolon, not her. But Hernan had begun pursuing her by then.

She clenched her fists tightly, drawing blood from her hands. She never tricked Hernan. The fairy magic bewitched him away from her. She took a deep breath. Once she'd severed the fairy magic hold Cytheria had over him, he would be hers again.

She turned to the mirror portal. On the other side lay the young woman who should have been her daughter. The young woman who looked so much like Hernan it made her heart break. She climbed up and slipped through, closing the connection behind her.

CHAPTER TWENTY

Allard pressed his forehead against the bars. He shut his eyes, running through everything that Ashlan told him. "Mortals fear to break.... Tools supplied?" He groaned. "What does that mean?"

He turned as he sank to the floor. Leaning against the bars, he stared at the closet resting in the middle of the cell. It looked like an oversized box, with its door hung open and cleaning supplies inside. He could use those somehow to get out.

He scrambled to his feet. He pulled out a broom, a mop and bucket, and a hand vacuum. He glanced around, wondering how he could use them to his advantage. He searched the cell for a power source, or even some water. As he passed the door again, something glimmered pink.

He stepped back. Pushed right up against the back on the shelf, sat a pink box. He stared at it. Pink definitely didn't seem to be a color Bryanna would be drawn to. He reached up and pulled it down.

White lace trimmed the bright pink box, with the letters, *EAD* painted in glitter on top.

"Hmm." He pulled off the lid.

Two thin rods about the length of his finger lay inside. He lifted them and immediately felt magic tingling in them. He slipped them in his pocket. They'd be useful, if he could figure out what they did. He wished Apolline could tell him. She would know. His conscious pricked. She could be dead, or in Bryanna's clutches, and he was at fault for it. He had to break free to save her and Elpida... somehow.

He looked into the box again and pulled out a yuckah hoof. It had to have some kind of magical properties, but again, he didn't know what. He shoved it into his pocket.

Last of all, he pulled out the globe he gave to Apolline, or at least, one that looked just like it. He turned it around, his throat clenching from the pain. Ashlan must have put the box here somehow, and she must have known about Apolline. Maybe she understood that once he had freed the princess, he wanted to be with Apolline. Maybe the globe was some kind of clue to lead him to her.

With nothing else to discover in the box or closet, he turned to the bars. The rods could probably pick the lock. He dug into his pocket, but instead of finding two rods, he found one and a small key. He brought the key out, stared at it for a moment, then slipped his arms through the bars. The key fit perfectly, and with a click, the door came open.

He pulled out the key and watched it shift back into a rod. "Nice."

He stepped out of the cell and glanced around warily. No one was in sight. He cautiously made his way out of the dungeon.

At the top of the stairs, the voices of several ogres arguing drifted through the doorway. He glanced around the corner to get a bearing on their positions and number. He counted seven of them, and a nest of rats slept by the far door. He looked at the rods, but they remained unchanged. He grabbed at his pockets, wondering if one of the other objects might help. The globe? No, that was practically useless. It just made him think of Apolline, and how, because of him, she faced great danger.

The yuckah hoof then? The yuckah were magical, so it could still have magic in it. He pulled it out and examined it. What did he know about them? Apolline hunted them. He shook his head. He had to focus.

His father told him that only those exposed to fairy magic could catch the beasts. Their magic made them swift, but the fairy magic acted like a drug and slowed them down. He moved the hoof around in his hands. Maybe the hoof could make him impossible to catch somehow. He had no idea what to do with it though.

"Wake up, little hoof," he whispered, but the hoof did nothing. He rubbed it, stroked it, threw it in the air, but still nothing. He groaned softly. He sat and let his arm dangle loosely beside him. As the hoof touched the ground, it came to life. He twisted and held the hoof firmly as it jolted around on the stone floor. He struggled to turn it, then whispered, "I need to get unnoticed through that door."

The hoof tugged him forward. He shot across the courtyard. He came to an abrupt halt and collapsed on the floor in a dark hallway. This magic nonsense made him dizzy. He glanced back to the courtyard through the doorway, but the ogres and rats hadn't noticed him. He looked at the hoof as it fell dormant again. He nodded, smiling, making a mental note to thank Ashlan.

One of the rods became heavier. He pulled it out to find it had become a small flashlight. He tucked the hoof back in his pocket.

He made his way down the corridor. Darkness consumed every hallway, and every corner he turned, he met more. The darkness turned out to be useful because it made approaching creatures noticeable. He'd see a light approaching, so carefully ducked into an empty room.

He'd heard of Mahkba. The planet had once been part of the Tyrone kingdom, until the royal fairy, Sophronia, moved it outside the galaxy. He found himself in awe that such power existed. But, as he made his way through the dark mansion, he wondered what the planet had been before becoming Bryanna's infamous prison. Built of stone, and in a similar style to that of mansions in Tyrone, it had to have some connection.

He walked around aimlessly. He wished he had more information on what to do or how to get out. Then, he thought of the palace of Tyrone. Since it looked similar, maybe it had the same shuttle bays on the roof.

He found a stairway and headed upward. New parts, different in design, met him as he ascended, as if added much later than the original estate. Level after level he climbed, but when he reached the roof, the darkness consumed him. Not even stars shone. He shuddered, and darted back inside. He listened, and, hearing nothing, began an aimless journey through the mansion again.

A roar echoed from far below, and the chattering rats seemed to surround him.

"The prince is free."

"Search the palace."

"Keep him away from the queen's mirror room."

Mirror. Maybe she had portals too. But where? He thought of the building's layout. It reflected a middle era design, except expanded. In the central parts it seemed perfectly normal, with living areas on the ground floor, and on the level above lay bedroom suites. Maybe the master suite held the mirrors? All the expanded parts seemed thrown together, like a magical fortress, cocooning the old estate. If her room lay in those parts, he would struggle to find it. The master suite was his best bet.

But with the creatures on the prowl, the journey proved difficult. He paused and pulled out the hoof again. He knelt down and set it on the floor, careful to keep a tight hold on it. It came to life.

"All right, hoof. Take me to the master suite on the second floor."

The hoof lurched forward, dragging Allard with it. It shot through the mansion as if searching for its destination. Allard flew by ogres, giants, rats, crows, and even wolves. He glanced back at the wolves when they howled, but the hoof dragged him onward too quickly to see.

A green glow appeared up ahead of him. The hoof pulled him right at the door and stopped. It fell lifeless again. He placed the hoof back in his pocket and pressed his ear against the wood, shocked that the master suite held something promising within it. He couldn't believe his luck!

A soft bubbling sound came through, but nothing else. He cautiously opened the door and glanced around. Finding the room abandoned, he stepped inside and shut himself in.

Dozens of mirrors filled the room. He examined the closest row. Each mirror had a label baring a planet's name on the top. A throne with a curved desk in front of it sat to his right, with a communicator resting on top. This had to be Bryanna's room.

He searched for the mirror labeled Mish, locating it in the first row. He stared at his reflection, wishing he knew how to make the mirror work so he could go through and check on Apolline. But he didn't, so he did the next best thing; he smashed it. He didn't want any way for Bryanna to get to Apolline if he could avoid it.

He turned and his heart jumped. A ghostly face gazed at him from within the mirror directly in front of the desk and throne. The disembodied male's appearance alarmed him, but when he said nothing, Allard approached the mirror. "Who are you?"

He didn't respond.

"Do you speak?"

Again, no answer. Allard turned his back to the mirror, focusing on the desk to find a way out of the castle. "Why must she have so many mirrors?" he muttered. "Is she so vain that she has to check every few seconds to make sure she is the most beautiful—?"

"Cytheria is the most beautiful."

Allard jumped and swung around as Cytheria's face appeared in the mirror.

"You show beautiful things?"

The mirror didn't answer.

"Do I need to ask the right question?"

Cytheria's face disappeared and the ghostly one reappeared and nodded.

"Who is the greatest sorcerer?"

"Bryanna." Her face appeared.

"Where is she?"

The mirror stayed silent.

Allard sighed. "How can I get back to Tyrone?"

The mirror didn't respond again, but a different mirror caught his attention as its surface began to swirl. He turned to the other mirror and watched the ballroom of the Tyrone palace form. He rushed over and, to his relief, found it had turned into a portal. He glanced back at the mirror for Mish, glad he had destroyed it. Then, he stepped through into Tyrone.

Bryanna watched the princess as she slept. She should have been her daughter. She stared at her face, unable to look away from the young woman. Bryanna couldn't help herself; the girl looked too much like Hernan. She could easily pass Apolline off as her own daughter once she'd done away with Cytheria. Apolline looked and behaved more like Hernan's daughter than Cytheria's. Smart, cunning, brave, all attributes of Hernan. How hadn't she noticed earlier?

She ran her fingers through Apolline's light brown hair. "All of this is your mother's fault," she whispered. "If she were to just give up and let me have Hernan back, I can pretend you are mine. I am growing too old to have children of my own."

She brushed her fingers over Apolline's cheek, and her gaze caught on the blue dress. She scowled. "Your eyes will betray you."

She stood, pulling the drapes closed again.

Someone called her name. She quickly walked to the window and looked down. On either side of the smashed spinning wheel, stood Fantine and Hernan. Fantine called her name again.

Bryanna's heart fluttered. Hernan wanted to speak to her, and he didn't have Cytheria at his side. He had Fantine. Fantine who had once... No. Fantine was bound to Cytheria. Even if Fantine did show some form of kindness once, her bond would prevent any now. But still...

Bryanna climbed unseen into the shuttle. She carefully maneuvered it across the courtyard, landed it just out of sight, and marched over to them.

Hernan turned to face her first and she caught her breath. Even looking aged, he still dazzled her. She breathed deeply, composing herself. "Your time has not yet passed."

"We know," Fantine said. "I just want my Apolline back."

"And I want that too," Hernan said, bowing his head. "I have never had a moment to know my daughter."

Bryanna turned away from them. "I'm not interested in pleas for mercy."

"Wait!" Hernan called.

She stopped, and slowly turned to him.

He came toward her, then grabbed her hand. "Bryanna, do you remember when we first met?"

She pulled her hand away from him warily. "Of course I do."

"You were something else. It took me all night to approach you at the reception, then it took all my courage to ask you to dance at the ball. No man could hold your attention because you were so superior. You were intelligent and stunning. It took me half the night to build up the courage to ask you." He chuckled, making her hard heart crack. "I almost backed out, but Miriam insisted."

Bryanna softened, the memories of her old friend and a time long gone bringing back a side to her she had forgotten. "You were the only one who could hold a decent conversation."

Hernan ran his hand through his hair, making her stomach fill with butterflies. "Well, you were very intimidating..."

CHAPTER TWENTY-ONE

Allard stepped into the ballroom. He scanned the room, relieved to find Tyrone unchanged. The dim light remained, and silence hung in the air. He hurried toward the mirror with the portal to the tower, walking soft footed because each step echoed around him.

He poked his head in, more cautious this time. When he decided it looked safe enough, he rushed to the window and threw one of his buttons at the shuttle, but it had gone. He turned and quickly checked the room again, but saw no signs of Bryanna.

Voices drifted up from the courtyard. Allard dashed to the window and peered down. Bryanna and King Hernan stood talking in the courtyard, barely more than a foot apart. They looked terribly intimate, and it made Allard curious. Once the pair had been in love. Could there be some residual feelings between them? That was highly unlikely for Hernan considering Bryanna had threatened to kill his daughter, but instead, had cursed the baby and forced him to give her up. But Bryanna...? Maybe.

A woman glanced up at him. She tilted her head, signaling for him to do what he needed to do.

He turned to the bed again. This time, he would see Princess Elpida. He walked over, his heart rate increasing. He fingered the curtains again. He needed to do it quickly. He didn't want to be disappointed, or let the faint glimmer of hope that she could be Apolline linger any longer.

He flung back the curtains. His eyes widened, a variety of emotions filling him at once. Disbelief, relief... He fell to his knees, stunned by who he beheld before him. Then his feelings turned to horror and rage at Bryanna. How could she do this to someone?

But finally, his heart soared. He leaned over and clasped Apolline's hand tightly, whispering, "Oh, Apolline! Thank goodness it's you! I don't know how I could have lived with my heart elsewhere."

He scrambled up and sat on the bed beside her. "I hoped it was you. I'm so glad it is you." He stroked her long, light brown hair tenderly and leaned forward. He could feel her breath against his lips as he whispered, "Now the real test... true love's kiss."

He softly pressed his lips against hers. Cold met his kiss, like death threatened to take her. He wished to warm them, bring her back so those lips would wear a smile again. It took a moment, but her lips pushed against his. Heat flooded into them, like someone had released death's grip.

He sat back, smiling as she scrunched her eyes and squirmed, lacking any grace whatsoever. But this was Apolline after all. If she woke daintily, he'd be disappointed. She yawned and stretched, before she opened her eyes...

Warmth spread from my lips, pulling me out of a bizarre dreaming state. I felt his presence beside me as I awoke. I found myself too afraid to look at him. He had to be the prince, so I kept my eyes shut, too nervous to look at royalty. What was I thinking? *I'm royalty...* as strange as that prospect was. Then, no longer able to avoid it, I tentatively opened my eyes. I shot up, my heart skipping a beat. "You!"

He smiled. "Yes, me."

"Where is the prince? Oh no, I'm in trouble aren't I?"

He laughed. "No." He turned his chest toward me. He wore the Oran royal crest on his chest, embroidered in gold.

"No!" I gasped.

"Oh yes, I am *Prince* Allard."

"But... I... you..." I touched his face as relief flooded over me.

He closed his eyes and grabbed my hand. "You want to know the best part for me?"

"What?" I whispered, staring into his face.

He looked into my eyes, lifting his hand to caress my cheek. "I know without a shadow of doubt that you are in love with me."

Heat rushed into my cheeks. "Oh, that kiss thing."

"Yes, that kiss thing gave it away." He leaned forward and kissed me.

I kissed him back, my heart skipping excitedly in my chest. I couldn't believe it was him! I had wanted it to be, but I didn't let myself believe it. All that time we had been together and he really had been my betrothed, and I his. We had resisted, but now it seemed worth it. He was mine, and my heart filled with joy. Then a thought dawned on me.

I pushed back from him. "Oh Ashlan! You sneaky fairy!"

"What?"

"Of course, she arranged for us to meet months ago. We needed to actually *fall* in love." I paused, blushing at my words, but he smiled at me warmly, reassuring me. "It was no coincidence you came to Mish and I was in town when you arrived. Ashlan never told me *not* to see you because she knew, she arranged it all."

"How do you know it was Ashlan, not one of the others?"

I leaned back and grinned. "The other two don't get romantic notions like that."

He touched my face. "Well, I'm glad it's you. I couldn't bear to live without you, and I'm glad you're safe."

My heart leaped in my chest. "And you. Bryanna told me she'd done away with you."

"Not me. I might not be as tough as you, but I can get out of a snag."

I let out a long breath, pressing my forehead against his. "You! I can't believe it's you."

He chuckled.

I looked into his eyes, all my desires and yearning for him suddenly allowed. I grabbed the back on his neck and kissed him.

He moaned softly as our mouths opened and he pulled me into his arms. My whole body responded to his lips against mine. I clung to him, taking his tongue into my mouth. He moaned again. He lifted me up and swung me around as we both laughed.

"I love you, Apolline," he whispered.

"I love you, Allard."

He grinned and kissed me again.

Bryanna's heart pounded. King Hernan smiled at her, inching closer. Maybe he did still have feelings for her, despite Cytheria, despite everything. She remembered the way he used to kiss her, look at her...

"I couldn't believe you let me talk to you," he said. "But Miriam pushed me. She told me I shouldn't be such a coward."

"Miriam." Bryanna whispered stepping back. "I didn't mean for her to be killed. You must know that. I loved her, so much. I would do anything to change that if I could."

Hernan hesitated, swallowing. "I wasn't sure. But now you've told me, I don't doubt it."

She brushed her hair behind her ear. Although suspicious, she wanted to hope he'd come back for her. "Elpida is yours. She looks just like you."

Hernan nodded, stretching out his hand. "Let me see her. Please."

She stared down at his hand. She lowered her hand, her fingers itching to touch his.

Her communicator beeped. She pulled it out and pressed it against her ear to hear the rat she sent with Prince Allard. "Mistress, the prince, he has gone missing."

"Excuse me?" she snarled.

"He is not in the cell and we have no idea where he has gone."

Her rage flared. She turned away from Hernan. "How did this happen?"

"All we found was a pink box—"

She threw the communicator on the ground. It broke into pieces against the cobblestone. "*Ashlan!*" she wailed. "Ashlan! You interfering little witch!"

She swung back around. Hernan's smile had changed to one of satisfaction. "Not going according to plan, Bree? What, has the prince escaped? He is a smart young man, you know."

Hot tears burned up in her eyes at his words. "You mock me now as well?"

He stared her down. "I'm not mocking you, Bryanna. But you could have been much more, you are so much better than this."

"But I'm not, because of *her*. She stole it all from me!"

"You did this to yourself. Now stop punishing us for your own self-pity."

Fantine rushed to Hernan's side. "I don't think..."

Bryanna's rage ignited inside her. Hernan had come to her as a distraction, nothing more. Cytheria must have sent him, to give Ashlan a chance to help the prince escape. Blackness poured out of her like oil and her eyes turned dark. The pain tore through her body at the endless betrayals. She lunged at Hernan.

Fantine flung up a magical shield. "Quickly, your highness, run!"

Hernan ran back into the palace. Just as he disappeared, Bryanna broke Fantine's shield. "You can't beat me, Fantine. You taught me what you know, and now I have surpassed you."

"I won't let you have Apolline!"

"I've already got her." She threw out the blackness in tentacles extending from her fingertips. It coiled around Fantine; the fairy glowed blue, struggling with all her magic to break free.

"Blue?" Bryanna laughed. "Your magic was red, like a rose, like Snow's lips. My, your heart has changed. You must love Cytheria beyond reason."

"It's Apolline I love," Fantine cried, pulling her arm free. She raised her wand. "She's like a daughter to me."

Fantine's wand lit up in a bright blue light. It shot out like a lightning bolt. Bryanna dodged, breaking free from the black tentacles. The tentacles, free of their master, encompassed Fantine. She stumbled, struggling against them as they pinned her arm down.

"No..." Bryanna watched, unable to stop them as they entered Fantine's mouth and nostrils and she collapsed onto the cobblestone. Bryanna gasped, and withdrew her power, returning to her normal appearance. She watched Fantine for a moment, until she saw her chest rise and fall. Still alive.

She rushed back to her shuttle. She shut the door, checked the cloaking, and took a deep breath. Hernan had played her! Cytheria's hold over him was as tight as ever. And Fantine, she could have killed her!

A sob escaped her, but she struggled against the emotions. Drawing a deep breath, she composed herself, and turned to the mirror portal to her castle.

"My queen," the rat said as she passed through into the dungeon. "We've searched the castle. The wolves say they smelled him and have been tracking his trail."

She didn't care. Hernan filled her thoughts. "Keep searching."

"Yes, my queen." The rat scurried off, leaving her alone.

She entered the cell to examine it. She crushed the box under her foot, certain upon seeing it that Ashlan planted it. Only she would use a pink lace box. Ashlan knew Bryanna would recognize her signature.

She lifted her hand, feeling for magic. Immediately, she felt its tingling sensation to her left. She rested her hand over the keyhole and the remnants of the power made her shudder.

"Fairy magic. Metal shape shifters." She sniffed the air. She smelled a magical creature, of the good variety. She turned back to the smashed box and bent over to look at it closely. "A yuckah hair." She sniffed again and began following her nose.

She reached the room where the ogres and rats nested. Most had gone to search the castle, but a handful remained, standing back with their gazes cast down. She looked at the ground at a single hoof print across the room in the dust.

"Very clever, Ashlan. I'm surprised the prince worked it out." She followed the hoof print into the corridor with the trail of magic in the air.

She traced the magic up to the roof, to the unused shuttle bays. Pausing, she touched the door handle, a hint of fear shooting up her arm. She kept her hand still, absorbing its power. When she turned back into the tower, a wolf met her.

"My queen," he said, bowing his head. "We have traced his scent. You must come at once."

Bryanna rushed after him, hoping the wolves hadn't ripped him to shreds. But the wolf led her to her mirror room. The pack stood by the door and bowed their heads as she burst in.

The mirror connecting to Mish sat askew and smashed. She glanced around, feeling violated. The prince entered her private domain, and by the cool look on her mirror's face, he'd spoken to it.

"What did you tell the prince?" she yelled.

The man in the mirror blinked.

She growled. She glanced around the room, seeing nothing else out of place. Except one mirror. She stepped toward the open portal that led to the ballroom of the Tyrone palace.

He had definitely gone through, and he knew how to get to the tower. He knew too much. He'd seen too much. Panic clutched at her chest.

CHAPTER TWENTY-TWO

*A*shlan!"

Bryanna's voice echoed around in my head. Allard grabbed my hand. "Come on, we've got to get out of here."

"But we need to stop her," I said, glancing around the room.

"Not from here." He tugged my hand. "We need to find weapons first. She will be here soon, especially if she finds out I've escaped."

"You escaped? From what?"

He pulled at me again and I followed. "I'll explain on the way."

He took me to a mirror. A ballroom reflected on its surface, except it didn't look reflective. He pulled me through and into the ballroom.

I glanced back at the room in the tower behind us. "She likes mirrors."

"I know. She has dozens of them in her castle."

"I'd be afraid of breaking one if I had too many."

"Why?"

"Because it's supposed to be bad luck, isn't it?"

Allard froze. "What was that?"

"Breaking a mirror is supposed to give you seven years bad luck."

He slapped his forehead. "Of course! It's so obvious!"

He darted back through the mirror. I watched as he pulled a mirror off the wall, smashing it on the floor.

"What are you doing?" I asked, poking my head through.

"Mirrors. Bad luck." He pulled another down, then another. Once he'd pulled all the mirrors down, smashing them, he stepped back through the mirror I'd poked my head through. He pushed me back, then reached through and pulled it off the wall. He quickly brought his arm back just as the mirror in the ballroom returned to a reflection of us standing there.

"What was that about?" I asked.

He grabbed my hand, pulling me into a run. "When Ashlan brought me here she told me; *to defeat the sorceress, you must destroy what humans avoid breaking for fear of misfortune.*"

"How did you *not* get mirrors from that?"

He glanced at me. "I wasn't exactly in the mood for riddles. I had just been dragged across space by a fairy, then saw that Bryanna had put you to sleep."

"Did you know it was me then?"

He glanced at me. "No."

"When did you know?"

"Right before I kissed you." He paused, glancing around a corner. "I have a question."

"Fire away."

He turned and faced me. "How did you *not* know I was the prince? You knew the prince is best friends with Beau White, my name is Allard, and everything I told you practically screamed my identity."

I shrugged. "It seemed farfetched."

"Really?"

"Yeah. You're not as hot as you think you are."

He gave me a sarcastic smirk. "You're funny."

"You're hotter."

He rolled his eyes but smiled. "By the way, your fairy called me hot."

"She has good taste."

He chuckled. "Good to know you don't feel threatened."

"Fairies don't marry." I reached out and touched his heart, remembering something. "Did she do this?"

He nodded.

"Hmm. Weird. She's done that to me lately too, except she says I'm warm."

"What does it mean?"

I shrugged. "I never bother trying to work her out."

We dashed through the palace and he filled me in on what happened in the couple of hours I had been asleep. We burst into a weapons storage room as he finished telling me what happened in Bryanna's castle. He impressed me with how quickly he escaped and figured out the objects. Then he pulled them out and showed me.

"The shape shifters Sophronia gave me!" I plucked them out of his hands to examine them. "These were Sophronia's. She gave them to me a few weeks ago, but took them away after our little... excursion."

He grinned. "I wish I'd known you were Elpida then. I would have made out with you like crazy."

I laughed. "I still can't believe *I'm* Elpida."

I picked up the yuckah hoof. "Fantine gave me this. I remember killing this stag. Who doesn't forget their first kill, right? Fantine insisted on keeping certain parts of it for her potions and medicines, and gave me all four hooves because they are handy for making speedy exits."

He handed me the globe. I brushed my fingers over the glass, smiling as I remembered staring at it and wishing for Allard to be my betrothed. I guess I got that wish.

"This is mine." I looked up at him. "Remember? You gave it to me."

He examined it. "Does it have magic?"

"Not that I know of." I frowned. "Why did she include this?"

We stared at it dumbfounded. I shrugged. "Who knows what Ashlan was thinking? It was probably meant to be a hint for you to say I'm Elpida."

I went to put it in my pocket, but realized I was wearing my dress. "I need to get changed."

"Why?" He turned to examine the weapons.

"Why? I can't run or fight in this. It's the only nice thing I own, and it's meant for the ball tonight."

"So? You're a princess now. You can replace it. "

I snorted, irritated. "Shut up. I'm getting changed."

"Fine, but let's load up first." He tossed a laser gun at me.

I tossed it aside and moved to the back of the storage room.

Allard stopped rummaging. "What are you doing?"

"Finding something more…" I paused to think of the right word. "Solid."

I searched for shotguns, rifles, handguns, or even bows and arrows. Eventually, right at the back, I found a handful of shelves that held the weapons I wanted. The dusty guns and ammunition appeared to have sat unused for many years. I grabbed a shotgun and examined it. "Should still work."

Allard approached me, tilting his head. "These are a little… old fashioned, don't you think?"

I clipped an old leather belt around my waist, slipped the globe in one of the pockets, and began loading the pouches up with shells. "No. Those laser guns are useless against Bryanna."

Allard glanced at the gun in his hand. "Why? They seem to have been doing just fine so far."

"Really? Is that why they managed to prevent so much destruction when she first started her rampage through the kingdoms?"

Allard hesitated. "What do you mean?"

I handed him a handgun in exchange for the laser gun in his hand. "Laser guns against magical creatures and beings are useless. The creatures just kind of absorb the energy. Bullets, on the other hand, are solid and harder to breakdown and deflect."

"How do you know that?"

I put my hand on my hip. "Do you enjoy questioning me? I know it because I have lived with fairies my whole life, and I tried once to use a laser gun for hunting and it had no effect on the yuckah whatsoever."

Allard dumped his laser guns and their ammunition, and loaded up with bullets for the handgun.

Handing him a rifle, I grabbed a revolver for myself and another handgun for back up. We then rushed back to the door.

Allard peeked out. "Where was your room?"

"I don't know. The east wing somewhere." I tried to describe what I remembered about it and the hallways I had walked through.

He grabbed my hand. "The east wing? Urgh. Seriously?"

"What is that supposed to mean?"

"It's just... old. Really old. It's the original palace. Hardly anyone goes down there anymore."

"Why does that matter?"

He smiled. "I know where we need to go."

He gave me a quick kiss, then pulled me into a sprint through the castle.

Just before we entered the courtyard, he stopped me and scanned the area. "Looks clear." He met my gaze. "What do you think? Can you tell if there is anything magical out there?"

I looked out and my stomach plummeted. Fantine lay unconscious on the cobblestone. I grabbed Allard's shirt. "Oh no! Fantine!" I dashed out and knelt over her. "Fantine, wake up!" I whispered desperately, as I felt for her pulse.

Allard rushed to me and grabbed me by the waist. "She'll be all right, it will wear off. But we can't stay here. It's too exposed."

"We need to at least move her—"

"She'll be fine. Look, there are people unconscious everywhere."

I glanced around to see people asleep all over the castle.

"Ashlan did it when you first fell asleep to prevent panic in the kingdoms." He lifted me to my feet. "Come on."

We dashed through the castle and burst into my room. We froze, startled by the sight of the king, queen, and Ashlan as they turned to face us.

"Allard! Elpida!" The queen rushed at us, hugging Allard. Then, carefully, she smiled at me. "I thought the worst had happened to you both. And Elpida, you are awake! We thought you had been—"

"I was," I muttered. "And it's Apolline."

Allard grabbed my elbow and pulled me closer. "Be nice. She's your mother."

I grunted and pulled away, heading to my clothes resting on the end of my bed.

Ashlan came over to me. "Why must you always be carrying a weapon? And what happened to your dress? It was purple before."

"Bryanna changed it." I glanced at Cytheria. "She said it was to remind people of the treacherous eyes."

Cytheria glanced away, flushing. A tear ran down her cheek.

"Apolline!" Allard said sharply. "Hernan and Cytheria have sacrificed a great deal to protect you."

I bit my lip and turned away from him, picking up my shirt. I felt conflicted. I wanted to know them. They obviously cared about me enough to sacrifice knowing me, and watching me grow to try and save me, but at the same time, I blamed them for the predicament I found myself in and for the life of lies I had led.

Hernan came up beside me and grabbed my shoulder. "Apolline, you are a smart young lady, and I know this is all a shock for you, so please be reasonable. You know the stories and events that led up to this, the fairies made sure of that, so you must know that your mother and I love you and did this to protect you."

I looked up at his face, fascinated by how much I looked like him, and wondered how no-one ever seemed to notice. I looked at Cytheria who was so stunningly beautiful that even Allard, as he followed my gaze, was struck by it.

I looked back to Hernan, sighing. "I know. It's just so much all at once. I need..." I paused and turned to face Ashlan. "Fantine! Fantine is—"

"We know," Ashlan said soothingly. "She will be fine."

I stared down at the shirt in my hand. "Help me out of this dress?"

Ashlan nodded and guided me behind a room divider. She untied my dress. "How is it going?"

"Ah... fine. I'm not unconscious."

She chuckled. "Did you like my surprise? Allard?"

"Very clever. But why didn't you say anything or get Sophronia to back off?"

"If I did that, they would have given you away. Bryanna watches him, Cytheria, Hernan. If you knew he was your betrothed, then you were obviously..."

"The princess." I pulled on my shirt, pants, and boots.

She handed me the belt with the guns and ammunition. I clipped it back around me.

Allard grinned as I stepped out. "Now that's the Apolline I know and love."

Cytheria and Hernan exchanged shocked looks.

"Wait," Hernan said. "You know each other?"

I squeezed Ashlan's hand and smiled. "Yes, we're well acquainted. Someone made sure of that."

They both looked to Ashlan who shrugged. "The spell was that true love's kiss would break the curse. So I'm a romantic. It was no different from your glass slippers and pumpkin space shuttle, Cytheria."

"Her what?" My gaze darted between the two as Cytheria flushed.

The whole castle shook. I grasped Allard's arm as dust fell around us. Screaming echoed up and down the corridors.

Bryanna gazed around the room. Shattered glass covered the floor. Mirror frames lay bent and broken. But her rage flared when she laid eyes on the empty bed. She rushed toward it, resting her hand on the pillow. She flinched away, and looked at the burns on her hand. How could a pillow get so hot and not ignite? She frowned. Magic. Good magic.

She retreated to her shuttle and snatched up her crystal. "Where is the prince?"

The green fog changed to pink. "Urgh! Ashlan!"

"Hello, Bryanna," Ashlan replied in a sing song voice. Her face appeared in the crystal. "Not going according to plan?"

"You're interfering."

"No, I'm not."

"You gave the prince magical items."

"No, I didn't. They all belonged to Apolline. Maybe you should be more careful where you leave empty closets."

"You put the box in there!"

"I promised Apolline I would keep them safe. So, I locked them in a lonely closet. It's not my fault the prince found them and knew how to use them."

"Where are they?"

"The items?"

"The prince and princess."

Ashlan smiled. "My, don't you know? I thought you had eyes everywhere."

"I hate you."

"I have never once interfered with you, Bryanna. Humans are capable of making their own choices. I never expected Cytheria to fall in love at the ball. I just wanted to make her happy."

"Shut up." Bryanna shook the ball, making Ashlan's image vanish.

Ashlan pushed Allard and I toward the door. "You can't be here. Bryanna will come here first. She will want to blame Cytheria and me, and will believe we're hiding you."

I resisted her. "We're ready to fight her." I picked up the shotgun from against the wall.

Cytheria whimpered.

Ashlan glanced at her, but said to us, "Not yet. She's too strong. You must destroy her power source."

"What is it?" I asked.

"I think you already know, Apolline," Allard said. He rushed to the mirror and smashed it.

We flinched back at the noise and glass spray. Ashlan nodded. "Very good, Allard. That will slow her down."

Allard grabbed my hand again and we rushed out of the room. He headed down the corridor checking each room for mirrors, and smashing every one we found.

With the mirrors gone, Bryanna needed to improvise. She pictured the room in the east wing and vaporized into it. She brought with her a darkness that poured out of her, dimming the corner of the room like an ominous storm cloud. "Where are they, Cytheria?"

Cytheria stared at her. "Who?"

Bryanna rushed at her. "Don't play coy with me! Your brat and that prince!"

"I thought you had them." Cytheria stared back firmly into her eyes.

Bryanna's eyes narrowed. "You've seen them." She turned to Ashlan. "You aren't supposed to interfere with humans."

"I told you, I haven't interfered, just guided and advised." Ashlan held up her chin. "I have never delegated or created a destiny."

A fire ignited in Bryanna's eyes. "You created mine by making Cytheria so bewitching, then tossing her in front of Hernan—"

"No, Bryanna. He made the choice to be with her."

Bryanna wailed and lifted her hand up to Cytheria. "Let me see you without fairy magic under your skin."

Cytheria recoiled as Bryanna's power ripped through her. Her bright, blonde hair dulled and lost its bounce, her skin lost its fullness and vibrant color, and wrinkles began to show. When she stopped changing, Bryanna stared at her in horror. "You are..."

Hernan rushed to Cytheria. "Cytheria, did she hurt you?"

"No," Cytheria replied softly, looking at her aged hands. "But I'm..."

Bryanna snarled and turned away from them. "Hernan, what do you think of her now?"

Hernan smiled at his wife. "She is still the loveliest woman I have ever met."

Bryanna stared at Cytheria who remained quite beautiful, but no longer striking. With wrinkles around her eyes, mouth and face, the years of strain tugged at her features without the magical shield. "She is no longer more beautiful than me."

Hernan turned on Bryanna. "She will always be more beautiful than you because of who she is, not what she looks like. Why don't you understand that?"

"Bryanna," Cytheria whispered.

Bryanna looked at her as the fairy magic took hold of her again.

As Cytheria slowly turned back to her usual appearance, she spoke, "We were close once, true sisters; why did that end? Why can't we have it back? I miss you."

Bryanna stepped back, stunned. The pain from the memories; her little sister smiling up at her, or crying when the girls bullied her. She stood up for her then. But...

She clenched her fists and vanished.

We reached the courtyard and stopped. Allard checked the path was clear again. He squeezed my hand. "We have to get to the ballroom before she does. There are enough mirrors in there to provide plenty of power."

I nodded.

We dashed out into the courtyard.

Bryanna vaporized in front of us, her emerald green dress emitting darkness, like her aura sucked light from around her. I gasped. Allard put his arm in front of me, pushing me behind him.

Bryanna laughed. "Ah, noble prince protecting his one true love. Very well, you can die now anyway."

She surged toward him.

I shoved him to the side, raising the shotgun, and fired. The force blew her back onto the cobblestone. But I hadn't hit her. As I lowered the gun, a green shimmering flickered around her. She glared up at me, winded from the impact.

"Stay down!" I raised my gun.

She let out a sinister laugh, and pushed off the ground. I fired another round. It knocked her back, the green shield shimmering as it took the brunt of the shot. Grabbing Allard's hand, we ran to the other end of the courtyard.

"You're still nuts!" Allard said.

"Nuts just saved you."

"I didn't say there's anything wrong with it."

I smiled.

We shattered several more mirrors on the way to the ballroom.

"Elpida!"

Allard looked back first, but it took me a moment to react. When I did, Allard pulled me into a sprint. I caught a glimpse of Bryanna, darkness surrounding her and filling the corridor.

"Allard!" I clung to his hand, frightened for my life.

He glanced at me, then, releasing my hand, swung around and fired off several shots.

The first shot hit her shield, making her stumble back. But then she pressed against the wall to dodge the rest. The darkness encompassed her.

"That's bad." Allard pulled me back into a sprint.

Up ahead lay the ballroom. We darted in.

I glanced around, realizing our mistake. "I don't think we should have come here."

"We need to—"

"Yes, but she's right behind us. This room will make her more powerful. We should lose her and come back."

He squeezed my hand and we ran to the far end. We climbed the stairs to a doorway. When we stood a few feet from the door, it rattled and locked. Allard threw himself at it to no avail. I swung around as Bryanna slowly walked toward us.

"I have you both now."

Allard turned to me, grasping my shoulders. "Apolline."

I gazed into his eyes. "At least it was you."

A determined look flashed onto his face. He bent down and kissed me. "Let's go down fighting."

He pulled out the handgun. Raising it and the rifle he already held, he pointed both weapons at the mirrors on the right side of the room. As he shot out the first two, I lifted my guns and shot at the mirrors on our left.

Bryanna knocked us both to the ground with her magic. We stumbled to the bottom of the stairs. But we rolled onto our knees and kept shooting. She let out a piercing, agonized scream.

Allard and I ran down the room, back to back, shooting mirror after mirror. Then, Bryanna pounced on me, pulling at my hair.

"You will die first, you brat!" She crushed my hand and I dropped the shotgun.

A shot whizzed by my ear. She let go of me and spun to face Allard. He raised his handgun and fired at her again.

She fell back, but charged him, overpowering him with her magic. "Or, you could go first, so she can watch."

He fell to the ground, wailing. His body twisted and contorted as she tortured him.

"Allard!" I swiveled to him, trying to reload the revolver.

Something strange in one of the mirrors caught my eye; a throne, a large desk, and a mirror with a face in it. I remembered the fairytale of the Whites. Snow's stepmother had used vanity to overpower people and bewitch them, perverting the magic mirror the fairies gave her. It dawned on me that the source of Bryanna's power came from that mirror specifically.

I lunged to my feet and ran to the portal, leaping over Allard as I ran.

"No!" Bryanna wailed.

"Elpida!" Cytheria screamed.

"Apolline, no!" Hernan and Allard called out in unison.

As the room in the mirror appeared around me, I turned to the mirror with the face in it. I looked back at my parents and Allard struggling to come after me.

The face in the mirror smiled at me. "Ask the question."

"What question?"

"Who is the bravest of them all?"

I raised my gun. "I don't care."

I pulled the trigger and the mirror shattered.

CHAPTER TWENTY-THREE

Apolline, no!" Allard, suddenly free from his magical restraints, rushed toward the mirror. He watched as Apolline raised her gun and shot at the face in the mirror.

"No!" He hit the mirror as it turned back to its normal reflective state. "Apolline! Apolline, no!"

He swung around. Bryanna, who knelt staring at her hands, began to laugh menacingly. Allard rushed at her and grabbed her. "Bring her back!"

Bryanna continued laughing.

"Bring her back!" Allard yelled.

Hernan slid up beside Allard, grabbing Bryanna's arm. "Bring my daughter back."

Her laughter lessened but she kept smiling. "I can't."

"Can't or won't?" Hernan asked with a snarl.

"Can't. She broke the mirror. I have no powers."

"Then why are you laughing?" Allard shook her.

"Why?" She laughed again. "She's in Mahkba, and without my magic, the creatures can't speak, and the ogres and giants can no longer get to their home worlds. They all know where the mirror is, so they will be heading right for her as we speak."

"Do something then!" Allard bellowed.

Bryanna shrugged. "Can't. It will be too late no matter what I do." She looked at Cytheria who had fallen to her knees. "Well, sister, I guess we're even."

Cytheria glared at her and stood. "It's not over, Bree. Apolline is my daughter after all, and she will find a way to free herself, just like I always did from your mother's restraints."

Bryanna's laughing stopped but her smile stayed. "There's no way out of there, Cytheria. Hernan's fairy made sure of that. I bet you're regretting the order to send the planet outside of the galaxy now."

Cytheria looked to Hernan. "Where's Sophronia?"

He shook his head. "I don't know."

Ashlan burst into the room. She glowed pink as she hurried straight to Allard and stared up at him intensely. She pressed her hand against Allard's chest. "Oh! So hot."

Allard frowned. "Hot?"

She nodded. "Love is a powerful emotion. Let me just..."

Allard stared at her as her pink glow brightened. "What's she doing?"

"Recharging," Bryanna answered.

Ashlan's eyes shot open. "Did you give her the globe?"

"The globe?" He stared down at her, confused. "Yes, a while ago. She found it in Charlie's store—"

"No, did you give it to her? Does she have it *now*?"

Allard checked his belt. He found the rods and the yuckah hoof, but not the globe. "She must have it."

Ashlan turned away from him and sat cross-legged in the middle of the room.

Bryanna watched her. "You aren't supposed to interfere, Ashlan!"

"I haven't. It's her globe." She gestured at Allard. "He gave it to her a few months ago."

"But what did you do to it?"

"I did nothing to it."

"Then what is it?"

"It's a globe with the Tyronian castle in it."

Allard spoke up. "It's magical, though, isn't it?"

Ashlan smiled, but didn't answer.

"You planted it in the store, didn't you? You knew she would like it and I would give it to her."

Her smile widened.

"What does it do?"

"You'll see." She shut her eyes.

"What do you mean by that?" Allard scurried over and looked into her face. "Ashlan, Apolline could die!"

She didn't respond.

"Ashlan!"

"She won't respond," Cytheria said. "She wants us to wait. She needs us to have faith."

Bryanna snorted.

Allard looked to Cytheria, growing desperate. "But Apolline…"

Cytheria sighed. "Ashlan knows best. I guess it's up to Elpida, ah, Apolline now."

The room fell into the deepest darkness I'd ever experienced. I froze, the sound of my breathing echoing in the silence. Fear gripped at my heart. The squeaks and scratching of rats rushed toward me. The snarling of ogres immobilized me. Hissing and rattling, crows' squawked, and the thumping of giants' feet sent my adrenalin shooting through me. The raucous noise drew closer and closer. An army approached, one ready to rip me to shreds.

Managing to regain some sense, I fumbled around in the dark toward where I saw the door. My fingers brushed against the wood. Feeling around, I found the knob and turned the lock. I felt around and found objects to pull in front of it, what they were, I had no idea. I just knew they were large and fairly heavy. I strained, groaning as the furniture scrapped the ground, but finally slid in front of the door.

Scratching sounded outside as the animals reached the room and tried to force their way in. I backed away, my hands shaking as I replaced the missing bullet in my revolver and pulled out my handgun.

The ogres reached the door and pounded on it. The lock buckled. The door jolted. I whimpered and raised my guns. The door pushed open a crack, and light burst into the room. Aside from rows of mirrors, nothing except the desk and throne would provide me cover.

The door jolted and an ogre's arm pushed through. I shot the arm and it pulled back. Instead, snakes and rats poured into the room. Howling of wolves echoed around me as I shot at the creatures sliding through the door. I backed to the desk and climbed onto it. My heart raced as I reloaded and kept shooting.

The door burst open. I fought not to panic and shot frantically at all the creatures rushing toward me. I kept shooting, reloading, shooting. I didn't want to die, except I had a bad feeling I didn't have enough bullets to kill what was coming for me. But I refused to just give up.

A rat crawled into my boot. I screeched, shaking my foot. An ogre grabbed my other leg and pulled it out from under me. I shot at him and he let go, but crows and snakes swarmed all over me.

No, no, no. This can't be it!

I grasped at the belt for another round for my guns, but clasped a glass ball instead. I swung it and hit several animals, freeing myself momentarily. I glanced at what I held; my globe. I honed in on the Tyronian castle inside. More than anything, I wanted to be there, with Allard as his soon-to-be wife, with the fairies as they watched me proudly, and with my parents who I barely found and now I would never know. They would be devastated after all they had done to protect me, but now I would die anyway.

I closed my eyes and wished for a spinning needle to put me to sleep so I wouldn't feel the ogres ripping me limb from limb or the tiny animals gnawing at my flesh. Allard would be heartbroken. After so much fighting against our love, we had found out we were meant to be... only now I would to die.

"I want to go home," I whispered, clasping tightly to the ball. "I want to see them all just one last time."

Everything went quiet. I opened my eyes. The scene in the room hung motionless around me. Animals midair, ogres with clubs raised, wolves with teeth bared. The room started to spin, the creatures becoming like a smear on a painting. I couldn't hold my eyes open. I found myself in a strange dreaming state again. Below me, the Tyrone castle drew nearer and nearer. Allard's voice surrounded me, echoing, but I couldn't make out what he said.

I soared over the courtyard and saw Fantine sitting up, holding her head. I shot through the palace to the ballroom and landed hard on the wooden floor.

I opened my eyes. *Ouch.* That had really happened, and I'd landed *hard.* My ribs and knees ached from the impact.

Ashlan smiled as she leaned over me, brushing my hair out of my face. "Good choice, Apolline."

Cytheria appeared at my side, clutching my shoulders. "Are you all right?"

Something stirred in my boot. I shot up and flung it off. The rat that had crawled in scurried over to Bryanna. We turned to face her as Allard restrained her.

Her eyes grew wide at the sight of me. "Tell me what it was, Ashlan!"

Ashlan gently took the globe from my hand and smiled. "It's very rare. It's a final wish giver, of elven making. It senses when the person who holds it is about to die and it fulfills their last wish."

Bryanna fell to her knees. "I have lost everything! All my planning, all those years! This was not how it was supposed to end!"

The rat bit Allard and Bryanna sprung free. She pounced on me and pinned me to the ground, her hands clasping down on my throat. "But I have one last trick up my sleeve."

Allard stood over her with a gun to her head. She froze.

"Let her go!" he said fiercely.

My gaze locked with Bryanna's as she glared down at me.

"Just because you lost your love, doesn't give you the right to take mine!" Allard pressed the gun firmly against the back of her head.

She winced at his words. Her hand loosened slightly from around my neck.

A thought occurred to me. I looked like Hernan, except my eyes. Maybe... I closed my eyes. She gasped, and one hand pulled away from my throat. She touched my face and a tear fell on my nose. "Hernan."

She pushed off me, and I opened my eyes. She faced Hernan with tears streaming down her face. "Did you love me, even just for a short while?"

His eyes widened. "I don't think that's—"

"Did you?"

"Answer her, Hernan," Cytheria said gently. "Answer her honestly."

He took a deep breath. "I did once. You were lovely then. But you changed. I tried to tell you at the ball, but you wouldn't listen, and then I met... I met Cytheria."

Bryanna gazed down at Cytheria. "You were always better than me, even before mother corrupted me against you."

"Bree, I..." Cytheria hung her head, her chin quivering.

Several guards rushed in and grabbed Bryanna. She didn't struggle, but stared at Cytheria as she allowed them to take her away. A solemn feeling came over us and we hung our heads. I stared after Bryanna, pitying her. She'd loved Hernan so much, but her misguided mother stole it from her by giving her dark magic.

But my pity vanished when I remembered how close to death I had come because of her. I had done nothing to her, but she wanted me dead.

The ballroom door burst open and a robust woman threw herself at me. "Oh, my Apolline! You're alive!"

I breathed in the strange smell of Fantine's hair as she gave me a crushing squeeze.

"Not if you keep that up, I won't be," I said breathlessly.

"Oh!" She pulled back and looked at me. "You are boiling over. Let me just..." She rested her hand over my heart and closed her eyes. "Mmm. True love is so rejuvenating."

Ashlan chuckled and touched her shoulder. "Is everyone waking up?"

"Oh, yes!" Fantine smiled. "They all look rather confused, but no one is the wiser."

The four of us stood.

Fantine turned to look at the prince. "Let's see this young chap you are to marry." She squinted at him. "You're familiar."

I fought to suppress a smile. "He's the young man who has been dropping into town; you and Sophronia told me to not to talk to him."

"He is?" She leaned closer, then her eyes widened. "You? You're the prince?"

Allard laughed. "I am."

She glared at Ashlan. "You could have told me."

"I'm sorry, Fantine, but I just couldn't." She shrugged with a delighted smirk.

Fantine shook her finger at her as she smiled. She wrapped her arm around my waist happily. "My dear, I'm glad this has turned out for you."

She scanned all the faces in the room, smiling with delight. "The family is all back together. Oh! I'm so happy. Grandchildren! Oh, grandchildren will come soon." She blinked, her smile falling. "Why are the mirrors smashed?"

Cytheria took her hand. "Just a minor skirmish. It's no big deal. We needed to redecorate anyway. All these mirrors make me a little uncomfortable."

CHAPTER TWENTY-FOUR

ytheria took my hand as we walked through the garden. Although it felt strange, I didn't pull away. I looked down at her and found her gazing up at me with tears in her eyes.

"Why are you crying?" I asked.

She chuckled. "I'm so happy. I was concerned that you hated me for letting you go."

I let out a long breath. "No. To be honest, I just can't believe I'm your daughter. I mean, look at me."

Cytheria's arm wrapped around my waist. "You're beautiful."

"Not like you."

Hernan draped his arm around Cytheria's shoulders, looking at me. "You are beautiful in the same way. You have such courage."

Cytheria smiled up at him. "She gets that from you."

He shook his head. "Apolline is completely unique."

My cheeks warmed. "Will I ever get used to this? I mean, my whole life I've known you as the king and queen, but never once did I consider the possibility you were my parents. I'm no princess."

"What do you think a princess is?" Hernan asked.

"Elegant, graceful, docile. I'm definitely not those."

"A princess is just a title," he said. "Something obtained through birth or marriage. What someone does with that title is completely up to them. You've been a princess your whole life, and soon you will be queen. Those titles will never change you unless you let them. A truly great princess and queen is true to herself. She is honest, caring, and wise. I believe you have all those attributes."

"Wise?" I raised an eyebrow.

Cytheria squeezed my waist. "You are. You're young, you'll see it eventually."

"Thankfully, I'll have Allard to keep me in line."

They exchanged smiles. That look told me they loved Allard and trusted him completely. My respect for him grew.

"Allard has been raised to rule and he can teach you many things," Hernan said. "But don't worry, we'll make sure you are taught what you need to know so you can rule just as competently at his side."

"A degree is in order."

Cytheria chuckled. "Yes."

"Oh well." I let out a long breath. "At least I won't feel inferior."

"Inferior?" Cytheria pulled me closer. "Why would you feel that way?"

"Allard's just so... perfect."

They both laughed.

"Ah, the blinders of love." Hernan sighed. "He's not perfect; you will learn that soon enough. But he is a good man... smart, compassionate, and patient. He sees the goodness in you, and I know he will do everything he can to uplift you and help you be the best queen you can be. So you're a little behind on the schooling, but you understand magic in a way he doesn't. You understand the everyday person in a way he never will.

"In many ways, I'm grateful for the life away from the palace you had forced upon you. It allowed you to be just you, and to understand life in a way you never could under the constant watch of tutors, the media, and those with certain expectations. Although I missed you and wished to have you returned to us every day, I do not regret it when I see the person you have become."

I stopped my stroll and looked down at my worn clothes and rough hands. "But... but what will people think of me? I'm just... me."

Cytheria touched my face. "That's why they will love you. You are just like them and will be a breath of fresh air. Allard will protect you from the aristocrats who will snub you, but even they will come around. Elpida means hope, and you have always been my hope. Soon, you will be theirs as well."

I ran my fingers through my hair over my shoulder. "I don't know if I could get used to being called Elpida."

"That's just fine." Hernan grasped my shoulder. "Apolline is your middle name; you were always meant to go by it. Elpida is your official name. I think strength suits you anyway."

"Strength?"

Cytheria nodded. "Your name; Elpida Apolline means hope and strength."

I let out a long breath. "And you're sure I'm your daughter?"

They both smiled.

"Of course," Hernan said.

I couldn't help it, I burst into tears.

Cytheria threw her arms around me. "Why are you crying?"

"I thought I was an orphan."

Hernan wrapped his arm around my waist as he softly placed a kiss on my head. "I'm sorry you had to live that lie."

"When Charlie accidentally told me I had a father, I didn't know what to think. But now I found out I've known about my parents all along. Fantine told me your stories, so I always felt like I knew you."

Cytheria brushed my tears away. "And now you always will. We will never let you go again."

I smiled and wrapped my arms around both of them.

We continued our walk through the gardens and talked endlessly. I learned that I more than just looked like my father, but our personalities synced up as well. It surprised me to find the respected and revered King Hernan had some serious sarcasm. I had picked up some of my mother's characteristics too—some of my gentler and tender attributes—which she was glad to see she had passed on.

As the time for the ball and wedding approached, I returned to my room to get ready. The three fairies waited inside for me. They rushed at me and hugged me.

"Apolline." Fantine squeezed me, forcing the air out of my lungs. "I can't believe this day is finally here. It came so fast, *too* fast. I expect children right away."

"Fantine." Ashlan touched her shoulder, shaking her head. "Let her breathe, literally and figuratively."

Fantine let me go and chuckled. "I'm sorry. I'm just so proud of her."

"As am I." Ashlan bowed her head. "Princess."

I chuckled uneasily. "Yup, that's still weird."

Sophronia huffed. "I wish I'd known that boy was *Prince* Allard."

"Don't be so bitter about it," Fantine said, adjusting Sophronia's military jacket.

Sophronia pushed her hands away and pulled at her pencil skirt.

Fantine grinned. "You're such a stiff."

"I am... fine, yes I am."

Ashlan giggled. "We all need to get dressed, especially Apolline."

She waved her wand. My clothes flew off and my dress slipped itself on. I shuddered at how easily she did that. She tapped her head and her hair twisted into an up style, and her plain brown and white dress turned into an elegant, pink, silky gown.

Fantine tapped her head as well, and her fuzzy hair braided itself back, and her floral print dress and apron turned into a chic, dark blue gown.

Fantine and Ashlan proceeded to fuss with my hair and zap several different sets of jewelry onto me, before finally settling with diamond earrings and necklace.

"But the dress," Ashlan said, tapping her chin with her wand. "Blue will not do. Blue is a symbol of Oran only." She tapped my shoulder with the wand. It looked like water pouring over the dress as the blue changed back to deep purple. "For royalty, and for the unity of two kingdoms, the red and the blue." She winked.

They walked me out to meet my parents who both greeted me warmly. Cytheria took my arm as the fairies went ahead to the ballroom that had undergone speedy repairs and decorated quickly with the help of the fairies.

Hernan softly kissed my forehead. "We're proud of you, Princess Elpida Apolline Diament of Tyrone."

We turned and they walked through the ballroom doors before me. I waited, forcing myself to breathe to remain composed. My name was called for my grand entrance and, as I stepped out, all eyes turned to me.

Allard straightened his dark blue coat. He couldn't believe how quickly the servants and fairies had fixed the ballroom. Where the mirrors had hung, now grand portraits of landscapes from all over the Tyrone kingdom took their place.

White curtains were draped from the ceiling, and chairs sat in rows, with just the red carpet up the middle, pointing to the altar. He walked to the altar, running his fingers over it, and wondering at how the fairy had managed to lead him to Apolline, his bride. He still found himself amazed that the woman he'd fallen in love with was in fact the Princess Elpida.

"Son."

Allard turned and grinned.

Brencis approached him with his arms open. They embraced, and Brencis squeezed him tight. "I'm so proud of you."

"Thank you, Father."

Brencis released him and looked into his face. "I have been told all that you both did. It sounds like we have a bright future ahead of us… and many grandchildren I hope."

Allard laughed. "One step at a time."

Brencis' grin widened. "Did you know she was the princess? Charles told me that the girl you were spotted with is her."

Allard shook his head. "I'm just as surprised as anyone else, including her. But I am relieved. She showed unwavering dedication to me, even when she didn't know who her betrothed was, so I know our marriage will be strong. She will keep me strong and humble."

"Your highness."

Allard turned his head toward Beau, wearing a coy grin. "Highness?"

"Yes, well, your father is right there. I don't want to seem rude."

Allard grinned. "That's never stopped you before."

Beau shrugged. "There's always a first."

"Allard!" Nathaniel slung his arm around Allard's shoulders. "So, you've seen the princess. How is she?" He winked.

Allard glanced at his father and they exchanged knowing grins. "She's better than I hoped."

Their sisters approached and bowed their heads to Brencis. Jamila stepped up and linked her arm through Beau's. "So, tell us about the princess, Allard."

He couldn't help feeling smug about how she'd react when she saw Apolline. She'd treated Apolline poorly, and looked down her nose at her when they met. "She's wonderful. When you meet her, you will be amazed."

Jamila's eyes lit up. "I'm excited to finally meet her. I'm sure we will be fast friends. We will see much of each other since I'm marrying your cousin and you spend so much time with Beau."

Allard forced back his urge to laugh. "I hope so too."

A man approached his father. A twinge of fear pulsed through Allard. Charlie, although cleaned up and wearing the black military uniform, still looked intimidating. Allard still saw the rough gunslinger from Mish.

Charlie's gaze met Allard's, and he bowed his head. Allard took a deep breath and stepped over, offering his hand. "I'm sorry I gave you such a scare."

Charlie's gaze lifted to his face. "Your highness, if I'd known—"

"Bryanna would have known." Allard grasped Charlie's hand. "Ashlan is clever. None of us knew what she'd done."

Charlie shook his hand firmly. "I feel like such a fool."

Allard smiled. "Don't. You did the right thing. How were you to know you were protecting her from me for me?"

"What does that mean?" Beau asked.

Charlie grinned at Allard. "Highness, you are in for a treat."

A trumpet sounded.

The crowd turned and looked up to the stairs as the three royal fairies descended. They each approached Allard, touching his heart. They bowed their heads and stepped to the side, a faint glow emitting from each.

Another trumpet sounded, and the herald announced King Hernan and Queen Cytheria. Allard's pulse increased and he took deep breaths. Apolline would appear soon, and they would be wed.

"Nervous?" Beau asked softly as the king and queen made their way down the aisle.

"No." Allard looked at Beau. "Excited."

"She's that good, huh?"

Allard smiled, meeting Cytheria's gaze. "Oh yes."

Cytheria kissed his cheek. "She's nervous."

"She is?"

Cytheria nodded. "She doesn't want to disappoint you."

Allard shook his head. "That's not possible."

Cytheria smiled. Beau sighed from beside Allard. Allard glanced over his shoulder, raising his eyebrow. Beau cleared his throat and looked away from Cytheria.

Hernan's hand wrapped firmly around Allard's, drawing his attention away from Beau. "You know, just because we arranged this, doesn't mean I won't be watching you closely to make sure you're treating her right."

"Hernan." Brencis grasped his shoulder.

Hernan shrugged. "She's my daughter. Do you expect anything less?"

Brencis grinned. "No, not at all." Brencis glared at Allard. "Treat her right."

"Thanks." Allard smirked.

"Elpida Apolline Diament, Princess of Tyrone."

Through the doors stepped the most beautiful woman Allard had ever beheld. Her long hair had been pinned back from her face so a crown could rest upon her head, but cascaded down her back in loose curls. Her dress, now purple, accentuated her curvy body.

Jamila gasped. "What...?"

Nathaniel stifled a laugh.

Beau clutched Allard's arm. "No way."

Allard grinned as his gaze met Apolline's.

Flashes blinded me as I descended the stairs. As I walked down the aisle, many aristocrats, courtiers, dukes, and duchesses, greeted me. Beau and Nathaniel rushed at me, ecstatic that I was in fact the princess. But Jamila hung back, her eyes hooded and her cheeks flushed. I stretched my hand out and gently grabbed hers. "Hey, no hard feelings?"

She glanced up at me. "I didn't know, I just thought—"

"I know, I get it." I gave her an understanding smile.

Her face lit up and she squeezed my hand. "Thank you. Let me make it up to you."

I nodded. "I do need some help learning to be ladylike."

She giggled. "I can help with that."

I squeezed her hand and moved on, coming face to face with Charlie. He grinned at me and I threw my arms around him. "You!"

He laughed. "We had some good times, didn't we?"

"I sure did, but I think I gave you more headaches than you bargained for, General."

He shrugged. "Yes, a teenage girl may seem easy compared to soldiers, but you proved that theory wrong."

I laughed and I finally reached King Brencis. He looked me over with his light blue eyes and a huge smile swept across his round face. "My dear, you are lovely, and brave too, I hear. My son is lucky to have you."

He stepped aside and my heart skipped a beat. Allard gazed at me, smiling, dressed in his deep blue formal royal suit. He looked so handsome I couldn't help blushing, which sent the photographers in a frenzy.

Allard gazed steadily into my eyes as he took my hand. "Are you ready?"

I leaned closer, the flashes increasing. "I've been ready since the day we met."

His smile widened. He moved to kiss me, but restrained himself.

He led me to the altar. Sophronia married us, to my surprise. When she pronounced us husband and wife, he wrapped his arms around me, holding me tightly as he kissed me. Holo-cameras flashed away, even after he pulled back.

Robots shot out and cleared the chairs for the ball. Allard didn't let go of me for one moment, not that I wanted him to. I looked up at him, but he gazed around, his chest out, looking mighty proud of himself.

"What are you thinking?" I whispered.

He looked down at me, his eyes softening. "I'm thinking about you and how lucky I am."

I blushed. Again, the cameras flashed all around me.

Finally the ballroom floor lay open for dancing. Allard looked into my eyes. "May I have this dance?"

I nodded.

On the dance floor, I felt strange as everyone watched us. "Don't you feel self-conscious? All these pictures, people staring at us?"

He glanced around. "Why does it matter if every person in the twin kingdoms is watching? I have you, and you are my princess."

I scrunched up my nose. "That was sweet, I guess, but a little—"

He bent down and kissed me. I felt like I was dreaming again. I pressed against him, completely focused on him, just him. All the people around us vanished. All that mattered was my true love's kiss with my husband, Allard.

CHAPTER TWENTY-FIVE

I **strolled down the main street of Mish, my hand in Allard's.** After several months of touring the United Empire, we deserved the time to rest and relax.

My parents disappeared into the newly opened tourist shop. I smiled, so glad to know them. I couldn't have wished for a more loving family.

Barnibos appeared out of Charlie's store and grinned. I waved and he headed right for us. "Apolline, or should I say, your highness?"

"Don't." I laughed and hugged him. "I'm still me, and apparently you knew all along."

"Not *all* along. I figured it out when you were sixteen. I'd acquired a portrait of King Hernan just before we stopped by and couldn't help noticing the resemblance. So I got the sheriff drunk, and grilled him. I found it harder than I anticipated to make him spill. The fairies set up some very powerful barriers, and swore most of the planet to secrecy."

"So everyone except me knew?"

He shrugged. "Not everyone. Your generation didn't, and many farmers didn't. That's why Sophronia wiped memories. Some people didn't pass security measures, so if they looked like they'd figured it out..."

I shuddered. "She never did it to me, did she?"

He grinned. "The king forbade it."

"Thank goodness."

Barnibos lifted a large bag of jerky. "You still owe me."

I grinned. "I'm headed there right now."

He stepped in beside me as Allard and I made our way to the store. "I'm glad Charlie decided to stay here."

"Me too. Allard was the one who thought he should be the mayor."

Allard's arm wrapped around my waist and squeezed.

"Considering this is now the royal vacation planet, it's probably for the best," Barnibos said. "Charlie can definitely civilize this place. Thankfully, he's still willing to let us drop by. I couldn't survive without his jerky and tobacco."

I chuckled.

We entered the store and found Charlie and Fantine arguing about the cost of her potions.

"King Allard?"

Allard and I both turned as the door flew open.

"Oh no." He dashed across to the storage room as the swarm of teenage girls ran at him. I laughed. Since his image had gone public, the swooning girls intensified.

"Ladies," I said as they all clambered at Charlie's counter, trying to break through. "King Allard is here on vacation. He would like some privacy."

The girls turned on me. "You're Queen Elpida."

I stepped back, sensing the vicious tone of her voice. This particular scenario had repeated over and over as we toured. Girls swarmed Allard like a rock star. He wished he'd kept his identity secret and, as I raised my hands, the girls advancing on me, I kind of did too.

"You don't deserve him! I do!" One of the girls attacked.

"Whoa!" I raised my hands, but they all froze.

Ashlan stepped into the store, a bright smile across her face. "Morning." She patted my cheek and turned to the frozen girls. "Leave."

They all hurried, stiff like robots, out the door.

Fantine sighed. "You need to start having babies."

Allard poked his head out the door. "Are they gone?"

"Yes," I answered.

Charlie turned on him, prodding his chest. "You just abandoned your wife to those... those... girls."

Ashlan giggled.

Allard looked at me. "Sorry."

I shrugged. "Last time they got hold of you, they ripped off most of your clothes. I prefer it if you just run. I can handle myself."

"I'm going to tighten security." Charlie disappeared into the storage room.

Fantine turned to me. "Apolline dear, could you deliver these potions for me?"

"Ahh..." I glanced at Ashlan and Allard. "Is it fine for me to do that?"

Allard stretched out his hand for the bag of potions. "We are just Apolline and Allard today, not the king and queen. Serving the people wouldn't be frowned upon anyway."

I nodded. "I'm still trying to work out what I can and can't do."

He kissed my forehead, wrapping his arm around my waist. "You're doing fine. The people love you, even with your... interesting moments."

I shoved him in the chest and he laughed.

"Except the single ladies of course." I grinned.

He grunted. "Everyone knows I'm married. Very married. Happily married. *Everyone.*"

"I keep telling you, have some babies," Fantine said.

Allard grinned and looked into my eyes. "I'm definitely working on it."

I pushed him off, my face growing hot.

He laughed and kissed my cheek. "Come on, let's deliver these."

We delivered the potions to Fantine's elderly clientele, heading toward the woods. When we reached the woods, Allard kept a firm grasp of my hand as I led him through to the cottage. When we arrived, he gazed around with wide eyes. "It's beautiful."

"Isn't it?" I smiled.

"You must have lived a charmed life."

"It's not the charmed life I thought the princess would live, but I definitely thought so."

Sophronia stepped out of the cottage, bowing as she approached. "Your majesties. I have secured the cottage and its perimeter. I must warn you though that a pack of Bryanna's wolves have immigrated into these woods. I am doing all I can to eliminate your scent, my king, from their memory. Until then, they will not be able to follow you here or find this location, and I advise against traveling in the woods after dark."

Allard cringed. "Duly noted."

"I have prepared the cottage for your stay with both your parents. Your room, my queen, is as you requested—unchanged except with a larger bed. My old study is now set up for King Hernan and Queen Cytheria, and my room for King Brencis."

"Won't you be staying?" I smiled.

She scowled. "I have important matters of business to attend to."

"No, you don't," Allard said.

She sniffed. "Bryanna still has not been judged, and the wolves must be seen to." She bowed. "Good day."

She reached out and touched our hearts, absorbing the energy of our love, before vanishing.

Allard and I entered the cottage and I told him about memories I held in each room and with different items. He smiled as he listened, but when we entered my room, he shut the door behind him.

EPILOGUE

Bryanna stared out the window of her cell. She wished she had her powers again. Her gaze dropped to her hands, trying to will her powers to return.

"Bryanna."

Bryanna looked up to Ashlan, Fantine, and Sophronia by the door. "Come to gloat?"

"No." Sophronia grasped the bars. "We would like to offer you something."

Bryanna sneered. "What could you possibly have to offer me?"

"Magic. Love," Ashlan said.

Bryanna's eyes narrowed. "What's the con?"

"No con," Sophronia said. "Except you will only be able to use good magic. We will teach you how to channel positive power."

Bryanna rolled her eyes, standing. "I am a mortal and became more powerful than you. That is because dark magic has more force."

"You never became more powerful than me," Ashlan said.

Bryanna frowned. She stood in front of them, folding her arms. "And why would I want to do this? I have nothing left worth living for. I might as well let the executioner have me."

"We know you are capable of love, great love," Fantine said. "We also have the ear of the kings and queens. Cytheria does not wish to see you dead, and if we present her with an alternative that will save you, she will take it. But you must agree."

Bryanna drummed her elbow, thinking carefully. "Where would I go? Mahkba has been seized, and all the creatures returned and sealed on their home planets. I would not be welcomed anywhere in the galaxy."

"We can arrange something," Sophronia said.

Bryanna pursed her lips. "I'll have to think about it."

Ashlan bowed her head. "Your sentencing isn't for another couple of weeks. You have until then. But once the sentence is made, we won't be able to make alternative arrangements."

"I understand." Bryanna turned her back on them and sighed. Death seemed like a welcomed friend. Hernan would never love her, she'd killed her best friend, and now the whole newly united empire despised her.

Except... She stared up at the barred window. A face flashed into her mind. A mischievous grin and gleaming pale blue eyes. Someone... someone named Horatio.

A rat's head appeared in the corner. She glanced down at it, and it scurried to her. The rodent bowed its head, squeaking frantically. She bent over and picked it up. "You were one of my servants."

The rat nodded.

"You must be frustrated, no longer able to speak."

It nodded again.

She stroked its head. Then paused. "But you can understand me still."

It nodded.

She smiled. "I think it's time I leave."

ACKNOWLEDGMENTS

The Princess of Tyrone has come a long way over the years. I first started writing it in high school, and it took me about five years to finish the first draft. Ever since then the story has evolved, and it became the first book in a series based around the "galaxy" in which it is set. Thanks to the Grimm Brothers and their morbid storytelling, combined with a slight obsession with *Firefly*, I was inspired to twist this once happy, overly sweet version of *Sleeping Beauty* everyone is so familiar with, into a gun-slinging space fantasy.

But, to thank the people involved, I'd really like to acknowledge Mara Valderran, who really has motivated me to work hard. She was my first eyes on this later version of the manuscript, and really helped me get it ready to go. I also want to thank Leigh Statham, who is always willing to listen and step in when I need some help.

I also want to thank Candis Rutterman, who reads all my books. Friends even when there's an ocean between us! Enjoy this one, hon!

And I always want to show my appreciate to my husband and kids. Writing can be time consuming, and often makes me a bit reclusive, but they always support me and understand. I love them so much!

I'd like to thank the team at Curiosity Quills. It's nice to work with them all again, as it's been a while since the Kiya Trilogy finished. But as usual, they are so professional, open, and hard working. I love that I found them and that they like me back.

Last of all, to my readers. I hope Princess of Tyrone gave you an escape to this lighthearted world, and that you will return for the next installment to meet Hansel and Gretel. Maybe later down the line, you will get to see Apolline and Allard again. *wink wink*

About the Author

Born and raised in Australia, Katie's early years of day dreaming in the "bush", and having her father tell her wild bedtime stories, inspired her passion for writing.

After graduating High School, she became a foreign exchange student where she met a young man who several years later she married. Now she lives in Arizona with her husband, daughter and their dog.

She has a diploma in travel and tourism which helps inspire her writing. She is currently at school studying English and Creative Writing.

Katie loves to out sing her friends and family, play sports and be a good wife and mother. She now works as a Clerk with a lien company in Arizona to help support her family and her schooling. She loves to write, and takes the few spare moments in her day to work on her novels.

THANK YOU FOR READING

© 2016 **Katie Hamstead**

http://kjhstories.blogspot.com

Please visit http://curiosityquills.com/reader-survey to
share your reading experience with the author of this book!

Kiya: Hope of the Pharaoh, by Katie Hamstead

To save her younger sisters from being taken, Naomi steps in to be a wife of the erratic Pharaoh. As Naomi rises through the ranks of the wives, Queen Nefertiti seeks to destroy her. To protect herself, Naomi charms the Pharaoh, who grows to love her. But when Naomi conceives his child, Nefertiti's lust for blood is turned against her.

Gyre, by Jessica Gunn

Trevor couldn't believe his eyes when Chelsea teleported onto SeaSatellite5. The miracle is Trevor's absolute worst nightmare. Chelsea is Atlantean, which would be fine if Trevor's family weren't Lemurian—enemies of Atlantis. Then SeaSatellite5 uncovers Atlantean ruins and stumbles into the crosshairs of an ancient war. The Lemurians want the artifacts inside the ruins, and Trevor's the only one onboard who recognizes the relics for what they really are: Link Pieces, tools used by ancient civilizations to wage their time-travel war. Chelsea and Trevor must brave the gyre of lies surrounding them. If they can't, Atlantis will be destroyed forever.

Broken Forest, by Eliza Tilton

Hopeless he'll never be more than the boy who didn't save his brother, 17-year-old Avikar accepts his life as the family stable boy, trying to forget the past. But when his sister, Jeslyn, is kidnapped, the thought of losing another sibling catapults him on a desperate quest. With his best friend by his side, and using the tracking skills he learned from his father, he discovers Jeslyn has been taken, kidnapped by one Lucino, the young lord of Daath, a mystical place thought only to exist in fables.

Artificial, by Jadah McCoy

In 2256, the only remnants of civilization on Earth's first colonized planet, Kepler, are the plant-covered buildings and the nocturnal, genetically spliced bug-people nesting within them: the Cull. And whoever engineered the Cull isn't done playing God. When Syl is abducted and spliced with Cull DNA, she must find a cure and stop the person responsible before the abomination spreads. For Bastion, being an android in the sex industry isn't so bad, as long as he can keep his emotions a secret. Crossing paths with Syl, Bastion must help the girl escape before he becomes victim to his too-human emotions.

CPSIA information can be obtained
at www.ICGtesting.com
Printed in the USA
FSOW02n2039010416
18742FS